EAGLE ONE

The Bugging Out Series: Book Two

NOAH MANN

Published By Schmuck & Underwood

ISBN-10: 1502811669
ISBN-13: 978-1502811660

All the great things are simple, and many can be expressed in a single word: freedom, justice, honor, duty, mercy, hope.

Winston Churchill

Prologue

I dreamed of things green.

Leaves. Grass. Avocados. Anything even remotely bearing that soothing shade. That hue of the old world.

I never set out to sample such things when sleep took hold. It simply happened. My mind, free of the real, let me slip back, back, back. To a time when I walked barefoot upon cool grass. Sat in the shade of a tree spread wide above me. Watched lush pines and firs bend in autumn winds.

Blue had once been my favorite color. No more.

Green...

Each dream of the planet alive came pleasant and warm. The sensations filled me as I slept. I heard sounds. Dogs barking. Crows screeching. The rhythmic stomping of horse hooves on dusty earth. I smelled summer. And winter. The fresh dampness of rain dripping from the broad leaves of oaks. The wafting scent of a Christmas tree in the corner of my living room. Spinach cooking on the stove. The pungent bite of cilantro.

All things good. All things alive. Things that thrived on the green earth.

I did not dream of the thing that had robbed me of this color. That had stolen it from the wider world. The blight found no quarter in my sleep. It had come, exploding from its appearance in a Polish farm field more than a year ago, spreading in all directions. Crossing oceans. Relentless as it destroyed every plant. Every tree. Every weed. And with them, all things that depended upon them for sustenance. For survival. Birds. Fish. Animals.

Humanity.

Shimmering deep pools of glacial lakes filled my head in the hours before dawn. Moss crept toward the shore. Lichen clung to jagged rocks. The Aurora shimmered green in the sky above. These were things I dreamed of. I suffered no nightmares in my sleep.

Those were plentiful when I was wide awake.

Part One

A New World

One

We heard the screams four miles from my refuge.

The second real snow of the season was threatening. You could feel it in the air. As Del said to me once, people had lost the ability to sense things like changes in the weather. He had been able to sense far more than things meteorological. I missed him.

Which made Neil's presence all the more comforting. I was no longer alone. Beyond that, his arrival nearly a month earlier, with Grace and her daughter, affirmed something Neil had said to me before the blight struck, before the Red Signal, before the world that was became what it was now—there was hope. People, good people, could survive.

Among them, though, there was a darkness. A cancer on what some called humanity. I'd seen it in Whitefish. In the dying eyes of Major Layton. And we were hearing it, rolling up the slope of the hill from a collection of old mining shacks long abandoned.

"Is that a woman?" Neil asked, instantly worried.

I watched him glance behind, up the slope. Hours behind us, Grace and Krista were safe at my refuge.

"A woman," I said. "And a man."

The cries rose from more than one. More than two, even. I thought I could make out three distinct voices calling out in terror. I looked to Neil, his tension dialed back down. It could not be Grace and Krista. But it was someone. Some people. Human beings. And they were being hurt.

Without any discussion we aimed ourselves at the sound and advanced, weapons ready. I carried my suppressed AR, and Neil a semi-auto Benelli 12 gauge, pistols on both our hips. Neil favored a plain Smith & Wesson .44 magnum, stainless, six shots of heavy lead ready to drop anything dumb or desperate enough to present a threat. I still carried my Springfield 1911. But beyond the armament, we had the will. Neil knew I had killed. I suspected that he had as well, though he'd still not detailed his journey from back east to my Montana hideaway. He'd simply told me that he wasn't ready to relive what he'd seen, and what he'd done. I could see it in him, though. He'd not come through unscathed.

Nearing the jumble of old mining shacks, we heard what neither of us wanted to—silence. The screams were gone. We stopped on a low rock outcropping, the leaning and weathered shacks partially visible below us past the naked trees, old timber frames sagging, roofs marked by holes.

Through one of those openings, the first wisps of smoke were rising from a small fire within. One set for warmth. Or for other obvious and hideous purposes.

"We don't have to involve ourselves in this," I said. "Whatever it is."

"We both know what it is."

Neil was right. But we still could back away and return to the safety of my refuge. Whoever was down there was unaware of our presence. They would likely soon finish what they were doing and move on.

And do again what they were, down there inside those four decrepit walls. To someone else.

"You've involved yourself before," Neil reminded me.

I had. Sharing the story of Layton, and Whitefish, and Del, had been partly cathartic, and partly instructive. Neil deserved to know what had happened. What I'd made happen. So he was right, I'd stepped in before. To stop something.

With just a moment's silent look between us, I knew I'd be doing so again.

We crept down the slope to a staggered line of trees, their grey bark hanging like scabs, colorless and cracking. Neil shifted left while I followed a gentle arc around the shacks until the weathered door of the one in question was in view. I looked and saw Neil in position at the rear. He gave me a thumbs up and I raised my AR, laying the sight's orange reticle on the entrance to the ramshackle structure.

"Come out!" I shouted, most of my body hidden behind a wide old pine. "With your hands empty! Now!"

There was no response. No sound at all. Just the hint of a low fire crackling within, its greyish ribbon of smoke rising through the roof and dissipating among the barren limbs above.

"If you need motivation, we can provide some!" I threatened.

A few seconds later, a rifle barrel poking through the shuttered window gave us our answer. I'd been shot before, and had no desire to repeat that event, nor the agony that followed. I adjusted my aim to where I expected the person wielding the weapon would be standing beyond the wooden wall and squeezed the trigger four times, the crack of each shot muffled by the suppressor. A sharp cry sounded from within the shack, followed by frantic scrambling. The person or persons within seemed to be scrambling about, but still did not reply or show signs of emerging.

Bang! Bang!

Two shotgun blasts to my left signaled that Neil was firing. Chunks of splintered wood blasted into the air from the back of the shack, the double-ought buck tearing pieces out of the old structure.

"You're not getting out!" Neil yelled, signaling an attempt to do so on his side.

"Come out now with your hands up or we fire everything we have at you!"

My final warning hung in the quiet woods for a moment, until the inevitability of the situation crystalized for those inside.

"Okay!" a man answered from within. "We're coming out!"

The shack's front door swung inward and three men slipped through the opening, two with both hands thrust skyward, the third managing to hold a single hand above his head, the other hanging limp, blood dripping from it. My shots had found their mark.

"Away from the shack," I ordered, staying behind cover. "Over there. There. Down on your knees."

The wounded man seemed to fold to the ground, landing on his knees, weight of his body coming to rest on his heels. His comrades planted themselves next to him, hands still raised. From the corner of my eye I could see Neil approaching the shack from the back, his shotty raised and ready.

"Keep your hands up," I reminded the men.

The wounded one tried, but his uninjured hand sagged and came to rest atop his head. His gaze began to swim as a puddle of blood gathered where his other hand lay on the ground next to his knee.

"He's hurt," one of the men said, spittle flecking the grizzled beard that mostly obscured his mouth. "He needs help."

"Yeah, maybe," I said.

Beyond the men, Neil appeared from the far side of the shack, standing upright, his shotty slung. He approached the door and stood in the opening for a moment, staring in. The hint of the fire within dappled his face with a warm glow that seemed alien to the surroundings. And to his being at that moment.

"Neil..."

He didn't react to me. Just stood motionless as I covered the men we'd flushed from the shack.

"Neil," I repeated, fearing the response to what I said next. "What is it?"

He finally looked toward me, but just for an instant. His attention shifted almost immediately to the three men, their backs to him. Cold hate raged in his gaze. With a determined, fluid motion, he drew his revolver and walked toward the kneeling men, positioning himself to the side of the line they formed. He raised the six shooter and took aim at the nearest man's temple.

"Neil..."

But there were no words to stop him. He squeezed the trigger once and the left side of the man's head exploded, spraying blood and brain and shards of skull over his two friends. The wounded man screamed as the body tipped onto him. At the end of the line, his face covered in the horror of what had been his friend, the uninjured man began to sing softly. A hymn of some kind, I thought, his words never halting, even when Neil fired a bullet through the wounded man's brain, sending another bloody horror upon him. Finally it was his turn. He kept singing right until the .44 hollow point round tore the front of his head off.

Neil stood over the bodies for a moment. The last man's feet twitched for a few seconds, then stilled. As easily as he'd drawn the weapon, Neil holstered it again and looked to me.

I didn't know what to say. What I'd just witnessed shocked me, though not because of the act's clear brutality. A sick warmth sparkled in my gut because it was my friend I'd just watched carry out an execution, without a word spoken, to me or to those he'd condemned to death.

"You want to know why?" Neil asked me.

I said nothing. He looked at me for a moment longer, then turned and walked back toward the shack. I followed, stopping at the door where he had just a few minutes before. Looking in I could see by the light of a pit fire built at the center of the smallish space. Two rifles lay on the floor. One was leaned against the back wall near the holes Neil's shotgun blasts had created. Next to it hung the bodies of a woman and a man, stripped naked, their throats slit, hooks and ropes suspending them from old rafters. On a makeshift table next to the fire a third body lay, a man, similarly stripped, deep slice across his throat, his left leg gone.

But not missing. The long appendage, stripped of skin, sizzled on a wire rack over the fire.

I backed away from the door and turned toward my friend.

"There is no more law," Neil said. "Only justice."

Two

Grace sat next to Neil on the couch in my great room, both trying to suppress laughter as they watched Krista destroy me in a game of jacks.

"You're terrible at this," Krista said.

She wasn't wrong, watching as I bounced the small rubber ball and fumbled with the multi-point jacks, trying to scoop up three but managing a big fat goose egg before the ball fell to the floor again.

"Worst I've ever seen," Neil commented.

I glanced up to him, the both of us smiling. But there was something else in the look we exchanged. A knowing. An acceptance of what had happened earlier some distance from my refuge. We'd decided shortly after coming upon the horror, and ending those who'd perpetrated it, that we would not share what had happened with Grace. She didn't need to know what had transpired so close to where we felt safe. Nor did Krista deserve to become aware of it by happenstance. It was something Neil and I would share, alone.

"Winner!" Krista shouted, thrusting her hands in the air, the last few jacks fisted in them.

"You wiped me out," I said. "I need to seriously start training for these matches."

Krista picked the ball up and bounced it three times.

"One bouncy, two bouncy, three bouncy," she said, mocking me. "Whew! What a workout!"

Neil and Grace howled with laughter. I grabbed Krista and pulled her into a joking headlock where we sat, the light moment welcome, and normal.

And fleeting, the levity ending quickly as the lights dimmed, then flickered, then went out with a pop from down the hall. I jumped up and hurried to the back of the house, grabbing one of the strategically placed flashlights, its beam cutting the darkness. Neil followed, as did Grace and Krista, the three entering power central right behind me. It was the bedroom I'd turned into a space to house the deep cycle batteries and their associated equipment, all which worked to power much of my refuge once the sun went down. Except for now.

"I smell it," Neil said.

I nodded and shifted the flashlight beam to the inverter mounted on the wall next to the banks of batteries. We both approached it. Neil glanced back, exchanging a look with Grace.

"Let's go clean the jacks up so someone doesn't impale their foot on them," Grace told her daughter, the both of them disappearing down the hallway.

"It's shot," I said.

The heavy electrical scent hanging in the space was all the indication, and confirmation, of the statement I was making.

"There's still one at Del's place," Neil reminded me.

I nodded in the near darkness. The backup inverter I'd brought with me to my refuge over a year ago was what we were looking at. Its predecessor had failed just two weeks ago. The one remaining at Del's, older by years than those that had already failed, would have to do. It was one of the few items of use we hadn't transferred from my friend's house a scant mile through the dead woods, following the direction he'd given me soon after we'd met—to use whatever he had if anything happened to him. Still, carting off his radios, his remaining food, seemed some final act of indignity visited upon the man who'd sacrificed his life for me. Returning there, to the empty space, cold and quiet, devoid of his laugh or his wisdom, was a necessity I did not relish.

"Yeah, we hook that up and it'll last how long?" I asked, the question more commentary than query. "There's something wrong with the distribution controller."

That piece of temperamental technology, unfortunately, had no spare, and was putting a strain on the inverter, which took DC current from the bank of batteries and converted it to AC power for the house's plugs and lights. The life of the inverters, which should be measured in decades, had dwindled to weeks in my failing electrical system.

"If it lasts a month, that's thirty days closer to spring," Neil said.

Spring...

That was when we'd decided to move. The winter's snow accumulation would be melting, and Neil had already sketched out a makeshift plow blade we could weld to the front of the truck he, Grace, and Krista had arrived in, a diesel beast that had seen better days, but had gotten them this far. We hoped it would take us the rest of the way on our journey, however far that might be.

Still, that journey wouldn't start in thirty days, if the inverter from Del's would even last that long. Any time beyond that would have to be survived with candles and fires and only necessary equipment wired directly into the generator, which, itself, was showing increasing signs that its best days were behind it.

"All right," I said. "In the morning."

"Eagle One, Eagle One, come in."

We heard the small voice from the great room, Krista's voice, and I returned to see her sitting at the collection of radios we'd transferred from Del's, the equipment wired directly to its own set of batteries charged every day from a dedicated solar panel.

"Eagle One, this is Big Sky Alpha, come in."

Grace lit a candle, then another, smiling at her daughter.

"Eagle One, please come in. We need your location."

Neil joined me in watching the child, working the radio's controls, dialing in frequencies, repeating the calls over and over, using the call sign she'd made up for our location.

"This is Big Sky Alpha, come in."

Del had avoided broadcasting, wary of anyone zeroing in on our little slice of peaceful existence. But Del was gone, and the things that we'd feared had either been eliminated, or likely died from the lingering effects of the blight. When Krista had asked if she could put a call out to Eagle One, which hadn't been heard from since before their arrival at my refuge, no harm was seen, and so she'd taken it upon herself for the past two weeks to seek out the location of the enigmatic signal. A place we knew we had to find.

"Eagle One, Eagle One, we know you're out there. Please come in."

Grace eased a candle across the dining table, which had become home to the radios. She watched her daughter, still smiling, but the expression was tempered. Krista was as eager as Neil, and as me, to start west. Her mother, though, seemed to hope that the winter was long and the snow deep. Reaching my refuge had been enough for her. The relative safety she and her daughter now enjoyed dimmed any desire to go further, regardless of the reality requiring that we would have to. The food would run out at some point. Power, as we were realizing, was a more tenuous commodity by the hour. Our time here would not be endless.

Yet it was here that Grace wanted to stay. In circumstances inching toward dire. What must have happened out there, on their journey here, that would make the certainty of starving and freezing to death in this place preferable to venturing onward?

"Big Sky Alpha requires your location, Eagle One. You helped us get this far. Please come in."

This far...

Del and I had wondered about the sporadic communications from Eagle One, some requesting that specific items be brought to them, mostly medical in nature. We'd puzzled over why anyone still alive in the wastelands would give a damn about some mysterious transmission seeking supplies. Only when Neil arrived did I learn why.

Food.

Mixed with the requests, in broadcasts that Del and I had missed, were directions. Instructions to points on the map where caches of food had been secured. Neil and Grace and Krista had traversed most of the country, from Virginia to Montana, moving from supply point to supply point, guided to coordinates shared over the airwaves. Some that they reached had already been cleaned out by others following Eagle One's directions. Enough, though, had been untouched that they were well supplied for the journey.

"We are good people, Eagle One. Big Sky Alpha wants to come to you."

I did. I knew that. If for no other reason than to come to some understanding of just what Eagle One was. Why did it need medical supplies? How did it know about the caches of food, mostly MREs, buried in large metal lockers under precisely twelve inches of earth? Not eleven inches, or thirteen, Neil had told me—an exact foot. In lockers that were, as detailed by my friend, freshly painted a bright red both inside and out.

Colored just like the Red Signal that had announced the beginning of the end.

"Please, Eagle One, we—"

A terrible, shrill screeching cut Krista off, the electronic wail screaming from the radio's speakers, overpowering her transmission. The young girl almost fell backward in her chair, jolted by the sound. I hurried to the equipment, Neil with me as Grace pulled Krista away.

"Feedback?" Neil asked, the grating sound pitching higher by the second, almost painful.

"Must be," I said, nearly shouting.

Neil dialed the volume down until near silence filled the space, just fire in the hearth crackling low. Bar graphs on the radio's signal processor display were peaked, something within the device likely failing.

"It's like it's overloaded," I said, adjusting the controls without any luck, the signal readout still off the chart.

"Not our day for electronics," Neil commented.

"Is it broken?" Krista asked, worried.

"I don't know," I said, about to explain to her what I thought was happening when the signal graph went dead flat.

Neil looked to me, puzzled, then the signal processor began registering again, tiny spikes showing on the readout. Not anything like what we'd just witnessed. He reached to the volume and slowly increased it.

"Big Sky Alpha, we hear you."

It was the voice. That voice. Of a child. A boy.

"It's Eagle One!" Krista nearly shouted, ebullient at what had come from the speakers.

Her joy lasted but a few seconds.

"Big Sky Alpha, cease transmitting," the child on the radio instructed, some urgency clear in their tone. "Cease transmitting immed—"

The screeching returned in force, even louder, drowning the admonition from Eagle One and spiking the readout again. Krista slammed her hands over her ears as Neil reached toward the radio, ignoring the volume control this time for the power switch. He flipped it off and the radio went dark, a final, electronic hiss leaping from the speakers as it shut down.

"It's okay, sweetie," Grace said, hugging her daughter from behind. "It stopped."

Krista slowly slid her hands from her ears and looked to Neil, then to me, her gaze seeking answers.

"Why did Eagle One tell us to stop?"

"That sounded like a warning," Grace said, her gaze shifting between us, worry plain in it.

I couldn't disagree with her.

"Why don't we leave the radio off," Neil suggested. "For a few days at least. Okay?"

Dejected by the suggestion, and by the abruptness from Eagle One, Krista nonetheless nodded, accepting what she knew she could not change.

* * *

Three a.m.

The time glared at me in blue numbers on the travel alarm clock I kept on the coffee table, within arm's reach of where I lay on the couch. I had one more set of batteries for it, maybe three months of nightly use. After that, with my wristwatch broken while clearing snow from the solar panels, I'd be down to estimating the time of day, or night. Back to eighteenth century living. Or would it be seventeenth? I wasn't sure, but it was brutally clear that, bit by bit, the blight was stripping away the trappings of the modern world. Progress was creeping in reverse. Maybe the end would be the last few survivors huddled in a cave around a fire, taking turns scrawling messages on the surrounding stone to tell the story of their world, their life, their demise. Little different from lost civilizations that had come and gone before.

Still, we were here. For now. On the opposite side of the low table Neil slept fitfully on the cot we set up each night for him. Krista and Grace had taken over my bedroom, at my insistence, a week after they'd arrived. I'd healed enough by then, and even in the wake of the horrors the blighted world had dumped upon us, manners and hospitality mattered. At least in my home.

"Jeez," Neil muttered softly, rolling on the cot's slack surface. "Next time I'm in the neighborhood, I'm finding better accommodations."

I smiled in the still night.

"Make sure you fill out a comment card when you check out," I shot back, our exchange in near whispers reminiscent of children yakking in their bunks at summer camp when they should be sleeping.

The fire burned in the hearth, stoked by a trio of logs added before we turned in for the night. It cut the chill a little less each night, requiring another comforter this week. The electric blanket system that Del had showed me how to construct still worked in my bedroom, keeping Grace and Krista warm enough through the increasingly cold nights.

Warmth was a problem. Food would soon be a problem. We could only hope that neither would be concerns when, and if, we reached Eagle One.

"Beds," Neil said softly. "That's what I hope they have there. Real beds. If the only food at this Eagle One place is cat food, I'll be fine, as long as there's a real mattress to sleep on."

My friend wasn't sleeping. I wondered if the same thoughts might be churning in his head as were in mine. Or, was there something else keeping him awake besides the cot? Maybe someone.

"You know she cares about you," I said.

Neil was silent for a moment. The topic I'd introduced finding a nerve. A raw spot that he had thought was hidden from view.

"It's obvious," I told him.

The looks. The glances. Her gaze finding him in simple moments. I hadn't noticed it in their first days at my refuge, but as I healed and the fog of pain and medicine left me, the connection that existed between my friend and Grace was beyond denying—at least to me. They tried, Neil more than her. In our silly time earlier, with Krista playing games with me on the floor, I'd glimpsed Grace shifting her eyes toward him. And I'd seen Neil avoiding the same with purpose. A too obvious exhibition of aloofness, making its opposite almost certain.

"Look, I don't know what happened with you two on your way here, but—"

"You're right," Neil interrupted, his head angling toward me. "You don't know."

More defensiveness. More confirmation that I was right. In the past I might have taken his resistance as a signal to let it be. To back off. But the past was gone. The here, the now, was what mattered. Opportunities that presented themselves could not be ignored. Every positive had to be grabbed onto, and held dearly. Every chance at living. Every morsel of happiness. Every bit of hope, however small.

"I just don't want to see you miss a chance at something good," I told my friend.

It wasn't even like Grace was grieving over a husband lost to the blight. He'd walked out on her and Krista when the girl was still in diapers. That much I'd been able to draw out of her when probing gently about the time *before*. But, like Neil, she held close most of what had happened on their way to join me.

And that made me wonder all the more on what they'd experienced. What they'd lived through. What they might have *survived*.

"Get some sleep, Fletch."

That was the last he said to me that night, and I pressed the issue no further. But his reluctance to even engage in discussion about Grace, and their journey, made me realize that, in one way, Neil had changed. Especially toward me, his oldest and closest friend.

He was keeping secrets.

Three

Del's near ancient inverter was bolted to one wall in the closet next to his radio room. I removed it with no trouble and returned to the living room where I'd left Neil. He'd said he wanted to have a look around for anything we might have missed, anything more to scrounge, but when I came back into the room I found him standing there, in the center of the space, staring at the recliner Del had favored as the pain from his cancer had intensified. It was something shared with Dieter Moore, Neil's father.

As it turned out, it wasn't the only thing.

"Got it," I said.

Neil didn't respond. Didn't move. Didn't glance my way. He simply stood and stared at the recliner. As if looking back into a memory.

"I left work and took my father from the nursing home," Neil said. "Took him home. By the time the signal was blasting everywhere a week later, we were at my camp."

His 'camp'. Neil had never referred to his own small refuge as what it was—a farm. Located in rolling hills and sparse woods of western Virginia, the ten acres were not as isolated as my refuge, but far enough from the hustle and bustle of everyday life to give the illusion of seclusion.

"We rode it out there for three weeks. He was getting weaker. He was hurting. I'd managed to scrounge enough pain meds, but he hated those pills. He hated feeling foggy, disconnected."

Neil glance to me. I had to smile. Not at the situation, but at the memory of what a tough old man he had.

"So he just swallowed it," Neil told me. "He took the pain."

He looked back to the chair again.

"Just sat in his big old chair by the window and stared out at the trees. They still had color then. Something other than grey."

Neil nodded. To himself.

"But he knew. He knew it was coming. I'd told him all I knew, but I think he...I don't know...*sensed* how bad things were going to get. I thought we were pretty safe where we were, but he didn't. He kept telling me to get moving. To head out and hook up with you up here. But I wasn't going to leave him. And he knew that." Neil considered the simple fact he'd just stated for an instant, the words weighted with some undeniable emotional gravity. "He knew."

My friend, my oldest friend, quieted, a darkness welling up from within.

"He was in bad shape," Neil went on. "But he could have made it another month or two. Maybe longer. Then trouble from the cities started getting closer and closer to my camp. The town market was looted and six people were killed. That was less than two miles from my front gate. He told me again to leave him and get out while there was still a chance to get clear of the chaos. I said no. So he did what he thought he had to do."

I sensed what was coming. For an instant, I considered telling Neil he didn't have to give the recollection voice. That he didn't have to relive it.

But I said nothing. I simply listened, knowing my friend had to share what had happened to set him on his journey here. To let out at least this part of what he'd endured.

"I was out by the barn splitting wood," Neil said, a skim of tears upon his eyes. "And I heard it. From inside. A gunshot."

Del had walked headlong into danger, sacrificing himself to take out those who'd come to eliminate the both of us. He'd done that so that I might live. Dieter Moore had done the same for his son.

"I didn't even run when I heard the shot," Neil said, some faded judgment in his tone. "It had started to snow that morning, and I stood in it. I'm not even sure how long. Five minutes. Twenty. I don't know. I think I didn't want to see what I knew I would."

I reached out and put my hand on Neil's shoulder.

"When I finally went inside I found a note on the counter by the back door. It was a piece of paper folded over, and on the outside he'd written in big letters READ THIS FIRST. I'd never been one to disobey the old guy, so I did. Do you know what he wrote?"

Neil glanced back at me and I shook my head.

"Just one word," he said. "*Go.*"

Shit...

I was gutted by what Neil had just shared. Imagining what he'd felt, at that moment, was impossible. It was something only he could comprehend. His cross to bear.

"Go..."

He repeated the word, soft, like a whispered prayer. The wet sheen that had glistened over his gaze spilled over, quiet tears drizzling down his cheeks.

"That's why I'm here. Because my father put a gun his mouth and removed the only reason I had to stay put."

"He did know you wouldn't leave him," I said.

"Yeah, he did. And if I'd stayed, I would have never made it. All the hell spilling out of D.C. would have rolled over me."

He stopped right there. Said no more about that string of moments in his past. Maybe he'd let it out, finally, so that it was done, no need to ever speak of it again.

"Neil..."

"Yeah?" he said, dragging a sleeve across his face.

"I'm glad you made it."

He sniffed away the burst of emotion that had come and allowed a smile.

"I am, too."

Four

I stopped, Del's house a few hundred yards behind, the sky an almost painful, brilliant blue beyond the dead trees above.

"What is it?"

Neil's question was tinged with recognition. With understanding that something had made me stop. Some sense of mine had gone on alert.

"Listen," I said, and we both quieted.

For a moment there was nothing. And then the sound rose again. Soft at first, but so alien in a landscape that was drenched in nothingness that it stood out, stark and singular, a hint of familiarity to its rhythmic, distant thrumping.

"Does that sound like a..."

"Helicopter," I said, finishing Neil's almost incredulous suggestion.

It did sound like that. Precisely like that. How long had it been since any craft had been seen or heard in the air above? More than a year, in my case.

"Is that from the south?" Neil asked.

The mountains and valleys played tricks with sound, but I thought he might be right. I put the inverter down on a rock poking from the calf-high snow and swung my AR around, bringing it to bear. Ready.

"We should be able to tell from the hill across the gully," I said.

Neil nodded, and we left the trail between Del's house and mine, making our way down the gentle slope, shallow drifts crunching beneath our boots. The sound of the helicopter rose and fell as we moved quickly through the thin layer of snow, leaping the dry gully, last skim of water at its base finally frozen solid. Beyond it, the southern hill rose, steep and nearly bare, decimated woods once thick upon it mostly toppled, leaving a jumble of snapped, grey trunks and limbs for Neil and I to navigate. We rolled and crawled over the biggest, ducking under others which had come to rest at precarious angles, just a stiff wind, or a dump of snow enough to send them crashing to a final rest upon the equally dead earth. As we neared the crest of the hill, the sound of the helicopter grew louder still. We moved now from cover to cover, staying low as we ducked behind the few remaining pines still erect, dead sentinels at attention atop the hill. From behind one just below the crest we looked across the colorless valley.

Lumbering up it, just above the dead forest, was the source of the noise. A helicopter. And even at the distance it was from us I could see that it was all black.

"It's flying low and slow," Neil said. "He's looking for something."

I took out my compact binoculars and focused in on the aircraft. It was a vintage Huey, workhorse of the Vietnam War era, every inch of it the color of rich coal.

"Is this like the one you told me about?" Neil asked.

I'd told him the story of the video the Denver station had played soon after the world began spinning toward anarchy, footage captured by a driver trying to flee from the mile high city with his family, only to have their route of escape cut off by a sleek black Apache attack helicopter that fired upon the convoy of civilian automobiles.

"This is an old warbird," I told him. "And he's not carry—"

What I glimpsed through the binoculars ended the incorrect observation I was about to convey. The Huey turned sharply, pointing north up the valley, giving a momentarily clear glimpse of its front in silhouette, revealing the pods hanging from stubby pylons on either side of its fuselage.

"Miniguns," I said.

I'd seen enough war movies and military documentaries to be fairly certain that the multi-barreled weapons mounted to either side of the aircraft were modern versions of the venerable Gatling gun, capable of spitting thousands of rounds per minute at a target. Chewing it to pieces from a distance.

Neil swung his shotgun around from his back and held it at the ready, an instinctive move. Or a fatalistic one. Going down without a fight was not in either of our natures.

But there was no fight, and no one was going down. Yet.

"It's still heading north," Neil observed.

I nodded against the binoculars, lowering them and looking to my friend as he shifted his gaze to me, the both of us realizing at that instant just where the black helicopter was heading.

My refuge.

We began running together, down the slope, cutting across the tangled, snowy landscape at an angle, racing straight for my house. Straight for Grace and Krista. Concealment worried us no more as we vaulted obstacles. The limbs of one felled pine snagged my foot as I attempted a running leap over it, sending me tumbling. I rolled down the slope twenty yards before recovering. When I was moving again at speed I was half a football field behind Neil. He was just visible through the trees at the base of the hill beyond the gully, scrambling up the slippery slope. I pushed hard to catch up, yelling at him to wait, but he was driven. On some personal mission to get there. To put himself between the black helicopter and those who'd traveled with him to my refuge. Before something terrible happened.

Neither of us, it turned out, was swift enough to prevent that.

We both heard it, a buzzing louder than the throbbing helicopter rotors. A whine like a beastly saw, spinning and screaming. Neil hesitated at the sound, looking in its direction. I did the same, just making out the faint outline of the aircraft, hovering now beyond ranks of rotting woods, streams of fire spitting from its sides.

"NO!" Neil screamed, his cry audible even above the maelstrom of violence a few hundred yards to our east.

It was shooting at my refuge. At Grace and Krista. Nothing mattered, to either Neil or me, except stopping that. As if connected psychically, we both shifted direction, aiming ourselves now at the black helicopter, Neil weaving through the trees on the far side of the gulley, and me on my side. The bird continued to fire in bursts, adjusting its position, seeming to spray an area with flaming bits of deadly lead. Ahead of me by only a few yards now, Neil nonetheless came into view of the chopper first, the thing hanging in the air three hundred feet away, and maybe half that above the grey canopy. He stopped at the first opportunity and brought his shotgun up, snugging it to his shoulder and firing, seven loads of double ought buck spraying uselessly toward the helicopter. But then, he had no illusion of doing it damage. He simply wanted to draw its attention.

And that he did.

Pellets from his fire ricocheted off the old Huey's metal skin, enough to draw the crew's attention. The fire directed at my refuge ceased and the aircraft swung left, its nose dipping as it repositioned itself, closing the distance as Neil ducked behind a thick stump, all that was left of a once mighty fir, and fed fresh rounds into his Benelli.

I ran along the slope of the southern hill, the screen of bare trees enough, for the moment, to shield me from the helicopter's view. It skimmed the top of the dead woods, almost directly over me. My turn had come. My best chance. Maybe my only hope. *Our* only hope. I took aim with my AR and fired at the belly of the Huey, suppressed rounds peppering it. Without effect. It flew on, no different than a hawk might through a swarm of gnats.

Brr-brrrrrrrrrr-brrrrrrrrrr-

The helicopter opened up on Neil as it banked, clouds of snow and earth and rock tossed into the air from the twin streams of 7.62 mm rounds digging into the landscape by the hundreds. Trees splintered as the torrent of fire dragged across the slope, shards of dead wood raining down, the stump where Neil had sought cover erupting in a shower of flame and dust as the crew found their mark.

I ran toward my friend as the helicopter swooped low over him. It swung hard around beyond the crest of the hill and lined up for another strafing run. Neil took advantage of the brief lull and rolled down the slope, sliding to a stop behind a cluster of jagged boulders just above the icy flats of the gully. I took aim and fired off rounds, ten or fifteen, I wasn't sure, the volley having no more effect than my previous attempt to do some damage to the craft.

It did, however, draw attention to me, and the helicopter slipped left, its nose tipping toward me as the miniguns opened up again. The ground around me exploded into the air, throwing a cloud of debris in my path as I ran toward the boulders shielding Neil. He popped up from cover as I neared and fired at the helicopter, buckshot spraying into the air as the bird roared overhead, miniguns quieting, the black craft disappearing over the crest of the hill.

I stumbled forward, collapsing next to my friend. He grabbed me by the coat and pulled me fully into the cover the angular rock pile afforded.

"Are you okay?"

I nodded, checking myself. No minigun rounds had found me. The worst I'd suffered was a burn on my neck from a piece of hot brass raining from the sky as the helicopter passed over. I reached to the collar of the shirt beneath my jacket and pulled the still-warm 7.62 mm shell casing from where it lay against my skin, tossing the expended round aside.

The sound of the helicopter rumbled beyond the hill, echoing within the shallow valley, shifting, to the left, the right, behind and ahead of us. But never retreating. It was still out there. Maneuvering for another run at us.

"We've got to get to Grace and Krista," Neil said.

"Yeah," I agreed. "Which means getting past that thing."

The throbbing of the bird's rotor blades changed, seeming sharper now. Clearly just to the east, from the same direction we'd first seen it.

"He's coming back," I said.

Neil reloaded again. I fed a fresh magazine into my AR.

"We've got to hit something vital on it," Neil said.

There was no disputing that. But that miracle shot, from a either a shotgun or my AR, finding something mechanical or human, would also have to happen while twin Gatling guns were spitting death at us. And now, I was realizing, rather than having two targets to deal with, the helicopter had only one. Coming to my friend had been the natural thing to do, but it had also been tactically wrong in this situation.

Brrrrrrrrrrrrr-brrrrrrrrr-brrrrrr-

The sound of the miniguns firing reached us at nearly the same instant as the smack of impacts against the boulders jolted us. Bits of rock, large and small, leapt into the air and fell upon us. We ducked closer to the back of the massive boulder, as if trying to crawl inside it for some ultimate shelter.

Then the hunk of ancient granite split in half, the relentless stream of fire taking its toll. A sizable portion on the downslope side broke free and tumbled a few yards below, crashing into the frozen gully. Half our cover was instantly gone.

"We've got to do something!" Neil shouted.

The fire continued in short, measured bursts. Chipping away at the fractured boulder. Soon we'd have nothing to shield us.

"Okay!" I said. "Next break between bursts, we take our shots!"

Neil nodded and readied his Benelli.

Brrrrrrrrrrr-brrrrrrrrrrr-

I shouldered my AR. As I did, the oddest thought rose. Neil's pronouncement to me, more than a year old now, shared on the cusp of the old world descending into the terrible new—'*there's always hope*'. One of us *could* make the shot. Could hit something, or someone, that would bring this to an end. It could happen, I told myself. It was possible.

Neil and I looked to each other, waiting for a break between bursts that was long enough to take our shots from cover. To momentarily expose ourselves. To play upon the hope that our aim would be true.

The miniguns fell silent. A long pause. We reacted, Neil popping up from behind the boulder as I leaned right, clearing myself around the sheared-off edge. It was time. Our time.

But neither of us fired a shot. Past the sights of our weapons we saw the dark helicopter pitching backward, executing an ungainly turn to the east, its tail wagging back and forth like a stinger swatting about.

"What the hell..."

Neil's comment about summed up my feeling at the moment as we watched the helicopter struggle awkwardly away from our position, lurching right and left.

"He's out of control," Neil said.

Both of us rose slightly behind the shattered boulder, watching the helicopter shudder into the distance, disappearing over the trees, losing altitude, our last sense of it being any sort of airworthy craft ending as a low *boooom* rolled over us from a place beyond my refuge. It was down.

"Maybe we hit it," I suggested, though our early volleys had seemed ineffective at the time.

"Maybe," Neil said.

Then, in an instant, the surprise of the moment was gone, and Neil's gaze shifted, slanting up the hill. In the direction of my refuge. Where Grace and Krista were.

He scrambled from behind the boulder and ran up the hill, slinging the Benelli across his back. I ran with him, half sprinting, half clawing my way up the incline. Grabbing at deadfall for handholds. Pushing off bits of stone poking from the slope. It took us five minutes to cover the distance.

What we found sent our hearts falling.

"Grace!" Neil shouted, almost stumbling from the dead woods toward what had been my refuge. "Krista!"

I followed. Slowly. Scanning the clearing where my house had stood for any sign of the girl and her mother. All I saw, though, was a pyre.

My refuge was ablaze. The structure collapsed, shredded by the minigun fire. A dozen yards away, the front half of the barn had folded in on itself, smaller flames sprouted there. Just beyond it, the truck that Neil and the others had arrived in rested low on the snowy ground, front tires flattened, windshield blown out. The tough old vehicle's hood had been twisted upward and off of one hinge by the impact of rounds from the helicopter.

"Grace!" Neil shouted again into the terrible silence. "Krista!"

Fire crackled. Timbers snapped. The sounds of destruction rose before us. And, beyond that, a voice.

"We're here."

It was Grace. She appeared beyond the flames, emerging from the naked grey pines between my refuge and the road, Del's rifle in one hand, the other holding Krista close.

Neil bolted toward them. Grace let the rifle slip from her grip as he reached them. Krista ran toward me, launching herself into my arms.

"Are you okay, sweetie?"

She nodded against my shoulder, face buried against my neck. Her warm tears trickled onto my skin.

"Mommy heard a sound and said we had to get out of the house," Krista told me.

"Everything's gonna be fine," I assured her, rubbing her back as I looked toward my friend.

Neil reached Grace and pulled her close, holding her. She eased her arms around him, a flood of relief seeming to wash over her as they embraced. Truly embraced.

But the relief lasted but a moment. In an instant, as if realizing he'd crossed some line of propriety, Neil let go of Grace and pried himself from her, stepping back, a look of abject shame upon his face. Or was it apology? He looked at her for a moment, then turned, avoiding my gaze altogether as he looked off over the barren woods. Toward the spot where the helicopter must have gone down, a thin ribbon of smoke rising from that unseen spot.

Neil stormed away from the smoldering ruins. Away from Grace. From Krista. From me. He swung his shotgun around and aimed himself at the gauzy black marker wafting into the sky.

"Wait!" He didn't react at all to my call. "Neil!"

Where fear had driven him a short time before, rage now filled his veins. The desire to do harm to any who had tried to bring harm to Grace and Krista. Or to see, with his own eyes, that they'd already paid the ultimate price.

I put Krista down and took off after my friend, following him into the decaying woods, toppled pines and snapped limbs laying a colorless weave of obstacles in our path. Neil dodged the deadfall, and from my position of pursuit some twenty yards behind, I could see he was losing his bearings, tracking to the left, more north than where the marker of the downed craft indicated it was. I didn't follow. Instead I maintained a course that I knew should bring me to that point, moving as fast as I could through the organic debris and intermittent drifts of snow, pushing to get to the crash site ahead of my friend.

I could never have imagined what, and who, I would end up finding there.

Five

The crumpled fuselage of the Huey lay across the road beyond my property, tail wrenched off, its nose buried halfway into a snowdrift rising out of the drainage ditch along the two lanes of asphalt mostly hidden beneath winter white.

I emerged from the woods and leveled my AR at the wreckage. Smoke swirled through holes torn in the aircraft's metal structure. What had been the rotor blades where shattered and snapped, lengths of the slender metal strewn across the roadway for a distance in either direction. The craft that had tried to kill us, all of us, had come in hard. Snatched from the sky for some reason and discarded here.

Movement. I heard it without seeing its cause. It might have been a loose bit of metal swinging about within the fuselage. A bare wire sparking. Or, I knew, it could be a survivor.

I advanced slowly, suppressed end of my AR shifting as I directed the muzzle toward openings in the craft. Through the crushed side door I could just make out the back of a seat in the cockpit, on the right side, some figure still and slumped there. A few steps more took me past that opening and near the torn left front of the cockpit, metal and side window ripped away. I inched forward now, wary, tilting my head as I looked past the sight of my rifle and saw, finally, the maker of the sounds I was hearing.

"Are they alive?!"

It was Neil. He'd realized his directional error and come out of the woods just a bit north of the crash. I looked toward him just in time to see him bring his Benelli up as he moved fast toward me and the downed helicopter.

"Back off," I told Neil.

He kept coming.

"Neil!"

"Get out of my way, Fletch."

Calm fury. That's how his voice came across, his demeanor little different than it had been when I'd watched him execute the three men ready to feast on their fellow man near my refuge. He was determined then, as he was now. The only thing that stood between him and another execution was me.

I stepped in front of Neil as he reached the wreckage and pushed the muzzle of his shotgun aside, shoving him back, away from the still living crewman.

"We need information!" I shouted. "Not revenge! Not now!"

Neil didn't calm. But he gave in, backing up, seething in silence.

"Stay back," I said, and he looked away.

I turned back to the helicopter and approached the twisted cockpit. Smoke drifted from the fuselage just above and behind the man in the left seat, what I could make out of his body covered in jet black coveralls lacking any insignia whatsoever. The man moved his head. Steamy breaths bubbled from his mouth mixed with frothy blood. Factoids from documentaries dribbled into my consciousness—he was the co-pilot. Maybe some sort of weapons officer, responsible for the mini-guns. The dead man to his right, windshield before him spider-webbed and torn from its frame, was the pilot. At least that's what I recalled, that, converse to airplanes, the pilot in command in a helicopter sat in the right seat.

This man, I realized, was likely the one who'd pulled the trigger on us.

"Who are you?"

The man shifted his head in my direction, weight of the bulbous helmet atop it pulling his neck to the right. His gaze found me, one swollen eye and one uninjured. There was no overt visual plea for mercy. For help. In fact, what I thought I saw in both his eyes, and on his lips as they curled slightly, was disdain. Maybe pity.

"Why did you try to kill us?" I pressed.

The look upon his face now came plain and caustic. A sneer. An expression of unwavering derision directed at me. For all of us, I assumed.

"Who sent you?"

He chuckled now, breath and bluster wet with blood. I could feel Neil drawing close again behind, and I glanced over my shoulder. His Benelli was lowered, but his gaze was locked on the man beyond me. He stopped a few steps back and advanced no further.

I looked to the crewman again, raising my AR this time, putting the business end of the suppressor against the side of his helmet.

—"Your last chance to answer," I warned him. "Who sent you?"

Another chuckle slipped out, and the sneer turned to a grin, and then the words came.

Words I could not understand. A language I did not understand, but that I knew. That I recognized. As did Neil.

"Is that..."

I nodded, never looking away from the crewman as his gaze dimmed and his face went slack. The weight of his helmet pushed his chin against his chest as the life left him.

"What the hell is going on, Fletch?"

I brought my AR away from the dead man and turned to my friend.

"I don't know," I said.

All I did know was that we'd both heard the unmistakable. The accent. The soft inflection.

"That was French," Neil said.

He was right. And it made no damn sense at all.

Six

We made our way back to the ruins of my refuge. Grace and Krista stood close to a burning beam, soaking in the warmth, a small collection of items on the ground nearby.

"I salvaged what I could," Grace said, eyeing the neat pile.

A singed blanket. Two metal cups. A knife. Two boxes of 12 gauge shells. That was what remained of the place that had sheltered me. That had sheltered us.

Neil approached, standing closer to me than to Grace.

"Do you speak French?" I asked her.

Grace puzzled at the question for a moment.

"No. Why?"

Neil had taken Spanish in high school. I'd opted for German, entirely to be close to a girl who'd later turned me down when I'd mustered the courage to ask her out. Even if I had chosen to go the Francophile route, I doubted I would have retained enough to make a dent in deciphering the few words the crewman had uttered before drawing his last breath.

"It's nothing," Neil told her.

She wasn't buying that.

"Hey," Grace said, snugging the slung rifle on her shoulder. "You don't just ask that question now, after what happened, without some reason. I'm neck deep in this with the both of you."

She had a point. Neil knew that. I could tell. But, for some reason, he didn't offer the explanation that Grace sought.

"One of the crewmen was alive when we got there," I explained. "And he said something. Just before he died. But it was in French."

"French?" she parroted, puzzled.

I nodded.

"It was probably gibberish," Neil said. "He was on his way out."

I sensed little conviction in my friend's words. Or possibly it was a desire to move on from the subject. To keep as much of what we'd seen from Grace, as we had other things.

"A Quebecer, maybe," Grace suggested.

Some murderous mercenary from the French speaking province of our northern neighbor? Possible, I thought. But not likely.

"The accent was different," I said. "I know...I knew someone from Montreal. He was a guide I used on a few hunting trips up there. There's just a difference between someone from Quebec speaking and someone from France. He said as much. His joke was that Quebecers were redneck Parisians."

"Does it really matter?" Neil asked, a hint of agitation about him. "What if he spoke Afrikaner? Or Russian? Maybe German?"

I supposed it didn't matter. His mini-tirade, though, suggested otherwise. Still, knowing his secretiveness of late, pushing him for some explanation would be pointless. And, besides, there was another question to deal with. One that began to coalesce when I noted the rifle slung on Grace's shoulder.

"You grabbed Del's rifle on your way out?"

She nodded at my question. I recalled the right side of the Huey's windshield. Cracked and spider-webbed, those radial fissures emanating from a pair of distinct round holes. Penetrations made by one thing—bullets.

"You shot it down," I said, smoke from the remains of my house drifting past us.

Neil reacted to my assertion, vaguely incredulous. Until he saw that Grace was not scoffing at the notion.

"I shot at it," she told me.

"Two shots," I specified. "Perfectly placed."

"Three," Grace corrected. "The last one missed. It turned away from us and was shooting at something else."

"That was us," Neil said.

"I know," she said. "I found a clearing just down the hill and did what I had to."

I stared at her. Krista stared at her. Neil look, a moment ago flavored with doubt, now bubbled with some surprise, bust mostly admiration.

"My father taught me when I was a kid. When I was Krista's age. Rabbits mostly. A couple deer when I was a teenager."

Krista looked up, processing the morsel of the past her mother had just shared.

"Will you teach me to shoot, mommy?"

Grace looked to her child, her joy, and nodded, a subtle sadness in the gesture. As if she knew that, were the world to remain as it was, and if they, if *we* were to survive, her sweet, precious daughter would not be shooting at rabbits in due course. She would be firing upon predators. The most dangerous kind.

And that's when I understood, more than I did a moment before, when I'd doubted within that she'd acquired her degree of marksmanship from dropping bunnies. Crossing the country, maybe before she and Neil had met up, she'd held her own, because that was what she had to do. For herself, and for her child.

"I imagine you had more practice in the past year," I said.

Grace nodded.

"How did you get out?" Neil asked, the churn of emotions that had been working on him, seeming settled now.

"I heard the helicopter coming," Grace said. "And the first thing I thought of was that sound on the radio, and the warning."

Neil looked to me and nodded.

"They zeroed in on the transmission," he said.

"That feedback could have been jamming," I said.

"Jamming?" Grace asked. "Who would do that?"

"It was Eagle One," Krista said, every adult around her considering what she was suggesting. "They knew. They tried to stop us from using the radio because that would lead the bad people to us. They warned us."

How the hell a kid on the radio could know some black helicopter was coming for us was beyond me, but I couldn't find any flaw in what the child was proposing.

"Why?" I asked. "Who are we threatening?"

That was a question whose answer none of us could yet conceive.

"Someone's willing to kill to keep people from getting to Eagle One," Neil said, looking to Grace. "I'd say that makes it a place we should find. Don't you?"

She hesitated, though not as long as she might have a few hours ago. Finally, Grace nodded.

"We have to get there," she said.

But there was a more pressing move to make.

"We have to get away from here," I said. "Fast."

"Why?" Grace asked, curious and concerned.

Neil thought for just a moment on what I'd said, his gaze registering recognition of the facts quickly.

"Because they weren't coming after us on their own," he said. "Someone's going to come looking when that helicopter doesn't return."

"They might be already," I added. "If they put out a mayday..."

Grace drew a long breath and looked to the remnants of the truck, an unpleasant realization rising.

"We're going to have to go on foot," she said, then glanced to the hodgepodge of materials she had pulled from the ruins of my house. "This isn't much to get us anywhere."

She was right. The situation seemed dire. But that wasn't necessarily so.

Seven

Neil and I found a pair of shovels at the back of the barn, partially buried beneath the half collapsed structure. Tools hidden by circumstance.

Two hundred yards from the smoking rubble of my refuge, we dug for things hidden by design.

"We need to put some miles between us and this place before dark," Neil said as he stabbed the spear-like end of the shovel again and again into the cold, hard earth. "But which way?"

We knew we were going to try and make it to Eagle One, which meant, first, *finding* Eagle One. With the scant information we had to guide us, a vaguely certain directive to head west, our journey, beginning far sooner than the springtime launch we'd anticipated, would have to be refined as we made progress. But there was no way we could make a headlong rush due west. Mountains, and the building winter accumulation of snow sure to materialize, made that not only inadvisable, but suicidal.

"South," I told my friend, scooping and scraping dirt from the hole I was digging, some three yards from his. "Down to Kalispell, past Flathead Lake, and onto Missoula before turning west."

"Interstate Ninety?" Neil asked, uncertainty and resignation in his words. "I guess that's the best play we have. But even the interstate won't have been maintained. It's been over a year. No repairs, no plowing."

"Life's tough," I said, smiling and savoring the mirrored expression my friend gave back.

"Be tougher," he said, our high school football coach's wise words truer now than they'd ever been.

Cthunk...

The solid jab of metal against something hard signaled that Neil had hit pay dirt first. A few jabs into the earth later I received the same satisfying sound from the hole before me.

We dropped to our knees and began clearing the chunky soil from what we'd hit, revealing the hard black plastic lids of barrels I'd buried within the first weeks after arriving at my refuge.

"Give me a hand," I said, and Neil joined me at the hole I'd cleared, grabbing at the handles molded into the container's top.

"Jeez," he grunted, struggling with the heft of the fifty-five gallon container. "Did you bury lead in here?"

"Some," I said.

More than some, actually, if one considered the business end of a couple thousand rounds of pistol and rifle ammo to be 'lead'. Added to that I'd secreted away several small weapons, clothing, food for a month, and various other survival items that would allow me to bug out of my bug out location should it be compromised. Being shot to pieces by some makeshift helicopter gunship qualified as that, I imagined.

It took us thirty minutes to open and remove the contents of the caches I'd buried. We sorted through the items, prioritizing and choosing only those things that would allow us to make a go at getting far away from our present location. What we'd selected we shoved into two backpacks I'd cached, leaving what wouldn't fit slung in the sagging hollow of a blanket we held between us as we returned to my rubbled house.

"I found a few more things," Grace said as we approached and put what we'd retrieved on the ground. "Krista's backpack was still in the truck, behind the front seat."

She held the small pink pack in hand. Neil smiled and took it, crouching and holding it out to Krista.

"We're going to need you to carry some stuff," he said, firm and, yes, fatherly.

"I know," Krista said. "I can do it."

Neil handed her the pack and stood, facing me and Grace again.

"Let's load up."

I nodded at my friend. It was time. Time to burden our shoulders with what would carry us away from this place. From my refuge. My home.

Twice now since the world spun down toward chaos I'd left the place where I'd built a life. First from Missoula. Now from here. I would walk away, certain to never return. It was like shedding a skin. An outer layer of 'me' that I'd come to know. That I'd grown comfortable in.

Now, as we loaded the packs and readied ourselves for the journey, I wondered for a moment who the next 'me' would be. In my old life when the world was green and whole, I'd been the solid citizen, working hard, paying taxes, enjoying the fruits of my labor. When that world disintegrated, I became what I had to, a survivor. A hardened believer in the hope that would carry me through the most difficult times. And now...

Now I was going to face the new world in a way I never had, with no safe haven to fall back upon. With no knowledge of what existed beyond the horizon. I was about to be a toddler again, stumbling through the unfamiliar, grasping for holds wherever possible to keep from falling.

"You ready, Fletch?"

But I would not be alone. That, too, was different. And it was good.

"I'm ready," I told Neil, and shouldered my pack.

"Does that feel alright, sweetie?" Grace asked her daughter.

Krista shifted the straps of the small pink backpack and gave a solid nod.

"Okay," Grace said, the word almost a breath, like some necessity acknowledged with dread reluctance.

It was my place to lead us away. I knew the most promising route to take through the landscape skimmed with winter white. But for a moment I hesitated, staring at the ground a few yards ahead, in the direction we would soon be traveling.

"You okay, Fletch?"

I wasn't. Neil knew that. The question he posed was almost rhetorical. None of us were 'okay' in any sense that was once normal. But it was not some emotional malady that help me in place right then—it was the pull of an unwanted gesture. The desire to look behind. Back to what remained of the home I'd made after leaving my real home. I felt the tug. My head wanted to turn. But I did not let it.

"Let's go," I said, and began walking.

Grace and Krista followed, Neil close behind them. I heard their boots and shoes crunch lightly through the veneer of early snow. That's how I knew they were there. Because I never looked, not even once, back as we made our way through the dead woods.

We were on our way to Eagle One.

Part Two

The Lie

Eight

We skirted the highway after setting out, a broken ceiling of clouds above. Winter's bite reached down from them, chilling us as we pressed southward. The afternoon hung frigid, sun still low, south wind at our faces, the cold blow rolling north from the Flathead.

"How far is it?" Krista asked, bundled against the elements, small pink backpack jostling between her shoulders with each step. "To this Kalispell place?"

We'd decided to shoot for the next spot on the map past Whitefish to spend the night before pressing on. To go further would mean taxing ourselves beyond what was prudent.

"Probably ten miles," I told her. "Maybe a little more."

She considered the answer for a moment, then nodded to herself.

"I can do that," she assured me.

Every few hundred yards we'd pause for a minute or so in whatever cover we could find, letting the space around us still as we listened, for any distant chop of rotor blades cutting through the air. For the sound of engines. Gunshots. Voices. Anything that might signal hostility.

In this new world, just about anything held that potential.

Krista never complained. She kept the gentle pace we'd set, Neil and I carrying most of the load in two full backpacks. Grace had crafted a large sling that held a portion of the food and extra clothes on her left, Del's rifle held in her right. She seemed on edge. Vigilant. As a stranger was in wild lands.

"Christ..."

Neil's exclamation stopped us as we crested a low hill. It was a spot I remembered. If I'd wanted to, I was certain I could search the surrounding area and find the handheld radio I'd discarded in the spot just months ago. With it I'd triggered the explosion that turned the tank car I'd sent down into Whitefish into a tool of destruction. A rolling bomb that flattened most of the town, burning it and everyone in it to a cinder, and allowing me to bring a deserving end to Major James Layton.

"I had no idea," Neil said.

Neil had guided Grace and Krista to my refuge from the north after a short detour through Canada. This was his first time laying eyes on the devastation I'd caused.

I, too, was seeing it with somewhat fresh eyes. At that moment, when I'd pressed the button on the makeshift detonator, I'd been in the grip of a desire for vengeance against the man who'd turned the once picturesque town into an armed camp. His own dictatorial fiefdom. My friend Del had given his life to protect me from Layton's thugs. The charred hell a mile distant was how I'd satisfied my bloodlust.

To my right I could feel Grace looking at me, sideways. Maybe wary. Afraid to take in the sight of me directly. I'd wanted to kill every living soul in Whitefish. I might have succeeded. In relative terms, my body count was likely higher than Layton's. He was Genghis Khan. I was the black death.

"Did anyone get out?" Grace asked.

I didn't look at her to answer.

"I don't know."

I started off again, moving down the hill, keeping to a snowy trail that kept us clear of the burned out burg. The others followed, but Grace hung back, further now than when we'd set out. She might have just been tiring, but I doubted that. The brutality she'd not thought me capable of, perhaps, was haunting her. Creating an aversion to my presence. Until little more than a month ago I'd been a stranger to her. I'd told her and Neil about what I'd done, but now it was real to her. I was a killer.

Except for the child, we all were.

* * *

We made it two miles past Whitefish. That was when we heard it.

Boooooooooom.

The sound was low and thick. Like some distant firework exploding. It rolled in from the south, maybe the southwest, passing over us and dissipating in the hills and mountains behind. The sensation of it clung to us, though, like some auditory stench, dark and ominous. It was no feat of nature. What we'd heard was made by the hand of man.

"Was that thunder?" Krista asked, squinting at the harsh, flat light bleeding through the grey sky.

"I don't think so," Grace told her daughter.

"That's the way we're heading," Neil said.

"Probably."

I couldn't fully agree. The hills, the terrain, they could play with sound. Bouncing it. Twisting it. But my friend was almost certainly not wrong. Something was out there, in our path.

We moved to cover and stopped, listening, for minutes that seemed like hours.

"What do you think?" Neil asked.

The quiet vexed any answer. Nothing had followed the blast. Not a sound.

"I think someone's out there," I said.

The words weren't comforting. Grace eased Krista away and helped her out of her backpack, rubbing the child's shoulders through the thick coat she wore.

"We've got maybe two hours of daylight," I said, focusing on what I thought was the brightest part of the grey sky. "I think we stop for the night. Keep our ears open. Then move again in the morning."

Neil considered the suggestion, nodding his agreement.

"Let's set camp in that gulley."

Neil pointed to a low spot beyond the leading edge of the once green woods. It would be cold in the depression, but the terrain would shield us from view and allow a fire.

"Okay."

He went to tell Grace and Krista, then led them to the spot we'd chosen. I held my position, in sight of the road, its surface blanketed with snow. From the vantage point I had I could see the pristine dusting covering the two lanes of asphalt. There was not a footprint to be seen. Not a tire track. Not a mark at all. Nothing, no one, had traveled the road in weeks. That should mean that we were alone.

But we weren't.

Nine

Neil glanced toward Grace. She sat away from us, Krista pulled close next to her, a shared, thick blanket around their shoulders. She held a book between them, her daughter's attention fixed on it, reading by headlamp, some effort at learning that was both hopeful and heartbreaking. It implied that some future where knowledge still mattered might exist, the uncertainty of that adding bitter to the sweet.

"She's tough," Neil said.

I laid a final two pieces of wood on the pile I'd arranged for a fire. The night would be cold, but manageable.

"You wouldn't think it to look at that," he said.

"She shot down a helicopter," I responded. "I believe it."

He looked away from mother and child, to me, smiling lightly.

"Damn smart, too," Neil told me, a true admiration in his words. "Do you know you don't have to boil water to make it safe? I mean, if you're not sure of the source."

I shook my head. I'd always thought a rolling boil was what killed the nasty pathogens that might lurk in water taken from places such as back country streams.

"You just need to get it to one hundred and fifty degrees for a few minutes," Neil explained. "Like pasteurizing milk. That's how Grace explained it."

"I'll stick to a full boil," I said.

"Suit yourself. But we had to purify water on our way to your place plenty of times. She had this thermometer she carried and she'd stick it in the water over the fire, like taking its temperature. It was..."

He stopped, beaming. The smile full and true. Somehow, the memory, that simple recollection of their time together, seemed on the verge of overwhelming him. Of taking him to an emotional place he could not visit. Or would not.

He looked off, to the dimming sky above the trees, and drew a long breath. Then another. Before he could stop himself he was smiling again.

"I thought we'd die before we ever got to you," Neil said, chuckling softly at himself. "I mean, I thought—no plants, no oxygen to breathe. We'd all just suffocate from the carbon dioxide without photosynthesis happening, right?"

I took a breath. The fear he was expressing had never crossed my mind. I wondered if it should have.

"Grace went into this long description of the carbon cycle, and how there was less carbon dioxide being produced because everything that did was dying from lack of food, and how the ocean interacts with the atmosphere, and, well, it was all above my pay grade."

"Mine, too," I agreed.

He looked to her again, openly, if quietly, marveling at the woman who sat on a felled tree twenty yards away. I wanted to say something to him again. About her. About the possibility of *them*. But I didn't. I'd gone down that conversational road with my friend already and was assured then that it was a dead end. I did not believe that for a minute, but I had to respect him. He had his reasons.

"You want the last bit?" I asked, holding the package of MRE crackers out to Neil.

He shook his head without looking away from Grace and Krista. I'd made us a passable dinner from a mix of

Meals Ready To Eat. Krista hadn't loved the Stroganoff, but devoured the brownie that came after. And the one that came after that, courtesy of Neil surrendering his.

"It's not right," Neil said, still smiling at mother and child. "What is life going to be like for Krista? What is she going to face?"

I noted that he didn't say 'fair'. 'Right' was another term altogether. Life was never fair, but the possibility of having a decent life, through work and perseverance, was always there. Or it had been. Now, for Krista, for any other children who might have survived, that hill to climb was steep beyond imagination. And the concept of a decent life to be had was now so degraded that mere subsistence was a matter for celebration. Goals and dreams were diluted down to the most basic hope—to live.

There's always hope...

Neil's words from before the world fell apart bubbled up in my thoughts again. But there had to be more than just surviving. There had to be the ability to really *live*, to *thrive*. If there wasn't...

Neil stood from where we sat by the fire and looked to me, a sullen determination about him. Like he was about to cross a river that was too deep, with no chance of ever reaching the far shore.

"I'm going to go sit with them for a while."

I nodded and watched my friend join those he'd crossed the country with. Krista snuggled up to him as he sat next to her. He took one side of the book in hand, Grace still holding the other as the girl read to the both of them.

I didn't know what kind of life Krista would face in the time ahead. But I did know, I was certain, it would be better if Neil was a part of it.

* * *

I woke, the cold night heavy above, its darkness flecked through parted clouds with the light of distant stars, countless of their number certainly dead. The twinkles they offered were just ghostly echoes of what they'd once been, nothing more now than a celestial tease that spun across the heavens above.

Something had pulled me from sleep. Not some sound. Not the soft crackle of the low fire. No gust of wind. No crack of a withered tree limb snapping from its wasting host. Instead it was a feeling. That sensation of presence.

My gaze tracked over the space around me and immediately found the origin of the silent, subtle disturbance.

Grace stood over Neil and Krista. Gazing down upon them. Her daughter was curled up against my friend, his body shielding her from the bitter chill. He'd shifted the sleeping bag meant for him over her, doubling her protection from the elements.

I eased up to a sit, the motion drawing Grace's attention. She turned to me. Her expression, verging on melancholy, hurt to look upon. It was as though she'd just witnessed some loss, not the tender moment that I saw it as.

Saying nothing, she turned and walked away from the fire. Away from our campsite. Into the darkness filling the dead woods.

I slipped out of the blanket I'd wrapped around my upper half and stood, making my way quietly past Neil and Krista. Past the fire. Into the dark cluster of barren trees surrounding us. A few dozen yards into the once lush forest, where the trees thinned and the land opened to a rolling grey plain, I found her. She stood at the edge of the vast clearing, arms pulled tight across her chest, collar of her coat rolled against her neck, the knit cap above stretched over her ears. In the thin drizzle of moonlight I could see her breath, slow puffs of misty white rolling out, dissipating in the night. All about her seemed both lost and content, an impossible mix, the weight of it evident as she stared out, contemplating the landscape before her.

"Are you all right?"

She glanced back to me, offering no answer one way or the other, then looked again to the fields stretching south.

"He doesn't want you to know," Grace said.

I could have prompted her to explain, but I sensed that was coming, regardless of any desire on my part to know. Perhaps the uneasiness between them, his stumbling and fumbling when physically close to her, followed by interludes of calm togetherness, had reached a tipping point, its reasons no longer containable, the first bits of revelation about to spill.

"We were in a town outside of Memphis," she began, seeming to pause for a moment as that time, and whatever events had charged it, came flooding back. "It was just me and Krista then. Two months and two days after it all started. We lived in Birmingham, Alabama, but we had to get out. The city was falling apart. The police just gave up, there was shooting everywhere. I had to get Krista someplace safe. So we headed west."

"Eagle One?"

She shook her head.

"We didn't learn about that until later. I just figured that getting to somewhere in the middle of the country would be safer. I don't know why I thought that, but I did, and I made the decision to leave."

"It had to be difficult with just the two of you," I said.

"What's that saying? You don't know how strong you are until you have to be?" She quieted then for a moment. "Until you have to be."

She seemed unable to go on. I took a step closer and stood next to her.

"You don't have to do this," I told her.

For a moment she considered that. Then she nodded and did go on.

"We'd avoided cities," Grace said. "But Krista was sick. She had a fever, her head was hurting. I thought it was an ear infection, and I thought it would go away. I prayed it would go away. But it didn't. The fever wouldn't break. She kept getting worse. I had to do something."

I understood. From my own experience.

"You went into the city for medicine."

She nodded at my informed guess.

"Antibiotics," Grace specified. "It wasn't safe, or it might not be safe. By that time, there were a lot of dead, but the ones who'd hung on they...they weren't all like you."

She hesitated there, and I couldn't tell if she was searching for some detail that eluded her, or for the will to even dredge rest from memory.

"We moved through back yards, alleys," Grace described. "I was carrying Krista. She was weak, sleeping and waking. The fever was...I was afraid it was killing her. But finally we reached a neighborhood just off some boulevard. I could see a pharmacy mixed in among the dry cleaners and bars. That was where I had to go. But it was out in the open, and in the distance every few minutes there would be a burst of gunfire. I couldn't expose Krista to that. I couldn't put her at risk."

"What did you do?"

"The hardest thing I'd ever done," Grace told me, then realized that wasn't quite accurate. "The hardest thing I'd done to that point."

She looked out to the darkened clearing again. Stared off at a place, a time, that wasn't here. Wasn't now.

"I left her," Grace said. "In a house close to the boulevard. It was empty, trashed, but I fixed a bed for her and covered her. She started to wake a little, and I told her I'd be right back. That's when she got scared, and begged me not to leave her. She begged me."

Grace turned to face me again. The pain of that moment, long ago when measured by time, but not by memory, flared in her gaze.

"But I had to," Grace said, hurting. "I made her promise to stay right where she was, and then I left. I had this old revolver that my father had insisted I keep when I went away to college. It was this stubby little thing. That was all the protection I had, just some pea shooter shoved in my back pocket. I didn't even take it out when I started across the boulevard. I didn't want to even imagine that I'd need it."

I tensed where I stood, beginning to fear where this was leading.

"I wasn't five steps inside the pharmacy when they grabbed me."

'*No,*' was all I could think, and I said nothing aloud. I need only listen to her. That was what she wanted.

"There were three of them..."

In that instant a memory flashed. Some deeper part of my consciousness making connections between places and people and events. It was an image of Neil. Images, really. Shuttering in my mind like some staccato montage as he walked from the old mining shed and executed the cannibals we'd come across near my refuge. Then, that moment was gone, and I was listening to Grace once more.

"...and they pulled me to the back of the pharmacy. Dragged me over toppled shelves and broken bottles. I tried to get to my gun, but one of them found it before I could. Then they...they pinned me to the floor and one of them took out a knife."

Her gaze ticked off of me, just a few inches, so that she wasn't looking me in the eye.

"They started to laugh, and the one with the knife, he put the blade to my neck and told me to go ahead and scream, because it was more fun that way."

She looked back to me again. It hurt to meet her gaze. To know, to imagine what she'd gone through in that place.

"But I wouldn't scream. I couldn't. If I did, and Krista heard me, she'd come. She'd try to find me, and that would mean she'd find them."

She took a breath, and I could see that the visuals, the sensations of that moment, were flooding back to her. Her back straightened. The tip of her chin rose. A muted defiance swelled within.

"Then the one with the knife grabbed my shirt and ripped it open."

I could only think again, *'No'*.

"And he slipped the blade between my skin and my bra," Grace said, as dispassionately as one could. "I knew what was coming. I felt that steel against my skin. That was when his head exploded."

I'm certain my reaction was a visible *'What?'*

"Blood, everything sprayed all over me. All over everything. He fell over me and I screamed. Then there were two more shots. They were loud, and they were close. The other two, they both flopped backward. I got a quick look at one—his whole chest was opened up. Everything inside was pouring out. I shoved the one with the knife off of me and scooted away until my back was against the counter. That's when I saw Neil."

The tension, the fear, the pain of the previous moments withered as she spoke his name. She smiled, soft and true.

"He was standing there with his shotgun. The barrel was still smoking. He stepped over the bodies toward me and reached his hand out. I took it. I can still feel how wonderful and strong and reassuring his touch was."

"He saved you," I said, stating the obvious.

"He did. I told him I had to get back to my daughter, but he said I couldn't see her the way I looked. He helped me clean up and gave me a shirt from his backpack. I tried to find the medicine I'd come for, but I was too shaky, so he dug through every box and bottle in the place to find the amoxicillin I needed. Then he walked me back to the house where I'd Krista, and he stayed. Just sat in the front room while I gave her the medicine and cooled her down. He said he'd make sure nothing bad would happen to us."

"He's a good guy," I said. "Best guy I know."

She nodded complete agreement with my appraisal.

"For three days he stayed," Grace said. "Just sat in that front room watching over us. He gave us food that he had. Anything we needed, he saw to it. When it was time to move again, he asked if we'd like him to come along. That was about two seconds before I was going to ask him the same thing."

How such a horrific tale could, at that moment, come to a point where the purest joy warmed Grace's face was beyond my ability to comprehend. But it did. Her next words confirmed why that was.

"I love him. I think he loves me, too."

"I more than think he does," I said. "You and Krista."

She, too, knew there was a certainty to his feelings toward her. But voicing that, making it real through statement, might be too big a step for her to take. Admitting it, implying a hope that it might become real, would put her in a place of vulnerability. A place of expectation, with no assurance of satisfaction. In the purest, simplest sense, she wanted a happy ending. Such a thing could exist in this new world. I believed that. I believed that for them, and I wished it would come to be.

"He won't cross that line from platonic," Grace said. "After seeing what those men tried to do to me, I think he just can't find a way to let himself get close. I think he sees that as some boundary he shouldn't cross. It's like he feels stained by what *they* did."

"Guilt by gender?"

She nodded at my suggestion. It was precisely what she'd been sensing from Neil.

"I know he just needs time," she said. "But I'm worried. The longer we're together without being together, it's tearing at him. Inside. I can see it."

"I can, too."

She smiled and looked to me and reached out her hand. I took it in mine and felt her squeeze it tightly, a gesture of thanks. For listening. For being there. For being a friend. All three, I suspected.

"If—"

Only that word slipped past her lips before a flash in the southern sky drew our attention. We looked up and watched a bright object carve a hot white streak across the heavens, a trail of fire briefly flourishing behind it before fading to nothing against the black tapestry of the universe.

"A shooting star," Grace said, choosing the colloquial over the correct.

It was a meteor. Nothing more. Just a fist-size rock plummeting through the atmosphere and burning up.

"Wow," Grace exclaimed softly.

I smiled. It was such an ordinary moment in a darkly extraordinary time. But it was also proof that there was a constant. Rocks still fell from above. And people could, if they wanted, still rise to meet what challenged them. To cross divides that existed between them.

"He'll see the light," I said to Grace.

She nodded, still looking to the sparkling night above. There was hope in the gesture. No more, no less. That was fine by me. The belief that good, that right, would triumph had sustained me this far. It had carried us all to this place and time. Neil would see that, in Grace, there was a future full of that goodness. He would. He had to.

We stood for a few moments and waited for more stars to fall.

Ten

We woke early and moved south, keeping our distance when we reached Kalispell, staying on the fringes of the town, peering into it from places of cover. Behind old buildings collapsed by the previous winter's snow. From an overturned bus on its side across the highway. Through binoculars we glassed the avenues reaching into the city. We scanned buildings. Homes. Abandoned cars.

No sign of life presented itself. No hint of what had caused the explosion we'd heard.

"It looks clear," Neil said.

I could have nodded, but I didn't. A scant few months ago, Major James Layton had held Whitefish in his grip. Word was that Kalispell was similarly under his thumb. It was possible that that had simply been a lie. A rumor. Or it might have held true until Layton had met his fate in the inferno I'd unleashed upon the whole of Whitefish. His people here might have scattered. They might lie dead in town, starved out, any supplies that Layton had promised never to come.

"It probably is," I said.

"If we could get a car running," Neil suggested. "Better yet a truck."

Hoofing it through the mountains to the west was not going to be easy. Getting some wheels under us would definitely be worth the effort of trying to get one of the heaps actually moving, if possible. But to have any chance at that being worthwhile, it would have to happen soon.

The day at hand was mostly clear, but winter, which had laid a thin layer of white upon the landscape so far, would soon arrive in force, making travel that was already difficult all the more so. Even deadly.

"Anything that moves," I agreed, knowing we had to get transport.

We emerged from cover and moved in a staggered line, Grace and Krista at the rear, Kalispell drawing closer with each step. When we reached the city and walked its streets we knew, we could sense, that we had entered a ghost town.

"It's so quiet," Krista said.

It was. There was the expected hush of a breeze flowing between the buildings, and the crackle of small stones and broken glass beneath our feet. The torn awning above a storefront flapped gently like an afterthought. All the things that once had filled the place with noise, with activity, with real life, were long gone. If there were survivors in Kalispell, they'd burrowed themselves away somewhere, either trying to live, or waiting to die.

"There's less to choose from than I'd hoped," Neil said.

A few cars were parked at curbs, or half pulled into driveways, but not a single truck of any size was visible. That told me one thing in particular—any men who'd been loyal to Layton, if they ever were here, had gone, taking with them the modified pickups his cadre of followers had preferred in Whitefish. Seeing no vehicle with a machinegun mounted above its cab was a relief. Not finding any unarmed sibling of one was not.

"We're going to have to make the best of the pickings," I said.

"Nothing out here's going to be roadworthy," Neil commented.

One look at any of the cars we could see confirmed that. Tires were flat. Windows were broken out to the weather, snow mounded on exposed seats within. If any actually had gas in the tank, and if, by some miracle, that fuel was uncontaminated by moisture and hadn't deteriorated, the batteries necessary to crank the engine would be dead and drained by now. We had to find a car that had been somewhat protected from the elements.

I stopped at the intersection with a residential street and looked right. Neil looked left.

"Grace," I said, "You and Krista go with Neil."

Before Grace could get half a nod out, her daughter looked sharply up at her and grabbed my free hand.

"I want to go with Fletch!"

I should have looked to Grace for approval. Instead, my gaze shifted to Neil, sensing his level of comfort with the idea of being with Grace. Alone.

"We'll check it out down that way," Neil said, turning to Grace.

She nodded, then looked to her daughter.

"Stay with Eric," Grace said, preferring, as she had since first meeting me, the formal over the nick Neil had branded me with in our youth. "Okay?"

"I will," Krista assured her mother, then looked up at, determined. "Come on. Let's go!"

"I've been drafted," I said, and followed the tug on my hand.

When we were halfway down the block I glanced back. Grace and Neil were walking in the opposite direction. Next to each other, but clear daylight between them.

* * *

I stopped in front of a small house, the blue paint that had once trimmed its porch beginning to peel. Not as fast as others we'd passed. This house, this home, had been tended to until the very end.

"Why'd you stop?" Krista asked.

Why, indeed?

It was the look of the place. The imagined qualities that it had once displayed to the world. Qualities that reminded me of someone.

"My grandmother's house looked like this," I said. "Well, what this must have looked like before."

The little girl studied the house from our place just off the sidewalk, admiring the simple home. Gardens that had once flourished near the porch now lay bare, layered with patchy snow, not even the dried stem of a rose left. All had gone to dust.

"I think we should look here," I said, and Krista puzzled at me.

"There's no car here," she said, pointing to the house on its narrow lot. "There's not even a garage."

"I'll bet you the next candy bar we come across that there is a garage," I said. "You just can't see it yet."

She doubted me with a look.

"Come on," I said, and led her up the snow-covered walkway.

The porch boards uttered not a sound as we stepped upon them. No creak, no groan. Sheltered by the overhanging roof, the approach to the front door was solid, its surface still hinting at the varnish regularly applied, until events interceded. The front windows were unbroken, curtains pulled beyond glass. Most houses on the street seemed unmolested by forced intrusion. Somehow, those who'd lived here through the most chaotic of times, had managed to avoid wholesale destruction. Other than some refuse scattered about the street and yards, tossed about by recurring gusts, it almost appeared that the inhabitants of this particular block had up and left, as if departed for some group vacation.

Out of some ingrained habit, and harboring only the faintest possibility that it might be answered, I knocked on the door.

"Hello?"

No response came to my rapping or my greeting. I took the doorknob in hand and twisted it, expecting it to jiggle against the lock that surely secured it. I was wrong. The small round of brass turned fully and the latch clicked, the door it might have secured popping inward a few inches as if was released.

A burst of stale air washed out past us. The home had been sealed up for months. Maybe a year or more. I let my hand rest atop my holstered pistol and pushed the door open fully.

What we saw seemed already like some sort of time capsule. We waded into a slice of the past preserved, revealed to us now, living room immaculately clean and ordered. No furniture was upended. Framed pictures still hung on the wall. Grandchildren gathered around a beaming older woman.

I instinctively closed the door behind us, partly out of politeness, but mostly, I knew, because I realized that once we were gone, what we stood in the midst of should be allowed to last as long as possible. To leave it open to early demise from the elements was unnecessary. Someone had cared for this place.

And maybe for more.

"Stay right here," I said to Krista.

She followed my directive as I moved quickly through the house, finding little out of the ordinary, and nothing unexpected. The pantry cabinet and refrigerator were empty. In the main bedroom, the bed was neatly made, and soft light filtered through drawn shades. A sewing machine sat in the only other bedroom. The bathroom was clean. When I rejoined Krista in the living room, I looked down a hallway past the kitchen. At its end there was a windowed door.

"You want to see the garage?" I asked.

"You're going to owe me candy, you know."

"We'll see about that."

I led the child down the hallway and shifted the curtain aside that hung over the window set into the door, making sure there would be no surprises beyond.

"You open it," I said.

Krista eyed me for a moment, wondering what I was up to, then took the knob in hand and twisted it.

The yard that lay beyond it must have, at one time, been no less lovely than its brethren in the front of the house. Even with miniature drifts of snow gathered against the side fences, the meandering border of garden beds was easily seen. How it must have looked, and smelled, in this place, this home, when spring came.

"You see it?" I asked.

Krista looked over the yard, her doubting expression changing, some flash of surprise replacing it.

"You knew it would be back here!"

I did. The garage sat back on the lot, yard between it and the house. There would be an alley beyond. Down the side of the narrow structure a walkway led from the yard to the alley beyond, a barren trellis and wooden gate blocking the view of that lane.

"Do you want to bet whether there's a car in the garage?" I asked.

Krista's gaze swelled with a devious delight.

"Yes! I bet there *will* be one."

"Let's check it out," I said.

We crossed the yard and approached a simple door on the side of the garage. It opened without any effort to a dark interior. But even in the din, the little light that slipped past us revealed what filled the space.

"A car!"

The girl's shout echoed within the cramped structure. She ran to the car and pressed her face to the driver's side windows, squinting to see within.

"It's empty," Krista said, looking back to me and beaming. "It's not even dirty!"

She squeezed between the front of the car and the garage door to get to the other side. I approached the vehicle, an old boat of a car, a Buick Electra, probably from 1977. Some local mechanic had kept the beauty running for its owner for nearly forty years. It had newer paint, but that was to be expected in a place with a true winter climate. The worst I could say about the gorgeous hunk of American steel was that its tires looked a little low.

"Can we get in?" Krista asked, excited. "Can we?"

I looked to the door locks. All were up.

"Give it a try."

The little girl grabbed the handle on the front passenger side door and pulled it open, climbing in and shutting it behind. She came to her knees on the seat and bounced.

"Come on! Get in!"

I put my pack and my rifle on the back seat, then opened the driver's door and sat behind the wheel. There was no ignition key stashed obviously beneath the seat or tucked in the sun visor, and I hadn't noticed any in the house. Of course I hadn't searched specifically for any, and we could go back inside to look thoroughly for one, but that would not be necessary.

"Wait here for a minute," I said.

Krista stayed on her knees, leaning over the seat back and watching me through the rear window as I went to a small workbench behind the car and pawed through a modest collection of tools. It took less than a minute to find what I needed.

"What are you doing?" Krista asked, curious at why I had the stubby, flat blade screwdriver in my hand.

"This, Krista, is how you can start an old car without a key."

I jammed the point of the screwdriver into the keyhole and pushed, then levered it clockwise until I heard a snap!

"You broke it!" Krista almost shouted, worried.

"Not even close," I said, and turned the makeshift key further.

The engine coughed, starter spinning. It was a good sign. The battery still had juice. But it wasn't turning over.

"Come on," I implored it.

"Come on!" Krista joined in. "Start! Start!"

She thumped her fist on the dash. Again and again. The engine rumbled and started.

"It started!" Krista shouted. "I did it!"

"You sure did." I said, smiling and pulling the screwdriver from the ignition, stowing it beneath the front seat. "I'm going to open the garage door. Buckle up."

She plopped down on the seat and worked the seatbelt buckle as I got out and went to the wide door. It had an electric opener, obviously useless. I reached toward the mechanical device and pulled the release cord, freeing the door to be operated manually. There was a collapsed umbrella pole for an outdoor table leaning in the corner that I could use to prop the door open once I lifted it. But first I had to make sure there wasn't snow piled against it in the alley. A small window at its center, hardly larger than a folded newspaper, would let me confirm that. I slid between the front of the roughly idling car and the door and wiped dust from the glass, looking out.

Dear God...

I turned away from what I saw, calmly, not wanting to telegraph any distress to Krista. She beamed at me through the windshield, sitting tall, all buckled in. I thought for a moment, glancing back through the window before returning to the car, crouching at the open driver's door.

"I have an idea."

"What?" Krista asked.

"Do you want to play a joke on your mom and Neil?"

"Yes! What?"

"Okay, you unbuckle, and get down on the floor in front of the seat. Keep your head down, way down, and when we drive up to them you can pop up and scare them."

Her gaze ballooned with anticipatory delight. She undid the seatbelt buckle and followed my instructions, getting herself into a classic duck and cover position on the floor of the car.

"Now stay there, all the way down, and I'm going to open the garage door."

"Okay," she promised.

I went back to the garage door, grabbing the large umbrella pole. At the bottom of the door a bar was bolted as a handhold. I gripped it and both pushed and lifted, positioning the pole to support the slab-like door as it tilted out and up. It settled against the pole and stayed open, giving me a perfect, horrific view of the alley outside.

Bodies lay there. Piled atop each other. Some weathered and withered down to bone. Most, though, wore think skin suits beneath the tattered clothes that covered them. There were no predators left to beat decomposition to the punch. No swarms of flies to lay eggs and hatch maggots that would strip the bodies down to their skeletal selves.

I looked up and down the alley, the lane behind the houses dotted with similar piles of once vibrant beings. This had become a dumping ground of sorts, it seemed. A place to deposit the dead without any effort directed to burial. Here they were out of sight, out of mind. The woman whose car we were appropriating might, herself, rest among the corpses.

Who, I wondered, was the last alive in Kalispell? Who had seen to this? The bodies were of varying stages of decay, telling me they had died as time passed, not all at once. Put out like the trash as they expired. And none seemed ravaged by cannibalism. Limbs, faces, all appeared intact. Somehow this community, or part of it, had maintained its sanity, even as they died, one by one.

Maybe, I thought, that last person alive was here. Among those whose disposal they'd seen to. Perhaps they'd sensed their own coming demise and let themselves lay upon one of the piles. Performing the last task, at their last moment, with their final breath.

"Fletch, are we going?"

I looked back to the car. Krista was out of view, still hunched down.

"We are," I said. "Make sure you stay down."

I got back behind the wheel and closed the door, then shifted into gear. The car crept forward as I eased off the brake. I pulled out of the garage, maneuvering past the mounds of bodies, turning left at the end of the alley, and right again on the street we'd split up on. Neil and Grace were walking toward me along the curb, their pace quickened when they saw the transport we'd found.

The old Buick pulled to a stop next to them and Krista popped up like a coiled spring.

"Gotcha!"

Neil and Grace each managed a smile, but it was forced. They looked to me, and I knew. We'd all seen things we didn't want to see.

"I'm ready to get out of here," Grace said, and climbed into the back seat.

Krista crawled over the front seat and joined her mother. Neil slid in next to me.

"You okay?" he asked.

"No," I said, then pulled away from the curb.

Eleven

Just south of Kalispell we found ourselves cursing the Buick.

"A four by four would be nice about now," Neil said.

Damn straight it would, I thought, staring through the windshield at the chasm where a bridge had spanned Ashley Creek, cutting the main highway off from travel south to Flathead Lake. We'd already tried minor crossings over the creek, but each and every span both east and west had been taken down.

"This was deliberate," I said. "Someone didn't want people going south."

"Or something coming north," Grace said from the back seat.

I looked back to her and gave half a nod. One of us was right, but one over the other didn't get us across the creek.

"Four wheel drive and we could off road it carefully."

"This boat is about as far from four wheel drive as we can get," I told my friend. "We'd bottom out ten feet off the asphalt."

I wasn't even mentioning holes that might be covered by soft snow. Or rocks hidden by the same. Or, most important, the reality that we were traveling in a car that hadn't been serviced in well over a year. Abusing it was asking for trouble.

Our options, other than continuing on foot, were evaporating quickly.

"We backtrack," I said. "And go west on Highway Two."

"Two lanes through the mountains," Neil reminded me. "We could get thirty miles and find an avalanche."

"That's thirty miles closer than where we are."

It really wasn't up for discussion. Neil wasn't disputing the choice. He was just voicing the obvious—that having four wheels under us didn't guarantee anything.

"Three quarters of a tank," he said, glancing at the gauge on the dash. "We can just fill up once we get to Bonner's Ferry."

I laughed softly.

"I'm sure northern Idaho just caught a glancing blow from this blight thing," I said.

From the back seat, Grace reached forward, a credit card in hand.

"Gas is going to be my treat."

We all laughed now, Neil fixing on the rectangle of plastic Grace held.

"Why do you still have that thing?" he asked through a chuckle.

"Civilization is going to come roaring back someday," she said. "And I'm getting some shoes when that happens."

"Me, too!" Krista said.

The light moment was nice. And real. But it had to end. I backed the Buick into a reverse three point turn across the highway and got us moving again. We had miles to put behind us. As many as we could. If we were lucky, we could make it to Bonner's Ferry by nightfall.

We weren't lucky. Not in any way we could imagine.

Twelve

"Do you see that?"

I slowed just as we turned onto Highway 2 from the 93 Bypass on the western edge of Kalispell. Neil's question came almost exactly at the instant that I, too, saw the tire tracks in the snow.

"Yeah," I said.

Grace leaned forward and looked past us. Her mood darkened at the sight of multiple impressions on the roadway dusted white, all coming from the town.

"How many?" she asked.

"At least two," Neil said. "Going the same way we are."

He brought his Benelli up from where it rested against the seat and took it in hand. I looked to Grace and nodded toward my AR where I'd stowed it on the wide back seat. She passed it forward and I placed it next to me.

"How did we miss those on the way through here?" Neil asked. "We crossed twenty yards west of this spot."

He was nearly exact in his estimation. We had, just a few hours earlier, passed across Highway 2 as we paralleled the edge of the city.

"We weren't looking at the ground," I said. "We were looking at buildings. And for people."

He shook his head. Not in disagreement, but in disgust at our failure to spot such an obvious mark of human presence.

"Those can't be more than a couple days old," he said.

Grace looked between us, a thought rising.

"That explosion yesterday," she said. "Wouldn't this be about where it came from?"

"Maybe," I said. "Or west of here."

"The way we're going," Neil said once more.

"Wonderful," Grace said.

Neil glanced next to Grace, his gaze settling on Krista. She was buckled into the seat, book open on her lap.

"You be ready to get her down low," Neil said softly to Grace.

No acknowledgment came. None was needed. Grace sat back, closer to her daughter than before we'd stopped.

I started driving again, turning left onto the highway, following the tracks without wanting to, passing driveways and dirt roads leading to secluded homes and fallow farms.

"It's just two," Neil said, the tracks becoming more distinct in areas. "Both look like truck tires."

The wide profile now easily seen made that apparent, neither set of tracks leaving the highway for any of the turnoffs. We mirrored their path, weaving west, until, twenty miles from Kalispell, we could go no further.

"Stay sharp," I said

I pulled to a stop in the middle of the road where a jumble of towering pines had gone horizontal, snapped at their bases, dozens sprinkled across the roadway like toothpicks dropped from a box. Wind had come in from the north at some point and toppled the once mighty trees.

"The tracks are gone," Neil said.

He was right. Both sets had turned left off the roadway, disappearing down a gentle embankment. Had they gone around the blockage? Or were they hidden off in the grey woods, watching us?

Neil and I stepped from the car. Grace did the same, Krista just inside now, kneeling on the edge of the back seat.

"Ideas?" I said.

Neil walked to the right edge of the road and looked west, past the deadfall blocking our way. He turned back toward me and shook his head.

"Has to be half a mile covered with downed trees," he described.

I swore silently to myself. Traveling west on this route was out. We could no more take the Buick off road here to circumvent the fallen trees than we could when trying to head south from Kalispell.

"North into Canada, then west," I suggested, but my heart wasn't in that possibility. "The weather will be worse."

"Or impossible," I added.

"We're running out of options," Neil said. "We can't go east. Not a chance."

Neil had come that way. His emphatic denial of that route as a possibility spoke to what they'd gone through, beyond even what Grace had shared with me.

"We may have to give up the wheels," I said.

Hoofing it. That's what lay ahead of us. It would take days to reach Bonner's Ferry, and there was no guarantee we'd be able to resupply once there. Or at any of the smaller hamlets before that.

"What do you think?" I asked my friend.

"If we have to then we—"

"Wait," Grace said, interrupting, her head angled left, to the south. "Do you smell that?"

I walked to where she stood, next to the open passenger door. My gaze tracked hers, looking across a wide meadow beyond the road, greyed earth dotted with snow.

"Smell what?" Neil asked.

Her nose twitched, drawing in the cool air. And something thin upon it.

"I must be going food crazy," Grace said. "But I smell steak."

What we'd been reduced to eating shouldn't drive a person mad, I knew, but it was entirely conceivable that the absence of real food, of good food, could trigger some wanting memory. Some sensory ghost to trick the mind.

But here, it wasn't that. I knew so for certain as soon as I sampled the air. I smelled what she did. Beef. Steak. Being cooked.

I looked across the top of the car and knew that the same scent was now reaching Neil. Krista hopped from inside the car and clambered onto the roof of the Buick, sniffing the air manically, her head twisting like a weather vane, nose finally pointing the way we were all looking. South. Across the dead meadow. Precisely where the wind was coming from.

Neil came from the front of the car and stood next to me.

"That's beef, right? We're sure?"

I knew what he was gauging. How certain was I that what we were smelling was not what some had taken to cooking over open flame? That horror, I knew, had a distinct aroma. It was not appealing, and, more importantly, it was not this.

"Damn sure," I said, looking to my friend. "Someone's out there having a barbecue."

To think that, much less speak it, was absurd. This was a remnant of the old world. Picnics in parks and backyard get-togethers. The simpler time. The good time.

I retrieved my binoculars from the car and glassed the meadow. A thick line of greyed trees, most barren of empty limbs, bordered the field about a half mile off. And just above them, something was moving, dirty white and slender, appearing and disappearing in an arcing motion beyond the dead woods. Like the blades of a large propeller, spinning in the breeze.

"Windmill," I said, and handed the binoculars to Neil.

It took him just a second's look to affirm my observation.

"Looks like an old one," he said, scanning the area more closely now. "There's a dirt road up beyond the blockage. It leads past those trees."

He lowered the binoculars and looked to me, then to Grace.

"Those tire tracks head up that road," he added.

So the mystery vehicles hadn't simply gone off road to get past the fallen trees. They'd been traveling to this precise spot. To whatever lay back there, beyond the decaying woods.

"I think we should check it out," Neil said.

"You have no idea who—" Grace hesitated, rephrasing her worry. "No idea what's out there."

She was right. But so was Neil. And if there was a chance at food, real food, some impossibly true sustenance harkening back to the old world, I believed we had to face some risk to get to it.

"I'll go," I said, and grabbed my AR from where it lay on the front seat.

"You sure?" Neil asked. "It was my idea."

I checked that I had a round chambered in the AR, then gave the 1911 on my hip a once over before securing in its holster again.

"If I get over there and everything's okay, I'll fire a single shot," I said. "If there's trouble, I'll fire two."

Neil nodded. Grace reached up and helped Krista down from the roof of the car.

"I can't see down here," Krista protested.

"We're going to stay here," Grace said, taking Del's rifle from the back seat. "Behind the car. It's safe here."

That was a hope, I knew. A reasonable one, but still tinged with an element of doubt. 'Safe' was thin proclamation to make in the new world.

Thirteen

Past the tangle of fallen trees blocking our way, I reached the dirt road, the wide path mostly covered by snow, clearly neglected. But not unused. The two sets of tire tracks that had left the highway made this plain.

I paused before continuing, studying the tread impressions in the snow, greater definition here on soil than there had been atop the snowy asphalt. One set appeared older than the other, by several days, or at least before the most recent snowfall. The other had been made within the last day, maybe two. Hardly a sign of any debris existed in the crisp, jagged impressions, made by fat, sturdy tires. I let my gaze track them back to where they'd left the road before the blockage. Whoever had come through and gone up the road did so in beefy four by fours. Going off road hadn't concerned them a bit.

"Everything okay?" Neil shouted toward me.

I looked back to him and nodded, then looked to the snowy dirt path ahead and began walking.

Several minutes later, as I neared the thick stand of withered pines, the almost soothing *whop whop whop* of the spinning windmill blades began to rise. But with it came a painful screeching, metal scraping on metal. To me it sounded like a bearing going bad. The windmill, neglected, seemed on its last legs, its spinning shaft ready to seize.

I eased around the finger of dead woods and paused. A clearing opened up before me. In and beyond it I saw several things. Farthest, across the whitened field, a house sat beyond a fence, the single story ranch little different than a hundred others within twenty miles. What did set the scene before me apart was the decimated truck laying in pieces on a blackened spot near the fence where the snow seemed to have been blasted away. I felt with my thumb to verify that the safety was off on my AR, then approached the scene of destruction nearer the house, stopping to survey the carnage.

The front half of the vehicle rested upside down, the cab crumpled, an arm sticking out from within, nearly pinched off between the door frame and the crushed roof. The hand at the end lay open, skin on the palm showing no sign of decay. This was a fresh death.

Or, as I was about to learn, a fresh kill.

"It would be best if you lowered your weapon."

The male voice came from someplace impossibly close, but was tinged with a slight electronic hollowness. My gaze tracked toward it and found a metal speaker box mounted atop a fencepost, skim of snow atop it.

"You can't see me," the voice said. "But I sure as hell can see you."

I looked toward the house. The man was there. Probably eyeing me through a telescopic sight, with a finger on the trigger of a rifle that could put an end to me before I'd have time to blink.

"I'm not here to cause you any harm," I said, hoping that the speaker had some way of picking up sound and carrying my assurance to the man threatening me.

"I believe they would have made the same claim," the man said.

They...

I glanced to the blasted truck, each half of it on opposite sides of a shallow crater. Some sort of mine had taken them out. A homemade IED, little different from the improvised explosive devices soldiers had faced in hostile nations across the sea. Now, the hostility was here. If it was that at all.

For some reason the four by four, and those who'd been in control of it, had made the man behind the speaker take action. If he was simply out to kill, he clearly could have sent me to my maker already, no warning necessary, making me wonder if I had come upon a scene of death for death's sake, or for purposes of self-defense.

"Truly, I mean you no harm," I said loudly. "We smelled...something back at the road. That's all. I was coming to see if we'd all just gone crazy or if it was real."

Silence hung for a moment. I almost felt the man looking at me past crosshairs. There was no reason for him to trust me.

Unless I gave him one.

I lowered my AR and slung it so that it hung across my back. A few seconds later the speaker crackled once again.

"Come on up to the house," the man said.

I looked behind. The road was out of view, Neil, Grace, and Krista could not see me. They had no idea what I was about to do. Or what I might be walking into.

"All right," I said, facing the house again. "I'm coming up."

The stench of new death washed over me as I moved past the upended cab of the pickup. On the far side of it I could no longer see the arm and the hand. But I could take in, in all its pure horror, a pair of bodies that had been thrown from the four by four, likely as it was launched into the air and ripped apart. They lay together, almost intimately, a man and a woman, their emaciated faces almost touching. His eyes were closed. Hers were open and fixed upward, sad and serene, as if she'd reluctantly welcomed her end.

I continued on, through an opening in the fence, my hands free of weapons and my own eyes, bright and alive still, fixed on the house as the front door opened and a man stepped out, rifle in hand.

Fourteen

"That's far enough."

I stopped maybe five yards from the porch, the man who'd exited holding a hand out to emphasize the direction. His other held the rifle, finger just outside the trigger guard.

"My name's Eric Fletcher," I said. "From Missoula, but I've been up at my place north of Whitefish since everything..."

There was no need to give the event description. Any living, breathing creature with a brain larger than a walnut knew what had happened to the world. And the same creature could, from where I stood, smell the impossible.

"We're not crazy, are we?"

The man looked me up and down. Appraising what stood before him. Maybe deciding if I was friend or foe, or some acceptable uncertainty in between.

"You're not crazy," the man said, then put his rifle down, leaning it against the porch railing before coming down the steps and offering me his hand. "I'm Jack Miner. You want to see what's cooking?"

I almost laughed, but managed a nod, and followed the man as he walked along the front of his house and turned down the side, stopping next to a large stone barbecue, chunks of wood burning red hot beneath a long grill, large strip of meat sizzling upon the blackened lace of metalwork.

"I don't understand," I said, regarding both the steak and the man I'd just met as one might a mirage.

"This is my ranch," Jack Miner said, gesturing to the land around us, fields and hills rising toward peaks in the distance. "If you'd been here two years ago you'd be looking out over three hundred head of cattle."

That might be true, I knew, but now the expanse was nothing more than a snowy landscape dotted with clusters of dead trees. How the beasts he spoke of transitioned to the single slab of meat cooking was unclear. At least it was to me. And obviously so.

"You look like you need a little context," Jack observed, not incorrect in the least. "Come on. I'll show you."

"Show me what?"

He smiled and took the sizzling steak off the grill.

"Come see for yourself."

The man led off toward the collapsed façade of an old outbuilding at the base of a small hill not far beyond the back of his house. I followed, passing near the creaking windmill, my gaze taking note of oddities about the structure. It bore the appearance of something near ancient, rust scabbing the metal and bits of old rope hanging from cross beams. Wood supports seemed tacked in place like an afterthought, as if nothing more than window dressing. Even the rhythmic whine of the turning blades came with a hint of falsity, the sound too precise. Too concocted. A good look upward as I skirted the tower only reinforced what I was thinking—suspended just below the bladed generator housing was a smaller fan, nearly hidden within the structure, whirling lazily along with its larger sibling, the distressed screeching coming from it.

The windmill, all of it, was in perfect working order. It had only been made to seem abandoned.

"Right over here," Jack said, wrenching the broken door up from its tilted frame, the portal of the fallen shed opening at a steep angle.

He paused at the opening, just darkness beyond and below. Above me the windmill screamed its lie. I felt the AR against my back. I could have it in hand in two seconds, the pistol on my hip in one. But Jack Miner stood before me unarmed. Calm. Even understanding.

"I'll go first," he said, smiling at my hesitance.

I nodded and he stepped through the opening, ducking. I heard something move. Something metallic. A handle, maybe, followed by a quick hiss of air and then a weak light built within the darkness.

"Come on in," Jack said.

I kept my hand on my pistol and moved toward the light.

Fifteen

Through the old door I came upon a small set of crude stairs, rotting planks over sculpted earth, and just a few steps from that descent was another door, insulated steel, open to a lighted space beyond. Jack Miner stood inside and motioned me through.

The chill hit me first, more than matching the wintry outside air. The size struck me next, the space long and narrow, like a shipping container. Except there'd been no such thing visible. Just the hill.

And that's when I understood. Or began to understand.

"You buried this," I said.

Jack smiled with pride. My eyes almost bugged at the shelves running down each side of the space, neatly wrapped cuts of meat stacked in every available space.

"If you're going to build a freezer, underground is the place to do it."

His explanation was spot on. But it didn't fully assuage my wondering.

"I've got two industrial chillers in the back," he said, pointing. "Air exchange vents come up in the hollows of some trees out the back side of the hill. Power comes from the windmill, and a solar array I've got out on the field behind some trees."

"Batteries?" I guessed aloud.

"Plenty to run things for a couple days at least, and through the nights. But there's almost always wind. And the units I put in are the most efficient you can get. The best that dirty paper could buy."

I chuckled, recalling my own spending spree after Neil's warning. When I'd accepted the reality of what was to come and liquidated my business credit to provision my refuge. I'd had the advantage of some inside information to allow me the luxury of preparing. In a similar way, Jack Miner had been clued in as to coming events.

"How'd you know to do this?"

He thought for a moment. As if he'd already discarded that moment of realization.

"I'm not sure. My son JJ and I were hearing a lot from cattle ranchers in Brazil. They were slaughtering their herds when the grass went bad. The price to buy feed went through the roof. We knew if it spread up here, it'd be too late to...to manage the loss."

I looked over the supply of beef crammed into the space, easily enough food for years.

"You slaughtered your herd," I said.

"A good portion of it. The rest we traded, sold. That allowed us to prep this freezer and lay in a supply and make it as invisible as possible. So that anyone chancing by here would see nothing special once we left."

"Left?"

"We have this place, a couple farms in the Midwest. We decided that back there would be the best place to ride out the beginning. Maybe the whole thing. We just didn't know how long it would last."

"No one did," I said.

"A few of us, at least, saw enough to hang on. To keep on..."

"Fighting," I finished the statement for him.

"I was going to say living, but those seem to be the same thing nowadays," he said, looking up and out the door. "Those fools in the truck wouldn't listen. They tracked me from town, I figure. Saw when I arrived, waited a few days, then decided to pay me a visit. I told them to stay back. They decided not to."

"You have some good defenses set up," I told him, realizing now that the distant boom we'd heard the night before was the makeshift mine taking out the truck encroaching on the man's property.

"JJ's doing," Jack said. "He figured we might need some protection beyond just the guns."

"Can't wait to meet him," I said, and knew immediately from the look on Jack's face, and his lack of any immediate response, that I'd broached a subject fraught with pain. "I'm sorry."

"Nothing to be sorry about. He'll find his way back here. He will."

They were hopeless words of hope. The kind any father would speak.

"Jack..."

"Yes?"

"Why did you trust me?"

His face shrugged.

"Why did *you* trust *me*?"

I had about as good an answer as I imagined he did.

"I had a feeling," I said.

"Me, too. Now, do you have some way to signal your friends?"

"I do."

"I've got steaks already thawing for the next few days," Jack said. "Why don't you go tell them to join us for a proper meal?"

I smiled, then, with probably too much haste, left the confines of the freezer and walked a few yards away and drew my pistol, firing a single shot into the grey sky.

Sixteen

We ate in silence. Not because of any sense of discomfort with our host. We simply hadn't eaten this well in more than a year.

"I can't begin to describe how incredible this tastes," Grace said.

"It is soooooo good," Krista agreed, cutting another bit of steak off and forking it into her mouth.

I cut into the perfectly cut and exquisitely grilled piece of meat. A rib eye, it was, and my knife sliced into its tenderness, juices flowing, separating another piece that my fork stabbed and slipped into my mouth. I savored the taste, the texture, the memory brought forward from a past I'd known as lost. All thanks to one man.

At the head of the table, Jack Miner sat, taking in the sight of four relative strangers basking in his hospitality. I glanced up from the rib eye I was devouring and noted the look about the man. A smile was plain on his face, but it was subdued, like a light dimmed. He caught me looking and the expression brightened a bit.

"This feels almost normal," he said, lifting his glass of cabernet and taking a small sip. "Like life used to be. People around the table. Eating. Talking. Well, more talking usually, but..."

"We are ravenous guests," Neil said after a swallow.

"I'm glad for the company," Jack said, the truth in his words impossible to miss. "Just the presence of others is so...odd. And realizing that that's odd makes you understand what we've lost."

Grace paused her enjoyment of the meal as Jack spoke, sensing the tinge of melancholy creeping into the conversation, and noting his gaze settling on her daughter, regarding her fondly, like a memory he feared might fade. My fork and knife stilled, too, as did Neil's, the both of us picking up on what Grace was watching.

After a moment, Jack noticed the attention he was generating. He looked among us and smiled an apology.

"My granddaughter loved coming up here to the ranch," he said. "My daughter Frannie's little girl. A couple years younger than this fine young lady here."

Krista smiled with a mouthful of steak and kept eating.

"You don't know what happened to them?" Grace asked, the query offered gingerly, with the expectation of an answer that, at the very least, would be born of uncertainty.

"My son, JJ, he was going to fly down from our Minnesota place to pick them up," Jack explained. "We, my son and I, we were hunkered down at the northern property. His sister refused to leave with Jill, my granddaughter, unless her husband would come. But he thought he could ride it out down in Louisiana. They had a shrimping business there. I guess he thought the sea would provide for them."

"Did it?" Neil asked.

Jack shrugged, a painful acquiescence to the unknown.

"Neither my son or I had heard from Frannie since a few weeks after everything went to hell. We waited at the Minnesota place, hoping she'd make her way there with her family. She knew we would wait for her. Until we couldn't wait anymore."

The last statement he spoke like a man who'd surrendered the whole of his being, his soul, in some act fouled by the stench of personal failure.

"I should have never let her stay down there," Jack said.

"She's a grown woman," I said. "With her own family. How could you make her do what she didn't want to do?"

He had no answer to that.

"Our supplies were down to almost nothing," he explained. "JJ said we had to fall back to this place. If our little camouflage job did its trick, and if the chillers held out, we'd have enough beef to carry us through a couple years, at least. That and some other stuff we buried. Those peas you've got aren't half bad for being dehydrated and left under a few feet of dirt for the better part of two years."

"They're delicious," Grace said.

Jack smiled at the kind words, his eyes beginning to glisten over the expression.

"My granddaughter loves peas," Jack said. "I hated peas when I was a kid."

He reached up with his napkin and wiped his eyes.

"You said he flew down," I said. "You had a plane?"

"Two," Jack corrected. "I flew here when he didn't return to the Minnesota place with the others. I thought they might have had to make the flight out here instead. But they weren't here when I flew in. And there's no going back. Not enough fuel."

I looked to Neil, thoughts churning behind his eyes. The same thoughts as mine, I suspected.

"You have a plane here?" I asked.

"At the field in Kalispell," Jack answered.

Again Neil and I exchanged a wondering, obvious look.

"You fellas fly?"

I shook my head and tossed a thumb Neil's way.

"I started lessons a couple years ago," Neil said, discounting whatever thin ability he might have. "I never even did my solo."

Jack nodded at that and sipped his wine again, thinking.

"Why is it you're leaving your place?"

"We're going to Eagle One," Krista said after a quick swallow.

Jack puzzled at the answer.

"It's someplace to the west," I said. "It may be the place to be."

My attempt at explanation only seemed to deepen our host's wonder. I delved further into the reason, telling him of the radio broadcasts, and food caches across the country that people were guided to, and why we were setting out now instead of the spring.

"A helicopter," Jack said after hearing of the attack on my refuge, no question in the words whatsoever.

"It nearly killed us," Neil said, then he looked to Grace. "She saved our lives. Put two rounds into the cockpit. Took the pilot out."

"My grandfather taught my mommy to shoot," Krista said, beaming.

"Is that so?" Jack gave Krista a wink, then looked to me. "You know, when I was flying in earlier in the week, I saw a chopper on the ground down south of Flathead Lake. Looked like a makeshift landing pad, with a whole bunch of trucks and dozens and dozens of people around it."

"Everything painted black?" I asked, and Jack nodded.

"I'm not sure, but they might have taken some pot shots at me," he said. "I saw a few flashes and didn't hang around to see any more. Headed straight for Kalispell and landed. Found a hangar that was still standing—several weren't—and nosed in. Snagged myself a pickup and made my way here."

"South of the lake," Grace said, worried. "That was the way we were going to go to reach the interstate."

Jack took in the sudden concern that volleyed silently between us.

"That was your plan? To catch I Ninety?"

"Yeah," I confirmed, fixing on my friend next. "But there were bridges out. That's why we came this way."

"Those downed bridges might have saved you," Jack said.

"The roads west of here don't look promising," Neil said.

"Roads don't seem like they're going to be viable routes in any direction."

The implication of my addendum was plain to Neil. And to Jack.

"You're welcome to my plane," he said. "Don't know how far you can make it on what's left in the tank."

Neil looked between us all, incredulous and resistant.

"Wait a minute. You heard me say I've only had a few lessons, right?"

Krista focused in on the brewing disagreement, eating as she watched.

"Neil," I began, "you said yourself—we're just about out of options."

"I'd invite you to stay here," Jack said, "but I doubt you'd take me up on the offer."

"We need to make it out west," I said.

"We have to try," Grace said. "Right, Neil?"

The weight of our ability to pursue that goal had just shifted entirely onto my lifelong friend. He considered the necessity, the challenges, the chances of success. None of the negatives outweighed the reality that we simply had to get to Eagle One. The hope he'd professed to me so long ago now lived there. At least for me, it did. It was a somewhat irrational expectation that a place we knew nothing of, with people we knew even less of, had become some sort of touchstone. But it was.

"We don't even know where to fly to," Neil said.

"Biggest city to the west is Seattle," Jack said. "Decent chance of people hanging on there. That could be a good thing, or a bad thing."

"Depends on the people," I said, and Jack nodded.

Neil thought for a moment. This leg of our journey was becoming his responsibility. Decisions were on him to make.

"We have to start somewhere," Neil said. "Seattle."

Jack seemed impressed that we weren't anguishing over minutiae. There was a point on the map, and we were going to aim for it.

"Do you have maps?"

Neil and I looked at each other, each giving Jack a shake of the head.

"There's no navigation," Jack Miner told us.

"Nothing?" I asked.

"GPS is gone," he said.

"I had a handheld unit that was functioning six months ago," Neil said. "It broke, but the system was fine."

Jack nodded and sat back. He poured himself some more cabernet.

"It was working four weeks ago when I was back in Minnesota," Jack told us. "But when I tried to log a flight plan into the computer to head out here, it couldn't find any satellites."

The other beacons we might have depended upon, beamed out from ground-based transmitters, had been long silenced through lack of maintenance or operator presence, existing only now as bulbous, wasting radomes and rusting antenna towers. But the Global Positioning System, its satellites not dependent on earthbound power, should have been invulnerable to what the blight had wrought. Apparently, it was not.

"Could it just be your plane's receiver?" I asked.

"Maybe," Jack allowed, but without conviction. "Or maybe someone shut the satellite array down."

Shutting down an entire constellation of satellites, each more than 20,000 miles into space, seemed an act lacking any rationale.

"Why do that?" I asked. "And who could?"

"Normally, someone in the department of defense," Neil said. "But we left 'normal' in the rearview over a year ago. As to why...to make it harder for people to find their way."

If some bit of government still functioned, in some sealed and supplied bunker somewhere, it was possible they could have shut the entire GPS system down. Elements of the old organs of state had already shown a desire to restrict movement. Maybe this was just another example of that.

And I had an idea why.

"Eagle One," I said, my wondering thoughts reaching an inevitable conclusion.

"All those transmissions," Grace said, chiming in. "If we heard them, and others did, then the people who could shut the satellites certainly would have."

"You know," Jack began, "it could be that there's a valid reason not to head for this Eagle One place."

"What if there actually is a valid reason to keep people from looking for this Eagle One thing?" Jack asked, looking to me.

"Valid as defined by the people who abandoned every citizen under the rank of governor or four star general when this started?"

We'd considered the likelihood that some power, somewhere, was trying to keep us, to keep anyone, from finding and getting to the elusive and enigmatic place we'd come to know through the airwaves. The jamming of communications at my refuge. The helicopter attack following that. If the disabling of the worldwide GPS system was just another part of that effort, it would make sense. And, as the earlier acts had done, it only hardened my resolve to actually reach Eagle One.

"I'm not trying to dissuade you," Jack said. "It's just that, you've got precious cargo to think about."

We looked to Krista as he did.

"I understand your concern," I said, trying to walk back the slightly harsh delivery of my previous statement. "But she's one of the biggest reasons to do what we're doing."

Jack understood, nodding.

"Gotta keep fighting," he said. "The good fight."

We were going. No matter what. But doing so, under the situation Jack had clued us into, wasn't going to be as easy as it might have.

"How will we navigate?" I asked. "Without GPS?"

"I'd recommend getting some good maps that cover your route. Navigate by highway."

"Any place at the airport to scrounge what we'll need in that department?" Neil asked.

Jack shook his head.

"If there was, it's been looted to the floorboards," he said.

"Library," Grace said. "City that size has to have one."

"Not many people stealing books to stay alive," Neil said, agreeing.

That was one obstacle mostly dealt with. There was still another.

"How much fuel was left?" I asked Jack.

"Not a whole lot. Probably enough for two, three hundred miles. I carried cans of extra in the cabin to get me here."

"Three hundred miles won't get us to Seattle," Neil said.

"It'll get us over the mountains," I reminded him, then looked to our host. "Are you sure you want to give us your plane? We can never repay you."

The man fixed his gaze once again on Krista, carving down the last of her steak into bite size pieces, chewing and savoring every last morsel. He sampled it like a living memory, his own granddaughter having sat in the same spot before, doing exactly what our tiny traveling companion was.

"You already have," Jack said, then stood from the table and walked into an adjacent room, returning a moment later with a single key in hand. "She'll serve you well."

He held the key out to Neil. My friend took it.

"I locked the door," Jack said, chuckling lightly at himself. "Can you believe that?"

Krista reached to Grace and tugged at her sleeve.

"Mommy, are we going in a plane?"

"I think we are," Grace said.

"Cool!"

Krista's excitement warmed us for a moment. Then thoughts of what had to be done rose again.

"The people in the truck," I said to Jack. "Did you see any more like that in the city?"

"Did you see anyone at all?" Neil asked.

"Not a soul," Jack answered. "I didn't even see them."

I turned to Neil and Grace.

"There could be more," I said. "The longer that plane sits there, the more chance something happens to it."

"Not much daylight left," Jack reminded us. "Flying out today would not be a smart move."

That reality was disappointing. But being foolhardy could be fatal.

"If we're going to do this, I want to babysit that plane until we take off," I said.

"We can head into the city now," Neil suggested. "Go to the library, get the maps, then pull an all-nighter at the hangar."

By the look of her, Grace wasn't loving that idea.

"We're going to stay there tonight," she said, no questioning at all in her tone, only dread admission.

I nodded.

"We'll be fine," Neil assured her.

She accepted that and shook her head, smiling at us all, amused by some thought.

"It's odd," she said. "But being in a city, anyplace with buildings and roads, it makes me feel exposed. But out under the stars...we're safe there. It's silly, I know."

I smiled back at Grace. Our conversation the night before, her condensed detailing of the events that had shaped what still did not exist between Neil and her, had come in a relaxed, quiet moment beneath sparkling heavens. It made sense that the revelation had come there.

We had finished eating. Our plates were scraped clean, bellies full. Gathering our things took just a few moments, and, after offering sincere thanks for the hospitality, we walked through the front door of Jack Miner's house with maybe four hours of good daylight left.

"Hold on a minute," Jack said from inside.

The four of us stopped at the bottom of the porch steps and watched as our host came out, a small bag in hand. He passed it off to me and I looked inside.

"Something for tonight," he said.

The contents were simple. But in these times what he gave us was valued more than gold. A dozen MREs, some flavored drink mix, and two small cans of peas.

"I'm still not big on peas," he said.

"Thank you," I said, and shook the man's hand. "If nothing else, Jack, you're proof that good people still do exist."

He accepted the observation with a warm smile. But the expression dimmed ever so slightly, a wariness creeping settling upon his face.

"I hope you find the same where you're going," he said. "I truly do."

We waved as we walked away, Krista turning back again and again to smile at the man who'd invited us into his home. As we came around the stand of dead woods that hid his house from the highway beyond, the sight of him was no more.

The car started promptly once we reached it, and I turned us around. Kalispell was once again ahead of us. Jack Miner was behind, gone from our lives.

Forever.

Seventeen

It smelled of the old world. Dust and paper. Computers had been looted, tables that had supported them empty, network cables tangled and tossed, like a nest of dead multicolored snakes spread about. But books they'd left. Disregarded. Shelved and scattered across the floor.

"Can we look for a new book, mommy?"

Grace put a hand to her daughter's cheek.

"Absolutely," she said, then looked to Neil and me. "We'll be close."

"So will we," Neil said, the protectiveness plain in his delivery.

Grace and Krista walked off, maneuvering over toppled bookcases. Neil looked to a lopsided directory hanging on a wall nearby. We'd entered the library through glass doors that had long ago been broken, glass shards strewn within the space, bits grinding under my feet as I stepped close to the directory.

"All right, we've got map books back there," Neil said.

I nodded, still eyeing the directory. Still looking for something as Neil walked away, noticing after a few seconds I wasn't with him.

"You coming?"

"Go ahead," I told him. "I want to look at something."

He laid an incredulous look on me. That sort of *dumbshit* appraisal we'd volleyed back and forth as teenagers when the other would pull some bonehead move.

"You have a report due I didn't know about?"

"You know what you need to find," I said. "I just need a minute."

He puzzled at me for a moment, then shook off the exchange and made his way toward the back of the library, disappearing down an aisle. I followed the same path, but turned before he did, right instead of left, reaching a section with signage still clear upon the shelving—languages.

Wisps of light barely reached where I stood. I took a small flashlight from my pocket and moved its beam along the rows of books, turning it on every few seconds for just an instant, conserving the battery. At my refuge I'd laid in a plentiful stock of batteries, but most had gone up flames. Here I needed just enough to first find what I was looking for, then a bit more to read within what I hoped would bring some clarity for me.

German. Spanish. And, finally, French. Among the other dictionaries the object of my interest was revealed under the quick burst of light, and, in an instant, I was back in high school, in the nascent internet era, where assignments still required finding and opening an actual paper book to obtain whatever knowledge was required. I slipped the book from the shelf and thought for a moment before opening it, remembering. Recalling. The words that the French helicopter pilot had spoken.

L'enfant est un menteur...

Softly, I repeated it to myself.

"L'enfant est un menteur..."

That was what the dying man had said. That was what I'd heard. How accurate my mental transcription was, I didn't know. Not yet.

I opened the dictionary and flipped through the pages, searching for the first word—*l'enfant.* But it wasn't there. Or was it, I wondered, breaking down the word in my head. Maybe the first part, the '*l*' sound, was some addition to the rest, which sounded more familiar. Almost like 'infantry', except with an 'e' at the beginning.

I refocused my search, flipping to the correct section to get the English translation, finding precisely what I was looking for.

"Child..."

I spoke the word quietly, surprised. It was not some military term, which would have made sense considering the attack. It was an innocuous word. Not threatening in the least.

Child...

Not having time to completely immerse myself in French grammar, I made a leap of conjecture and assumed that the 'l' sound in combination with the word would roughly translate to 'The child'.

...est un menteur...

The second word I found on the very next page.

...is...

The child is...

Then the third word, skimming further on in the dictionary.

...un...

...a...

The child is a...

Finally, the last word, located near the middle of the book. No harder to find than any other. But when I laid eyes upon it, I stopped, not wanting to add it to what I'd already deciphered. Its meaning, taken whole, taken in context, chilled me.

I closed the dictionary and slipped it back onto the shelf, standing there, alone, refusing to speak the words aloud, even if only to myself. That expression I could control.

But what churned in my thoughts could not. The words, the phrase, played over and over, louder, until it was screaming within.

The child is a liar...

Part Three

Danger Close

Eighteen

The single engine Piper sat exactly where Jack Miner had told us it would be, nosed into an open hangar, the space invaded by the elements, small drifts of snow piled against the interior walls. I pulled the Buick in next to it, fully into the structure.

Ten minutes it took to drive from the library to where we now were. There, Grace and Krista had found a small armful of books to occupy and educate the girl. Neil, too, had secured a trio of maps and atlases covering the Pacific Northwest and the mountain states inland. I'd brought nothing from the place. Nothing physical. Just an answer. A knowing.

Neil had asked me what I'd gone in search of when I finally joined him where the maps and geographic books were shelved. I shrugged off the inquiry then, telling him that the smallish library didn't have what I'd hoped to find. On the surface, it wasn't a complete lie.

Lie...

The child is a liar...

"We can use the car to sleep in," Grace said as we climbed out.

"Absolutely," I said.

A liar...

There was only one child the French pilot could have been speaking of. The child whose voice we'd heard broadcasting from Eagle One. But why? Why would a foreign helo jock, flying on what was, or had been, United

States soil, use his dying breath to tell us that? What lie could that child tell to elicit an armed strike on those reaching out to Eagle One?

"Small fire at the back of the hangar sound okay?" Neil asked.

"Yeah," I nodded, transferring our gear from inside the car to atop its hood. "We can heat up some food."

I couldn't tell them. Any of them. If I were to breathe a word of the pilot's translated statement, it could be enough to embolden Grace's reluctance to head west. Enough, maybe, to even draw Neil toward the side of hesitance.

We had to get there. I felt that. It was a quiet compulsion that churned inside. Whether it turned out to be the ultimate destination, or just a way station, we...*I* had to find it. See it. Understand it.

"It's in good shape," Neil said.

I looked to my friend. He was at the plane, walking around it, performing a visual inspection of the exterior. Some sort of pre-flight check. There was a ritualistic feel to the process, his hand reaching out and touching specific points on the aircraft, feeling along the trailing edge of the wing, checking the tires, the windows.

"Feel better now that you've seen it?" I asked.

"I have every confidence in the aircraft," he said. "The pilot's just a bit sketchy for my liking."

"I thought I was the only one who felt that way," I said.

Neil tossed me a smile and walked to the tail end of the plane, then beyond it, until he stood just outside the hangar. I joined him, looking over the landscape beyond. The day's last light, peeking through slivered clouds to the west, dappled the snowy expanse with warm light. Were it not for a line of charred buildings on the far side of the runway, the scene would look serenely normal. The new world was like that. Bits of what remained, viewed under the right circumstances, at the perfect moment, seemed to echo the past. As if it still existed.

"We'll have to do something about the runway," Neil said.

"Too much snow?"

He shrugged. The layer of winter white upon the long strip of pavement wasn't deep, but I suspected it didn't need to be to cause issues with taking off.

"We're not going to find a plow," I said.

"We don't need one," he told me, glancing back to the Buick. "In the morning we just take that beast and drive up and down the runway, over and over. That should help. That should be enough."

I eyed my friend for a moment. He'd always been the kind to rise to a challenge, but what he was going to do here, when the sun rose on a new day...

"You are one cool cucumber, Neil."

"Yeah? I'd be a lot cooler if I'd finished those flying lessons."

"Life's tough, my friend."

He smiled.

"Guess I'll have to be tougher."

We joined Grace and Krista inside the hangar. An hour later, after getting a fire going and heating up our dinner, we sat on upturned buckets and cans, talking. Relaxing. Except for Neil. He spent a good two hours inside the Piper, in the pilot's seat, familiarizing himself with the controls, the systems, even starting the engine and running it for a few minutes. It was a process of preparation. Running through a mental checklist that had as much to do with himself as it did with the aircraft.

In the morning we would leave Montana, in all likelihood for the last time, but we weren't in any hurry. There was no schedule to keep. No alarm clock to set. We would wake when we woke and be on our way, heading west on our terms.

The rumble of truck engines just after dawn changed all that.

Nineteen

Grace nudged me with her foot. Before I could ask her why, I heard it.

"It's over there," she said. "On the highway."

I'd been sleeping by the fire, along with Neil, while Grace and Krista, as planned, sacked out in the car, mother and daughter curled up together in the back seat. My eyes opened wide at the sound and I sat up. A few feet away next to the embers smoldering low, Neil was just rousing as Grace jostled him.

"What is that?" he asked, shaking the sleep off.

I was already on my feet, reaching for my AR.

"We've got company," I said, and Neil bolted up, arming himself as I had.

By now the sound was the kind you could not only hear, but feel. It reached up through the soles of my feet like the constant low hum of a tuning fork. Neil and I ran to the edge of the hangar door and looked out across the runway. Beyond it, on the far side of burned and rubbled buildings, was the highway. The same one we'd tried to head south on, until the fallen spans crossing Ashley Creek had turned us back. Some distance beyond them, if what Jack Miner had told us was accurate, a sizeable force had been camped. At the time he'd flown over that force included a helicopter, which almost certainly was the one crashed near my refuge. He'd also seen trucks. Lots of trucks. Trucks now loaded with an armed force heading north to search for their missing comrades.

Neil turned fast back toward Grace. She had already kicked piles of dirty snow onto what little remained of the fire, quenching the remnant smoke it was generating.

"Get Krista ready to go," he told her, then looked to me. "It's gotta be now."

I glanced to the plane, and then to the runway. No more snow had fallen. But none had melted, either. It was still a thick, wet layer, several inches deep.

"We can't use the car to clear the runway," I said.

"I know," he said, his gaze swelling now. "We've gotta hurry."

He rushed to the plane as I looked back across the runway. No longer was it just sound alerting us to an approaching danger. The first of the trucks appeared between two collapsed buildings, just glimpses of them as the convoy trundled up the highway. They'd gone off road to get around the downed bridges, and were heading into town, but all it would take was a chance look, or a decision to search the airport, and we'd be found. Our journey west, and likely more, would be over.

"I'm taking the brakes off," Neil said. "We're going to have to push it back."

Without the luxury of being able to drop the aircraft into reverse, muscle would have to be used to get it out of the hangar. I took a position on the leading edge of the left wing, and Neil on the right. Grace hurried to the nose and planted her hands against center of the propeller, leaning hard as we pushed, and shoved, our feet slipping on the icy floor.

"Come on!" Neil half shouted. "Move! Move!"

But the aircraft barely rocked. Grace stepped back, eyeing the landing gear, her gaze fixing on the nose gear, snow having buried it as it plowed to a stop. She dropped to her knees under the nose and scooped away the piles of icy white until the nose wheel was visible—turned sharply to the right. Almost at a ninety degree angle to the plane's center.

"Turn the wheel!" Grace shouted to Neil.

He left the wing and climbed into the cockpit, cranking some control, the nose wheel inching left, and more left, until it was straight again.

"It's good!" Grace told him.

In a few seconds he was back on the front of the right wing, and after a quick look to each other to time our attempt, we put our full weight and strength against the plane in unison. At first it moved an inch and seemed stuck. We pushed harder. Neil yelled as he gave it every last ounce of strength he had. I made no sound. I simply drew a breath, held it, and pushed as though my life depended upon it.

Because it did. Krista's scream made that perfectly clear.

We all looked toward the child, standing just beyond the wingtip, still in the shelter of the hangar, her arms extended, finger pointed across the runway where a truck was barreling across a parking lot between destroyed buildings. Coming right at us.

"Now! Push!"

It was Grace urging us on now, and we pushed. Drawing on every reserve we could summon, the plane finally rolling backward. Steadily.

"Go get our gear," Neil told Grace. "Everything. Hurry!"

I looked over the wind as the plane continued to roll into the clear. The truck had left pavement and was sending up a rooster tail of snow as it sped across a field. It was close enough now to see that there were people in the open bed of the large vehicle. People holding weapons.

"That's far enough!" Neil said, and he threw the door open and climbed into the pilot's seat.

"Here!" Grace shouted, carrying and dragging our packs and weapons, Krista running at her side.

"Got it," I said, taking the gear and shoving it atop the back seats.

"Starting up," Neil said, the engine firing a second later, propeller spinning, the wash from it blasting over us.

"Get in!" I yelled above the suddenly thunderous noise. "Here!"

I reached my hand down and grabbed Krista as Grace lifted, almost throwing the little girl into the back seat.

"Come on!" Neil shouted.

Grace took hold of my hand next and I pulled, dragging her onto the wing. She climbed in back next to her daughter and wedged the gear bags and weapons between them as best she could.

"Close the door!" Neil said, the engines already revving.

I slipped into the right seat and pulled the door shut as my friend firewalled the throttle. Looking past him I saw the truck slide sideways a hundred yards from us, tipping almost over as half of its wheels slipped into a drainage culvert masked by snow. A handful of the people in its back tumbled out as the vehicle bogged down abruptly.

"This is going to be a short takeoff!" Neil shouted. "I don't want to pass over them!"

He sped the plane onto the taxiway, retracing the now faint tire impressions that Jack Miner had made when landing some days ago. At the intersection with the wider runway he swung the plane hard right, aiming us southeast.

"Here we go!"

I looked over the seat. Grace was buckling Krista in, her fingers fumbling with the belt latch. Past the child and through the left side window I could see the truck in the distance, and the now dismounted troops, which is what they clearly were. And from the group of identically uniformed fighters I began to see flashes.

"They're shooting!" I said loudly to Neil, leaning close.

Ahead of us, puffs of snow erupted into the air as rounds impacted the runway. The instinct was to swerve, but Neil kept us straight, accelerating along the slushy pavement.

"Faster, baby," Neil urged the aircraft. "Come on. Go. Go."

The landing gear churned through the snow, spinning faster, the speed increasing. But the end of the runway was racing at us. Fast. And rounds from the troops behind were still slicing past the aircraft, maybe even into it, a possibility that we might only discover too late.

"Fifty five knots," Neil said, reading out the speed. "Sixty. Come on."

There was no more time. Even skimmed with snow, the end of the runway was plain and abrupt, a ground level cliff that we were about to plunge off of.

"Sixty-five..."

"Neil..."

He drew the yoke back, gently, the nose shuddering as it lifted, then the rest of the aircraft rose from solid ground into the air. What shaking there had been subsided as we climbed. I looked to the instrument panel and found the speed indicator, passing ninety now, and climbing steadily. One hundred. One hundred and five.

We were on our way.

Twenty

We continued to gain altitude, rising into low, broken clouds, the clear blue sky above them warmed by the morning sun.

"We're okay," Neil said, glancing back to Grace, his chest still heaving, heart pounding. "We're okay."

She might not have heard him over the engine noise, but she smiled. She knew. Neil had saved us.

"Fletch," he said. "There are headsets back there, and one at your feet."

I nodded and leaned over the seat, fishing the items from the floor beneath the gear we'd had to quickly stow.

"Put these on," I told her.

There was a cord running from each, and jacks to plug them into so we could all hear one another over the constant drone of the engine. Grace slipped a headset over her daughter's ears and tipped the boom mike up, out of position. She looked at me as she tucked the end of the cord between the seats, and I understood—there might be things said that little ears need not hear.

I slipped into my headset, and Grace hers, Neil maneuvering his on as he maintained control of the aircraft. He looked over the instruments carefully, checking each.

"Gear is up, we're in good trim. Everything looks good. It looks really good."

From the seat behind me, Grace reached forward and across, putting a hand to Neil's shoulder. He acknowledged it with a soft smile at first, the expression for only himself. Grace could not see it, but I could.

I also saw what Neil did next, taking one hand from the yoke and reaching up to lay it atop Grace's. The contact was unsolicited, and likely unexpected. Had the barrier between them begun to crack? Maybe. But the divide wouldn't fully resolve itself in the skies over western Montana.

Grace slipped her hand from Neil's shoulder, letting him have full focus on the aircraft.

"This is so odd," Neil said, his words clear through the headsets.

"What?"

He replied to my question with a gesture to one of the small display screens on the instrument panel.

"The GPS is registering no satellites," he said. "None."

"Jack told us that," I reminded my friend.

"I know. I'm just trying to wrap my head around a complete shutdown of the system. Would they really do that just to keep people from reaching a place where a kid broadcasts over ham bands?"

It was a question with larger implications than might seem apparent. For one particular reason.

"I guess it depends on who 'they' are," I told my friend. *The child is a liar...*

The phrase rose again, without desire on my part. I had to remind myself that they were spoken by a man, a foreigner, who'd tried to kill us all. Men, woman, and child. Even if they were true, I had no way of knowing what the lie was. And I told myself, sailing through the clear air above my home state, that I would no longer entertain thoughts of it. Not until there was reason to.

"Can you get the maps from my pack?" Neil asked.

Hearing the request, Grace dug into his gear and had the small collection of atlases out almost before I reached back.

"I'm going to take us south over Flathead Lake until we pick up the interstate," Neil said.

I opened the large softcover book that was a compilation of maps covering the Pacific Northwest and most of the Rocky Mountain states, essentially the upper left corner of the continental United States.

"Once we reach that, we're going to follow it," Neil said. "We're back to the days of barnstorming. Flying by looking down. Following highways. Towns and cities are landmarks that take us west. I'm going to need you to keep me updated on what's ahead of us. Especially terrain."

The relevant map page was open on my lap. So was another. A larger representation of the route we'd be taking, with a scale at the lower right. I used that to estimate the distance we'd be covering following the route Neil had decided upon.

"How far did Jack say we could go with the fuel onboard?" I asked.

Before Neil answered he checked his fuel readout.

"He thought two or three hundred," Neil said. "I think it's closer to three."

"How far will we get on that?" Grace asked. "I mean, where will that get us?"

I used my thumb to transfer the scale approximation to the route that lay ahead of us.

"If we stay following I Ninety we'll make it past Spokane, Washington," I said. "But not by much."

"What do we have there, Fletch? If we make it past the city?"

I looked. In the old world there would have been two perfectly acceptable places to land. In the new world, we wouldn't know until we got there.

"We've got an Air Force Base, and before that, Spokane International Airport."

Neil seemed to chew on the information I'd just given him for a moment. Beyond the time it should take to pick one or the other.

"There's a chance," he began, "that we might be able to take this plane more than three hundred miles."

His suggestion led to only one possibility.

"You think we can refuel," I said.

'I think it's a chance we take," Neil said. "If we find fuel, we try it. Either the engine works, or it won't."

"What if it works for a while?" Grace asked. "Then stops once we're in the air because the fuel is bad?"

That, too, was a possibility that had to be considered. But in my friend's mind, it wasn't an insurmountable obstacle.

"If we refuel, we run the engine for ten minutes on the ground," he said. "If there's going to be an issue because of what we put in the tank, it'll happen by then."

Neil quieted for a moment, then gave a quick look to Grace and me.

"Of course, this all depends on me landing this thing."

There was a hint of humor in his words, but it was gallows humor, just enough potential truth in it to make outright laughter inappropriate.

* * *

For the next two and a half hours we flew. South, then west, finding the interstate and following it between and over mountains. The whitish winter landscape turned grey brown as the aircraft carried us out of Montana and over northern Idaho, then into the extreme east of Washington State. The season was not yet in full force, the moist air rolling in from the Pacific fighting with the chilled air, dropping more rain than snow, the Spokane River raging as we flew over its namesake city, mudflows from denuded slopes upstream choking the tributary.

"The city's half flooded," I said, looking below at inundated streets. "This shouldn't happen at this time of year."

"Welcome to the new normal," Neil said.

Gthunk—

The sound reverberated through the aircraft. It was akin to hitting a speed bump in the air, an instantaneous deceleration followed by an acceleration.

"What was that?" Grace asked, leaning forward.

Neil eyed the instruments, and as he did the sound repeated. It was coming from the front of the aircraft. I recognized it, or its earthbound twin, as something between and backfire and an engine not firing on all cylinders.

"Fletch, find me the airport," Neil said.

I'd been practicing my navigational skills as we progressed west and was ready. A quick look at the map on my lap, and an even quicker scan of the terrain below gave me the answer my friend needed.

"Left, heading two-fifty degrees."

Neil turned the aircraft, lining up on the bearing I'd given him. The engine sputtered again, louder this time. He lowered the landing gear, struts folding and wheels folding open beneath us.

"Mommy, what's wrong?"

Krista's worry sounded small through her mother's microphone, her own purposely left unplugged.

"It's going to be fine," Grace said. "Neil's going to land soon."

The engine coughed loudly, three times, the nose beginning to dip.

"There it is," I said, instinctively pointing forward toward the flat expanse beyond the city.

"Thank God," Neil said.

The relief he expressed lasted just a moment as the airport, once a minor hub of international traffic, came into clearer view.

"No..."

Neil's soft exasperation made me lean forward, closer to the windshield. Past the stuttering propeller I saw the runways, two of them, the length of each, and the taxiways that paralleled them, strewn with overturned cars, trucks, buses. Barriers were scattered about the lengths of concrete every hundred feet, creating an unusable patchwork of pavement.

I thought quickly, glancing down at the map.

"Fairchild Air Force Base, due west, four miles," I said, my heart throttling up.

"We can't make that," Neil said.

As if to emphasize the point Neil had made, the engine cut out completely, prop spinning down, coming to a stop, just a flat, still blade on the nose of the aircraft.

"We're going down!" Neil shouted.

Grace grabbed Krista and pulled her close. I braced myself, feet against the firewall, as the plane banked hard and nosed toward the earth.

Twenty One

"There!"

Neil didn't point as he yelled in the suddenly quiet aircraft cabin. But I tracked his gaze, finding a strip of roadway adjacent to the airport. It was long and straight, free of obstacles except for a string of power poles to one side.

"Can you make that? Look at the poles."

"No choice," he said.

He turned the aircraft, fighting the controls, lining up for a dead stick landing, adjusting the Piper left, then right, wingtips dipping in either direction before leveling out.

"Straight, baby, straight," Neil willed the plane.

The power poles drifted away from the roadway on the left, but a stand of dead trees encroached on the right.

"Trees," I said.

"Got 'em."

The aircraft wobbled, falling, nose aimed at asphalt, a double yellow line our centerline.

"Here we go," Neil said.

I stayed focused forward, but reached back between the front seats toward Krista. She took my hand and squeezed tight as her mother held onto her.

"You got this," I told my friend.

"Let's hope so," he said.

We were there. Lined up. Almost on terra firma. Just a fast, expensive glider now as Neil pulled the nose up, flaring the aircraft just an instant before the main gear touched down, hard but not harsh. A few seconds later the nose wheel slapped asphalt.

"Watch it!" I warned. "Watch it!"

To the right, the clearance was inches. The tip of the wing skimmed past the thick, grey trunks of barren fir trees. Neil steered left just a hair, keeping us clear of any disastrous contact, the Piper rolling silently down the road, dead center, brakes slowing us finally to a gentle stop.

The breath Neil let out was deep and loud, a lifetime he'd choked off in the last few minutes.

"I'd like to not do that again," he said, slipping his headset off.

"I'm glad you did, though," I said.

I shed my headset and leaned across the seat, giving my friend a fast shoulder hug. He looked to the back seat. Grace and Krista both flashed relieved, appreciative smiles at him.

"Let's get out of this thing," Neil said.

* * *

It was cold outside, not quite the chill we'd left in Montana, but close. We gathered near the front of the plane, taking in the landscape that surrounded us.

"I still can't get used to the quiet," Grace said.

Quiet wasn't quite the word. Where once we would have heard the roar of jet engines pushing planes into the air, there was hardly more than silence. Even the chirp of a bird would have been welcome to erase the hollow reminder of death. Or the bark of a dog. The honk of a horn.

There was none of that. Just the hush. The ever present scream of aloneness.

Neil and I did a walk around of the Piper, weapons slung. Grace had left Del's rifle—now hers—inside the plane, just a pistol on her hip as she watched over Krista, the little girl picking through colorful stones where the edge of the road dropped down into a gully.

"You didn't break it on landing," I said to Neil.

He gave no reply to my joke of admiration. I moved around to the side of the plane he was on and found him standing near the tail, gaze fixed on the vertical stabilizer.

"Look."

Even if my friend hadn't pointed a finger to direct me, I would have been able to see what he was—a trio of holes in the tail, closely spaced.

"They got us," I said, thankful that the damage, sustained during the volley of fire during takeoff, hadn't stopped us. "Is that going to be a problem?"

Neil put a hand to the punctured metal skin, testing the damage and shaking his head.

"It's clear of the rudder," he said. "I didn't notice any vibrations or control issues."

So we'd dodged a bullet while not dodging three of them. We could do with a continuation of luck of that sort.

"All we need now is fuel," Neil said, looking across the field toward the airport complex, easily half a mile to the nearest perimeter fence.

"You still want to try flying all the way?"

He scanned the road up and down, appraising the makeshift runway.

"Only thing stopping us is seventy-two gallons of fuel," he said.

"Barrel and a half," I estimated. "Piece of cake, right? Find the fuel, a couple empty drums, fill 'em, and edge roll 'em over here."

"With a hand pump," he added.

"Of course," I said. "Every post-apocalyptic flight across the country requires a hand pump."

My friend chuckled. It felt good to laugh, for both of us.

But ours was not the only expression of glee cutting through the quiet right then.

"Hehehehehehe..."

We heard the woman before we saw her. Laughing in the dead woods alongside the highway.

"Mom..."

Grace stepped toward Krista and pulled her daughter close with one arm, her free hand coming to grip her holstered pistol.

More laughter chattered, like a crazed bird. Neil and I came around the plane. He swung his shotgun around from where it was slung across his back. I took my pistol in hand.

"Just one?" I asked.

Neil nodded and brought his weapon up, tracking it toward the cackle growing louder. Drawing closer. Closer.

Then she appeared, stepping from between withered trees, long flowery skirt over thick work jeans and mismatched boots. Her upper body was thickened by three layers of coats. A long knit cap dragged behind her head and down her back like some misplaced tail. Those were obvious features to notice, though not as notable as the pair of clear ski goggles she wore, a trio of thin clear tubes penetrating the gasket that sealed it to her face, each disappearing into a gaudy orange and purple pouch slung on her left side.

"Hello!" she shouted, laughing again after the greeting, hands waving, boots clawing for purchase as she came out of the woods and worked her way toward us up the gully at the side of the road. "Hello!"

Neil kept his shotgun low and ready. I held my pistol at my side and kept an eye on the woman's hands. They were empty, just fingerless gloves, one black and one red, giving some protection against the cool morning. As she reached the crest of the roadway and scrambled to stand upright, I held a hand out toward her, palm flat, signaling her to keep her distance.

She ignored it and headed right for Grace.

"Hey!" I said, bringing my pistol up now. "Stop!"

"Oh, I'm no trouble to you," the woman said.

She never slowed, getting to Grace before Neil or I could do anything to stop her, short of shooting.

Krista ducked behind her mother as the woman stopped close to Grace and stared at her, wide eyed, planting her half-gloved hands gently upon the stranger's cheeks.

"Oh, you are so clean," the woman marveled, gaze gaping through the lenses. "So fresh and clean. And your skin is soft."

Rough fingers dragged over Grace's cheeks, and she reached both hands up, seizing the woman by the wrists, stopping the odd pawing.

"I'm no trouble to you," the woman assured once again.

"Who are you?"

The woman eased her hands away as Grace released her grip. She tucked the hands together under her chin and looked to each of us, smiling, those balloon eyes seeming perpetually in some state of astonishment behind the lenses.

"You don't know just how wonderful it is to see you," the woman said, almost giddy, her expression, her manner, turning almost child-like in a flash. "Everyone else is dead, you know. Dead and rotting, or dead and in tummies."

Krista closed her eyes and slipped fully behind her mother.

"What is your name?" Neil pressed.

"My name?" The woman puzzled for a moment at the question, those wide eyes swimming with uncertainty. "Name?"

Her face tipped toward the overcast sky and, in a flash, her left hand slipped into the pouch slung at her side.

"Hey!" I shouted, taking direct aim at the woman's head.

"Get your hand out where we can see it!" Neil ordered, his shotgun leveled for a clear center mass shot.

Slowly, her face settled toward us again, but the hand remained in the bag and seemed to clench, squeezing something within. As it did, a spray of thick liquid squirted within the goggles, directed at her unblinking eyes. Clear goo dribbled over the blue pupils and dripped slowly from small drainage holes on the underside of the goggles, rolling down the woman's reddened cheeks like slow motion tears.

I grabbed her left wrist and jerked her hand from the bag. In it she held a small, vaguely opaque plastic bladder, tubes jabbed into it like some odd IV bag. The goo within coursed through the tubing with each pump of her fist.

"What the hell is that?" Neil asked.

Just behind us, Grace stepped away from Krista, reassuring her daughter with a touch on the shoulder, approaching the woman.

"Let her go," Grace said.

I eased my grip and the woman drew her left hand back, bladder fisted in it, fingers stilled, the stream of tacky liquid no longer being pumped into the goggles.

"It's okay," Grace said to the woman. "I'm a nurse."

I glanced to Neil, and could tell from his look that neither of us had any idea what Grace was doing. What had drawn her to the strange woman. Why telling her she was a nurse would matter. Then she took hold of the goggles and gently lifted them, revealing the woman's eyes, and we knew. We saw.

Her eyes had no lids. All that remained of those protective flaps of skin were irregular scars above and below the eye where they'd once been attached to both brow and cheek.

Krista gasped and ran to Neil, huddling behind him.

"It's okay," Grace repeated, examining the healed wounds, smiling softly at the woman. "You have to keep them moist, don't you?"

The woman nodded and slipped the bladder back into her pouch.

"Did you do this?" Grace asked.

"Of course," the woman answered, the giddy demeanor she'd arrived with gone now, an embarrassed wariness washed in behind it. "You have to watch for them. Even when you sleep. If you don't, they'll get away."

Grace's hands were on the woman's cheeks, and felt them flush hot just as she drew her hand again from the pouch. A small, sharp knife was fisted in it.

Neil shoved Krista to the ground as Grace began to stumble back from the woman, blocking his weapon. I was the one with a clear shot as the woman slashed forward with the stubby blade, missing Grace by inches.

My shots, two of them, did not miss. One drilled through the left side of her chest, and the other the same side of her neck. She fell away from me and backward, tumbling into the gully, blood spraying as she rolled, arms flailing. At the bottom her body came to rest on its back, limbs askew, face smeared red from the arterial spray. She coughed once, then again, and then made no more sounds, her dead, wide eyes fixed on the darkening sky above.

Krista pulled her knees up and hugged them where she sat on the road near the nose wheel of the plane. Grace scrambled toward her, but Neil grabbed her by the arm and lifted, pulling until she stood, facing him.

"What the hell was that?" he demanded. "Why did you do that?"

"I was trying to help her!"

"You put yourself at risk!" Neil shouted back, then calmed a bit. "You can't do that. Not anymore. Not in this world."

Grace jerked her arm from him, angry and sad all at once.

"The world's not turning me cold," she told Neil. "Not if I can help it."

"She was trying to get close," I told Grace. "To kill you. To kill us."

Grace looked down the slope at the woman who'd sliced her own eyelids off.

"She was crazed," Grace said.

"You mean crazy," I said.

She shook her head.

"There's a difference," Grace said. "Crazy is. Crazed happens. She was driven to this state."

Neil shook his head, exasperated, taking a few steps away.

"You want to treat everyone we come across like a homicidal maniac?!"

With a sharpness I'd rarely seen in him, Neil whipped around toward Grace, shotgun leaning on his shoulder.

"Yes! Yes I do! Because that is what the world is now!"

I holstered my pistol and went to Krista, sitting next to her on the cold roadway and pulling her close. She slid her arms around my neck and sobbed dryly.

"We might want to tone it down a bit," I suggested.

Neil turned away again and stomped down the road, then down the far embankment and into a dirty field. He stopped halfway across it, chain link fence beyond, airport runway past that.

"He's wound too tight," Grace said, watching him. "I'm afraid he's going to snap."

"He'll be okay."

She looked down to me where I sat with her daughter, unconvinced.

"I've known him a long time," I assured her.

"He sees danger everywhere," she said.

"There is," I reminded her.

She quieted for a moment, a sullen truth seeming to weigh upon her.

"Then why are we even trying?" she asked. "And don't feed me that line about hope."

I studied her for a moment, my concern shattering the sudden aura of defeat that had enveloped her. She turned back toward Neil as Krista stood and joined her mother.

"He's so busy worrying about saving us that he's losing himself," Grace told me. "He can't go on like this. He can't."

She drew a breath, then looked to her daughter.

"Stay with Eric, sweetie," Grace said.

Krista nodded and shifted her position closer to me as her mother walked away from us and off the road, crossing into the wasted field where Neil stood. She approached him and stopped close, saying something too far away to hear.

"My mom really likes Neil," Krista said.

"He feels the same," I told her.

Then we watched without saying anything as Neil tried to turn away from Grace, but she would not let him. She took his face in her hands, palms to his cheeks, and held him as she spoke, still more words known only to them. His head bowed a bit, inching toward her. She brought her face up to meet his and they kissed.

"Finally," Krista said, tipping her head against my shoulder where we sat.

I had to agree, watching as the kiss, which lasted but a second or two, ended, my friend and Grace embracing once it was done. Holding each other, alone together as a cold wind blew.

Twenty Two

Neil and I found fuel at the airport. More than enough stored in a tanker that had been used to ram through a back gate by someone in a failed attempt at stealing the beast. Tires had blown in the process, leaving the beefy vehicle a useless wreck. Except for our purposes.

In a mechanics' bay we located a hand pump and filled a pair of empty drums pulled from one of the makeshift barriers blocking the runway, rolling them on their bottom edges a mile to where Grace and Krista waited for us at the aircraft. When we neared them, I could see that Grace had driven a small cross fashioned from fallen branches into the soft side of the roadway just above where the crazed woman had fallen.

The both of us stopped, taking in the sight of the simple memorial, mother and daughter standing near it, holding each other.

"Thank you, Fletch."

I looked to my friend, unsure of what his appreciation was offered for.

"For what?"

He never took his eyes off her as he told me, smiling soft and true through the answer.

"For knowing."

It was more the sentiment in what he was saying than the words that made me understand. I had nudged him to accept his feelings toward Grace. There was no belief on my part that what I'd said before we'd fled my refuge had brought them finally together. What was in their hearts had done that. My friend was simply glad that I had been there for him, even when he hadn't wanted me to be.

We continued on to the plane, placing the barrels near the wings and getting to the laborious process of hand pumping the fuel into the plane's tanks. By the time we'd topped them off, and Neil had fired up the engine, running it for the intended ten minutes to ensure its viability with the aged gas, we'd been on the ground for just over four hours.

"How long to Seattle?" Grace asked as we buckled into the Pipe and donned our headsets, the engine idling loud and perfect.

"Hour and a half," I said, assuming my position of navigator once again, map for the next and, hopefully, final leg of our journey open on my lap.

"Let's get there," Neil said, and throttled the engine up.

The Piper picked up speed along the roadway, the knots of dead trees that had encroached on the right side thinning out until the minor plot of woods was nothing more than a few toppled trunks taken down by wind and weather.

"How's it feel?" I asked.

"Good," Neil said, glancing at the speed indicator, the number climbing steadily. "I think we're okay, Fletch."

The road bumped beneath us, the aircraft riding over the slightly uneven surface without trouble, hardly jostling us within as Neil eased the yoke back again and took us into the air. The Piper climbed steadily, leveling off at a thousand feet above ground level, the interstate visible below, a building ceiling of clouds above.

"We might get some weather," I said.

"No," Neil countered. "No weather."

"You see what's above us, right?"

He did. It couldn't be missed.

"No weather," he repeated. "We're going to get there. Nothing's going to stop us. Not now."

It was more than determination driving my friend, I sensed. It was purpose. I looked to the back seat, meeting Grace's gaze, seeing Krista's smile, and the reason for his certainty was clear.

I turned back toward the windshield and flattened the map on my lap, working with my friend to get us to our destination.

* * *

Mt. Rainier rose into the afternoon sky to our left, and ahead, beyond the city coming into view, a collection of moonscape islands filled the sound. Once lush, they now lay there, dead and ashen.

But what I really noticed was what lay below us, four lanes of blacktop cutting through the wasting woods, the altitude not enough to obscure what stretched across it at varying intervals.

"Look," I said.

Neil glanced out his side of the plane, flying parallel to the interstate beneath us.

"Those aren't just random wrecks," he commented.

"Roadblocks," I said, looking out again. "That at least means there are people."

"Who might not be amenable to visitors," he said.

Grace leaned forward, trying to pick up on our conversation.

"Are we close?"

I nodded at her. We'd made it. Seattle was a building vision in the near distance.

"You want to try for King County Airport?" I asked Neil. "Closer to the city center than SeaTac."

Seattle-Tacoma International Airport was larger, but size mattered little now. We simply needed a runway that was clear of obstructions.

"King County it is," Neil said.

We left our direct adherence to following Interstate 90 and turned southwest, cruising over Lake Washington, crossing the southern tip of Mercer Island, the long runway we were shooting for just beyond the wide expanse of Interstate 5. In five minutes we would be on the ground, that much closer to finding Eagle One.

Then we saw the bright flashes on the ground near southern and western shore of the lake.

Twenty Three

The first burst blossomed in the air ahead of us like a black rose, expanding until it dissolved into the low, wispy clouds. Except for the concussion of its blast wave jolting the plane, the obvious shot of anti-aircraft fire was mesmerizing.

"They're shooting at us!" Grace shouted.

Another shell exploded to our right, then another, shaking the aircraft with a double punch as compressed atmosphere slammed into us.

But they weren't the explosions of movie familiarity. They were bursting in shades of coal black, and bright blue, with sparkles of yellow and orange and red spreading across the sky ahead.

"They're fireworks," I said. "Just fireworks."

"I don't care what they are," Neil said. "Any one of those hitting the right place can take us out."

We'd already taken fire when taking off from Kalispell, and been lucky that the hits we'd discovered later hadn't caused any serious damage. Counting on good fortune continually was far from a smart course of action to take.

"Get out of here!" Grace almost begged, Krista latched onto her, terrified. "Please!"

"I'm trying!"

He turned left, the plane banking sharply, a wall of clouds ahead. I looked out the right window as the aircraft leveled out and could see the ground below still erupting, rising from rooftops, from between buildings, streaks of fire rocketing skyward before blossoming, bright and dangerous.

"I guess that means we're not welcome," I said.

Behind, the last few blasts of aerial mortars faded, just distant thuds as we plunged into the clouds.

"Was that Eagle One doing that?" Krista asked, her petrified voice bleeding through the microphone on her mother's headset.

"No, sweetie," Grace said. "They wouldn't do that."

The child is a liar...

The promise I'd made myself to give those words no place in my waking moments was shattered by what had just happened, and by Krista's innocent wondering. Still, there was no obvious, or even logical link between our ultimate destination and the attack that we'd just evaded. We'd only hoped that reaching Seattle would lead us to Eagle One. There was no guarantee that it, whatever it was, would be there. West was the only direction of certainty we had to go on, and that had been offered to me by a dead man.

Del...

West, he'd said. That was where the broadcasts from Eagle One were coming from. I wondered what Del Drake would do now, if he was here, with us, flying blind toward an unknown. An unmarked place on the map.

Wait...

What *would* he do? It was a simple question, with a blindingly simple answer. He would do what he did—reach out to them. As they had to us.

"The radio," I said, turning to Neil. "Does the radio work on amateur frequencies?"

"Ham bands?" Neil said more than asked. "No. Aircraft frequencies are separate to avoid interference."

It wasn't the answer I wanted to hear. We needed some way, some chance, to reach out to Eagle One again. Just like Krista had from my refuge.

"There's no way to just broadcast into the open, hoping someone will hear?"

Neil shook his head at my suggestion. Just ahead, the clouds parted for a moment, a hint of terrain far below, highways snaking south, choked with wrecks.

"It doesn't work that way," he said. "Just like a ham radio you have to be dialed into a specific frequency. Something someone would be..."

In an instant my friend's demeanor changed, from resistant to energized.

"...listening to."

"What is it?" I asked.

Neil reached to the radio and turned it on before adjusting the frequency.

"One-twenty-one point five," he said. "International air distress frequency. Every airport monitors that."

"They're not an airport," I said.

"We don't know that," he countered. "And you don't have to be an airport. You can monitor aircraft frequencies on different radios."

Neil had a point. One that I hoped was more than just a shot in the dark.

"Eagle One, Eagle One, come in," Neil called out, pressing the transmit button on the yoke. "If you hear us, please come in."

My headset plugged into the co-pilot's jack, I could hear any reply that came. All I heard was the hush below static. White noise.

He put out the same call, with varying levels of pleading, but still received no response. To extend the range of the radio transmission, Neil climbed, taking the Piper up to near 10,000 feet, calling out again and again, listening and hoping.

"Nothing," he said, glancing back to Grace and Krista. "They're not answering us."

Us...

The thought struck me. His characterization of the failed attempt at communication was too broad. Eagle One, if they were listening, hadn't neglected to answer *us*—they'd simply not answered *him*.

"Neil, give Krista the headset," I said.

"What? Why?"

"Who was the last one to talk to them when they actually replied?"

My question was more answer than query, and he immediately understood, slipping out of the headset. I took it from him and stretched the cord between the front seats, slipping off the one Krista was already wearing and replacing it with Neil's.

"What are you doing?" Krista asked.

"We need you to call out to Eagle One," I said.

"Hey," she said brightly. "I can hear you through these things."

I smiled and positioned the boom mic close to her mouth.

"I'll tell you when to talk and when to stop," I said. "Okay? When I point to you you call out to them, and when I stop pointing you be quiet so we can listen for their answer. Got it?"

The little girl nodded. I leaned close to Neil, almost shouting above the engine noise.

"Press the transmit button when I put my hand on your shoulder."

He gave me a quick thumbs up.

"You ready, Krista?" I asked.

"What do I say?"

"Tell them we're trying to find them," I suggested.

Krista looked up to her mother.

"You got them to talk before," Grace told her daughter.

Krista straightened in her seat, pulling against the belts that secured her. She looked to me and gave a quick nod. I put my hand on Neil's shoulder and pointed to our newly drafted radio operator.

"Eagle One," she began, hesitating for a moment, a smile building confidently on her face. "Eagle One this is Big Sky Alpha, come in!"

I stopped pointing and took my hand from Neil's shoulder. We listened for a moment, but heard nothing still.

"Keep trying," I said, and pointed to Krista again as Neil began transmitting.

"Eagle One, this is Big Sky Alpha, we are in an airplane and we're trying to find you. Please help us find you."

Again she stopped, and we all listened, the whispering hiss of no reply dragging our hopes down. But we couldn't stop. Couldn't give up. I was about to put my hand to Neil's shoulder again to begin another transmission when we heard it.

"Big Sky Alpha, this is Eagle One, do you copy?"

Krista's eyes bugged, a wave of collective relief swirling about the aircraft cabin. It was the boy, the same boy, talking to us. To Krista.

"Sweetie, go ahead," Grace told her daughter.

"Eagle One, this is Big Sky Alpha, we hear you! We hear you! How do we get to you?"

"What is your location, Big Sky Alpha?"

"Tell him we're south of Seattle and flying south," I prompted her.

"We're flying south. We're south of Seattle."

There was a brief burst of silence, some contemplation or consideration taking place on the other end of the broadcast. As much as Eagle One was an enigma to us, we were the same to him, or to them.

"Big Sky Alpha, continue flying south. Stay near the coast. How far can you fly on your fuel?"

I relayed the question to Neil and passed his answer on to Krista.

"About five hundred miles, Eagle One," Krista said.

"Copy that, Big Sky Alpha. Keep flying until you see a beacon. It will be a rotating white light flashing twelve times a minute. When you see that, contact Eagle One again on this frequency for further instructions."

"Thank you Eagle One! We are coming to you!"

"Cease further transmissions until you are in sight of the beacon. Eagle One out."

Krista beamed. She threw her arms around her mother. I took Neil's headset from the girl and returned them to him.

"Okay," Neil said. "It's not a destination, but it's a way."

"Let's find it," I said.

Neil pushed the yoke forward and took us gently down, descending through broken clouds, the sun to our right, settling toward the western edge of the world.

"Before nightfall, hopefully," he said.

"Yeah," I agreed, knowing my friend had enough pressure in him keeping us alive up here without having to concern himself with doing it in the dark.

We leveled out at two thousand feet, long streaks of cloud cover above, just occasional puffs at our altitude. Neil flew a southwest course until we reached the coast, then followed the boundary between land and sea. Keeping track on the maps, I noted when we crossed into Oregon over the Columbia River, and reported the coastal towns below as we passed above each, the sky darkening with every landmark we left behind.

"How are we on fuel?" Grace asked from behind, Krista dozing next to her, ears covered by the unplugged headset once again.

"Fuel we're good on," he said. "Light is what we really need right now."

To the east it was already night, sky and land meshed in a wall of blackness reaching toward the stars above. Over my right shoulder, out beyond the blue-black sea, the edge of heaven and earth was a fading line of weak yellow and deep blue. The sun had dipped below the horizon, that half place between day and night existing now, twilight slipping toward full darkness.

"Not that there's anybody from FAA to care, but besides having no license, I've never flown at night."

"You're doing fine," Grace said.

He glanced back to her, a quick look, but one that meant so much more now than just hours before. Somehow this journey, marking a new start for all of us, marked that for them on an entirely different level. The love they suppressed was free now, and it both drove and calmed them. Especially Neil.

"Fletch..."

"Yeah?"

"Just off our nose to the left."

I followed my friend's direction, looking to the south, scanning the landscape, and almost immediately picking up on what he was.

"Rotating beacon," I said, trying to quell my excitement.

"Yeah," Neil said. "Just wanted to make sure I wasn't seeing things."

Grace leaned forward a bit, her head poking between the seats to witness what we were—a fulfillment of what Eagle One had said would happen. This was no lie.

"Thank God," Grace said.

"You think they'll talk to me?" Neil asked.

Krista was asleep. We wanted her to stay that way until it was time to land. Until we knew it was going to be safe and smooth.

"Give it a shot," I said.

Neil readied himself and thumbed the transmit button on the yoke.

"Eagle One, this is Big Sky Alpha, we see your beacon. Come in."

There was no break this time. No silence between call and reply. Someone was waiting for us.

Someone that was clearly not the boy we'd heard from before.

"Big Sky Alpha," a man said, his voice flat and direct. "What are you bringing us?"

Neil glanced to me, and to Grace, who put the pieces together quickly from all that we knew of Eagle One. The transmissions. The requests.

"They promised sanctuary in exchange for medical supplies," she said.

Del had heard the same. The boy broadcasting from Eagle One reading off a list of items they needed, all things a doctor or hospital might need.

"What do I tell them?"

"Big Sky Alpha, respond. You will not be allowed to land without revealing what you are bringing."

Tell us or take a hike. That was the ultimatum just delivered. The problem was, we had nothing of substance to offer, outside some bandages and a suture kit in Grace's backpack.

Neil looked to me, the thought plain in his gaze. It was no different than the one we'd shared when younger, much younger, when caught by his father or mine in some childish transgression. The choice then had been the same as now—lie, or fess up. Then, the stakes had been the loss of some cherished activity. Or, at worst, a stiff hand across the backside.

Here the consequences would be far worse.

"The light's gone," Grace said.

Both Neil and I looked. Beyond the windshield, the darkening earth looked flat and featureless. But it wasn't. There were obstacles. Hills. Buildings. Dead trees stabbing at the sky. Without some guidance, both to get us to the airport and to mark the runway, making it down in one piece was beyond doubtful. Not even taking into account the thick, soupy wall of grey rolling in from the Pacific.

"Fog," I said.

There was virtually no time for a decision. Both Neil and I knew what had to be done.

"Eagle One, we have a defibrillator unit and a supply of epinephrine."

We waited through silent seconds after Neil's transmission, hearing nothing from Eagle One, but getting acceptance of our feigned offering in the darkness ahead.

"Runway lights," I said.

The twin strip of glowing markers stretched out, laying a path upon the black earth for us. But the bright white spots spaced along the runway began to dim, their welcome brilliance fading almost as soon as it had appeared.

"It's the fog," Neil said.

"Please," Grace said, her gaze lifting in silent prayer.

"Eagle One, we're coming in," Neil said, lowering the landing gear.

"Big Sky Alpha, wind is five knots from the west."

The report from the airport, which, from looking at the map, was hardly more than a narrow strip of asphalt just south of the town limits, was welcome. Five knots was a manageable breeze I knew, even without any flight training whatsoever.

"One more time," Neil said, mostly to himself. "I just have to do this one more time."

Getting on the ground was what he meant. In one piece, actually. The deteriorating visual conditions as we descended were going to be a challenge. A test of my friend's skill, and his nerves.

"One hundred feet," Neil called out.

Grace sat back in her seat and reached a hand across to rest upon her slumbering daughter's lap. Krista stirred, her eyes fluttering open.

"Are we there?" the girl asked.

None of us could hear her over the unplugged headset. But Grace smiled at the light of her life and nodded, pulling her into a side hug.

"Fletch," Neil said, and looked to him. "I'm losing the lights."

The mist thickened, blotting out the markers that had been lit for us.

"It's down there," I said.

"I know. But I can't see the runway."

Were we going to come this far only to slam into an already dead pine to the left or right of the landing strip? Or clip the top of a building and tumble out of control?

No. I told myself that. And I told my friend the same.

"You've got this, Neil."

"I can't see it."

"You were lined up," I assured him. "You still are."

"Fifty feet," he said.

The ashen tip of a pine whipped past the right side of the plane, its spear-like tip just missing the end of the wing.

"Come on," Neil nearly begged, easing the Piper left.

Whoosh...

The sound of the engines reverberated off an antenna tower it rocketed past on the left.

"I'm too far left," Neil said, shifting right again.

'Lights!' I shouted, stabbing a finger at the windshield.

Neil was right. We'd been too far left. He slipped right even more, the fog thinning nearer the ground as we were finally over asphalt, the runway's faded white centerline right beneath the spinning prop.

"Ten feet," Neil said.

Then we felt it, for the second time that day, our craft of the sky returning to earth. Wheels slapping pavement.

Behind me, Krista clapped, filled with joy. I was, too. For the moment. But as the Piper slowed, that overwhelming sense of relief was washed away by what resolved through the mist outside.

Twenty Four

The aircraft rolled to a stop halfway down the runway, blinding lights coming on, vehicles speeding toward us from every direction. Six vehicles, I counted. They slowed and stopped, surrounding us.

"I'm guessing we've got some guns pointed at us," I said.

Neil killed the engine and shut the aircraft's systems down. We slipped our headsets off.

"What's our play here?" he asked.

"I think that depends on theirs," I answered.

"EXIT WITH YOUR HANDS EMPTY!"

The command came over a loudspeaker, penetrating the aircraft cabin with ease.

"Not much of a choice," I said, then looked back to Krista. "Hey, we're going to be fine. They probably want to make sure we're good people."

"We are good people," Krista said.

"That's right," I told her. "And they'll see that."

"EXIT NOW!"

I couldn't be certain, but the voice on the loudspeaker seemed to be the same one that had communicated with us over the radio as we approached the airport. The directness I'd sensed then was now dialed up to something approaching a demand.

"Let's go," I said.

Neil opened his door first, pistol still on his hip. I followed out my side of the aircraft, helping Grace and

Krista out and onto the solid runway, a damp chill washing over us.

"KEEP YOUR HANDS WHERE WE CAN SEE THEM! DO NOT MOVE!"

I put my hands to my front, as did Neil and Grace. Past the blinding headlights, diffused to wide spots of harsh white through the shifting fog, silhouettes appeared. People approaching us. One man and one woman.

The woman, her hair dark and short, moved right at me, a stubby MP5 sub machinegun tucked close to her side, business end pointed at my gut, one hand wielding it while the other took the Springfield from my holster and set it on the wing.

"Anything else on you?"

"Knife in my right cargo pocket," I told her.

She fished it out and placed it next to the pistol before looking to Grace.

"Anything on you?"

"I left my weapons in the plane," Grace told her.

The woman shifted her gaze to Krista, the little girl latched onto her mother's leg. She stared at the child for a moment. A long moment that unnerved Grace.

"She doesn't have anything," Grace said.

The woman looked up from the little girl, meeting Grace's protective gaze.

"Jackets off," Elaine said. "Down to your shirts. Everybody."

We followed the instruction, dropping our coats where we stood. All but Krista.

"It's cold," Grace said to Elaine.

"What about the kid's coat?!" Elaine asked loudly, half looking over her shoulder.

"Everyone!"

The voice answered from near the vehicles. That same voice, no longer on the loudspeaker. Clearly someone with command in their blood. And little compassion in their heart.

Elaine looked to Grace, but didn't have to say anything.

"Let's slip this off for right now," Grace said, and Krista did as told, hugging herself, the chill already taking a bite.

"Elaine?!"

"They're clear!" Elaine reported, and took a few steps back away from us, keeping her weapon directed at me.

On the other side of the airplane, where I was certain Neil had undergone the same disarming procedure that we just had, I heard a man affirm that the pilot had been cleared of weapons. His name was Mikey.

Then another figure stepped through the fog, his form cutting the glare of the headlights. He stopped short of the plane, AK slung on his left.

"Bring 'em up," he ordered.

Elaine motioned for us to move. We walked the few steps to the front of the Piper and stopped, Neil already there, his guard, and ours, taking up positions behind.

"My name is Burke Stovich," the man said. "I'm chief of security for the town of Bandon. Where are the materials you brought for us?"

I could feel Neil wanting to glance my way, but knew he wouldn't.

"Well?" Burke pressed when our silence dragged on, his attention focusing on Neil now. "You're the pilot?"

"I am."

"Where are the items you said you had?"

Neil might have been ready to answer. I didn't let him.

"We lied."

Burke's gaze shifted to me. His jaw tightened. But he said nothing to me. Did not strike out. After a moment's consideration of my admission he looked over his shoulder toward the vehicles.

"Load 'em up."

Beyond him, a door opened, metal hinges squealing. The man stepped aside.

"Move," Mikey said from his position behind Neil, the command for all of us.

We walked toward the vehicles, threading between two of the, past the blinding lights, their scattered glow revealing the door I'd heard. It hung open at the back of a van, windowless interior within.

"Get in," Elaine said.

I hesitated and looked back to her. The muzzle of her MP5 rose until it was pointed directly at my face.

"Let's go, Fletch."

Neil stepped in first, helping Krista and Grace up over the rear bumper.

"You don't have a choice," Elaine told me.

She was wrong. There was always a choice. Only here that option other than compliance was death.

I chose to live. To ride this out and see where it would lead us. They could have executed us as we stepped from the plane, or immediately when I'd confirmed our lie. But they didn't.

"Okay," I said, and climbed in the back, sitting on a metal bench bolted to the van's floor on the left side.

Elaine reached out and closed the door. Through the sheet metal I could hear a padlock being clicked shut. We were, in essence, prisoners. There was no view out the sides, the back or to the driver's compartment up front. Just a weak light affixed to the roof allowed us to see each other.

"Fletch," Neil said.

He sat across from me, on the bench bolted to the right side of the compartment, his arm around Grace, and hers stroking Krista's hair to comfort her as the van engine started and we began to move.

"What?"

His gaze shifted, off of me, directing my attention toward the end of my bench closest to the front of the vehicle. I looked, and saw immediately what had caught his eye.

A spot, dark and irregular, both on the worn white painted surface of the bench, and on the bare metal floor of the van. It bore the appearance of some liquid that had spilled and dripped onto the floor. A colored liquid, the tinge of deep, crusted crimson still apparent against the pale top of the bench.

Blood.

Twenty Five

The van stopped after just a few minutes, vehicle brakes screeching behind us, signaling that the convoy which had accompanied us from the airport had stopped. Voices consulted beyond the locked rear door for a moment, and then it opened.

There were guards everywhere. Men and women. Bearing arms that any big city tactical team would take for granted. Only the dress was different. Ninja black was traded here for hunter camo and sturdy work wear, load-bearing vests over all, mag pouches bulging, wires running from earpieces to radios. They were connected. To each other.

And to someone else. Someone calling the shots.

We were ordered out of the back and directed to walk north. Six of the guards escorted us down a narrow street, then between buildings, a stiff sea breeze whipping between the structures, the fog that had made our landing sketchy rolling in from the ocean in fat white waves. They'd stripped us of everything but our first layer of clothes at the airport, jackets taken and piled. The bite of the wintry ocean air stung.

"Mom, I'm cold," Krista said.

Grace pulled her daughter closer as they walked and glanced back to Elaine. She was probably about Grace's age. There was a hardness about her. An absolute conviction.

Still, she was a woman. Maybe a mother. If not now, then once.

"It's freezing out here," Grace said to her.

Elaine, her MP5 pointed at the ground now, considered the plea as they walked, then looked to Krista.

"We're almost there," Elaine said. "It'll be warm. I promise."

A touch of humanity, it seemed. But what about the others? All I knew about them so far were a smattering of names that I'd learned through introduction, or heard in the chatter back at the airfield. Burke. Jeff. Jenny.

And Martin. That name I'd heard more than one of our welcoming committee speak, though not in any direct way. There was no 'Martin' among them, but there was most definitely someone of that name they were speaking of. Speaking in strict tones. Not quite reverence, but close. Respect, if we were lucky. Anything beyond that and I feared we'd have another Major Layton on our hands.

"Up there," Burke told us, pointing to a small warehouse, a pair of guards waiting at its door.

"The child is a liar," Neil said quietly, looking to me as we walked.

I half-turned my head toward him, angry and incredulous. He knew. He'd understood what the dying crewman had said, right then and there, and he'd kept it to himself.

"You don't work around diplomats for years and not pick up a bit of the major languages," he said.

"So you just decided to keep that from me? From us?"

"Like you decided to after your trip to the foreign dictionary section of the Kalispell library?" he fired back, blunting my challenge.

So we both knew. And we both feared that letting on might dull our collective determination to get to Eagle One.

Yet we were here. Whatever 'here' was, beyond a mark on the map. Beyond a collection of people who seemed less than happy we'd dropped in on them, despite offering urgings to come and directions to guide us.

As we neared the old structure, corrugated metal sides tinged a solid rust red, one of the guards pulled the door open, a dimly lit interior beyond. But before we stepped through I noticed something else. A neatly stenciled sign next to the entrance. One that had the appearance of being freshly painted again and again, no hint of weathering or corrosion upon it. An innocuous descriptor of the building we were about to enter—Meeting Hall.

"Inside," Burke told us, his AK at the ready now, no longer slung, finger just outside the trigger guard.

There was no point objecting or hesitating. We'd come this far. It was time to finish the journey.

I looked to my friends and then stepped through the doorway.

Part Four

Micah

Twenty Six

The door closed behind us and the six guards led us to the center of the space, an old, small warehouse, single light fixture suspended from the ceiling. Just enough light emanated from it that I could make out dozens and dozens of folding chairs stacked neatly on rolling carts pushed against the west wall of the structure, but nothing else. The room was otherwise bare. Besides the door we'd entered through, there was just one other, on the opposite wall of the space. It opened after we'd been waiting for a few minutes and someone came through, Krista gasping softly when she saw him.

He walked toward us, hissing through his mask, oval holes in the vintage respirator darkened, just a hint of eyes beyond the smoky glass. Black rubber gloves and boots covered his hands and feet, a loose white plastic jumpsuit everything else. A few feet from where we stood he stopped.

"What did you bring?"

The question he posed crackled past the mask's dull filter, like steamy spittle erupting from a leaking radiator.

"They didn't bring anything," Burke said.

The man in the respirator looked past us to the head of the guard detail. An instant of silence seemed to telegraph some annoyance that was impossible to see on his face.

"I asked *them*."

Burke offered no reaction to the verbal slap, standing mute behind us. Mute and armed.

"Nothing," I said.

Behind, two of the six guards who'd escorted us here lifted their rifles and put the muzzles at the back Neil's and my skull. Some not so gentle urging to come up with a better answer. Or else.

"That was not the information you gave when you were allowed to land," the man said.

"It was the only way you'd let us land," Neil said. "We tried Seattle, but the welcome they gave us included artillery."

"Seattle," the man parroted, laughing lightly behind the mask. "Yeah, that sounds about right for them."

"Pardon me for not finding humor in this," I said. "But the only difference I see between you and them is you look ready to shoot us on good old solid ground."

Beside me I could sense Krista's fear rising. Grace laid a harsh look on me.

"How about we just chill a bit?" she asked and suggested.

The man looked to her. Then to Krista. He took a step forward and crouched down, placing his masked face even with hers.

"How old are you?" the man asked.

Krista glanced up to her mother, seeking some permission to answer. To speak to the stranger. Grace hesitated, then nodded.

"I'm nine."

The man seemed to mull on the answer for a moment, then his head tipped upward, gaze angling to Grace, then Neil, and finally to me. He rose and drew a long, filtered breath.

"Come with me," he said.

The guards began to move as he turned, but he waved them off sharply.

"Just them," he said, nodding to the four of us. "Just our visitors."

It wasn't as if we had any choice in the matter. The men and women equipped for battle weren't following, but they would be close, I was certain. With only a brief hesitation stalling us, we followed the unknown man through the door he'd come in through and down a short hall, another door at its end, bits of muted light sneaking in around its edges. He pushed it open and an odd bright light filled the corridor, flat and filtered. We saw why as we emerged into an opaque tunnel, walls, floor, and ceiling all made of thick plastic stretched around a tubular metal frame, exterior floodlights bathing it from outside. It seemed to be affixed to the building we'd just exited, its length stretching across a narrow roadway, with steps at each side where street transitioned over curbs to sidewalks. Through the milky walls I could see people. A few to either side, the unmistakable silhouette of rifles in their hands. More guards, I thought. Securing this passage.

But a passage to where? To what?

The plastic tunnel reached a set of steps, the thick material following every tread and riser as we mounted them, landing on a porch, the tunnel pinched and gathered there to pass through a doorway minus the door. The masked man moved through the opening, leading us into a house. Or what had been one before every exposed inch was covered with the same sturdy plastic. Where there might have been furniture, a table, a television, in some past incarnation, the space, which certainly was the home's living room, now served only as some sort of way station, one way in behind us, and two ways out just ahead.

The masked man stopped and looked at us through the respirator's darkened lenses.

"Wait here until I call you back," he said, lifting a hand and stabbing a gloved finger toward the left exit, strips of plastic hanging over it to obscure the space beyond. "Go that way only."

He didn't wait for any acknowledgement, simply turning away and disappearing through the exit on the right side. A rustle of movement sounded beyond, then a wet hiss cut sharp through the house.

"Any guesses?" Neil asked.

"On what?" I asked back.

Neil gestured to the space that seemed not far from some mob murder room depicted in movies.

"It's a vestibule," Grace said. "For a clean room."

"A what?" Neil pressed her.

"A space to keep dirt out," Grace explained. "Or germs. The way he went is a decon chamber. That's the shower we're hearing."

"A decontamination chamber," Neil parroted, uncertain.

"That way allows access to the clean room," she said, pointing toward the shower sound.

"And this way?" I asked, gesturing toward the exit on the left.

The spray of water quieted and Grace looked to me.

"I think we're about to find out."

The slap of bare feet on a hard floor, then the rustle of clothes being slipped on, preceded a stillness. A silence. We waited.

"Come back," the man said, his muted voice seeming to have shifted, coming from beyond the narrow strips of plastic obscuring the way beyond the left exit.

"After you," Neil said.

I reached forward and pushed the plastic strips aside, leading us toward yet another unknown.

Twenty Seven

We came into a room that was cut in half, a plastic wall sealing one side from the other. Beyond the clear barrier I could see computers and wires and radio equipment arranged precisely atop a long table against the far wall. And above that, mounted to the plaster, was the thing that defined the place, for me at least—an American eagle, sculpted flat, the piece of art in relief seeming poised to spring off the wall.

"Eagle One," I said aloud.

"Welcome," the man said, stepping into the space beyond the barrier from a room to the right.

It was the man who'd been masked and bio-suited just minutes before. Now he wore jeans and sweatshirt, with pristine sneakers upon his feet, not the thick boots that had been mated with the bio suit.

"Just what is going on?" Neil asked.

"Just one moment," the man said, then walked across the space beyond the barrier and tapped on a door. "Micah, can you come out?"

"I'll be right out, dad."

Krista looked up at us, excited.

"That's him," the little girl said. "That's the voice."

The man approached the wall of soft plastic and smiled at Krista, no mask between them now.

"You're right," he said.

I looked above. A small speaker and microphone was mounted to the ceiling, and on the opposite side of the barrier an identical setup existed, allowing clear communication from one side to the other.

"I'm Martin Jay," the man said, introducing himself.

The door he'd tapped on opened, offering a glimpse of what lay beyond, a simple bedroom. A child's bedroom. And from it came a child. *The* child.

"Micah," Martin said. "Come meet our new arrivals."

He was young, but older than Krista, maybe by a year or two. His face was thin, but not the kind of thin we'd come to know. Not the starving, jarring state of emaciation so many had worn like sick costumes as death raced at them. It was a stature thing with the boy, I thought. In times long past he might have been referred to as sickly. With his lithe limbs wrapped in sweats and a long tee shirt, feet clad only in socks, he looked to have appropriated the appearance of a patient instead of a pre-teen.

I took in the sight, not only of the boy, but of the environs that confined him, and realized that he was sick.

"Will you do the introductions?" Martin asked, looking to me.

"Of course. I'm Eric Fletcher, this is my friend Neil Moore, his..." I stuttered for a moment as I considered what label to append to Grace's name, but realized it was their place to define the relationship, not mine. "...this is Grace. And this cute little bug is Grace's daughter, Krista."

Krista lifted her hand a bit and waved it shyly.

"Are you Eagle One?" the little girl asked.

"I am," Micah said. "How old are you?"

"I'm nine."

"I'm eleven," he told her, the conversation narrowing to just the two of them. "I remember your voice. You started calling out to me as Big Sky Alpha."

"I picked that name," Krista told him.

"Would you like me to show you my radio?"

Krista balked at the invitation, her gaze sweeping the clear barrier between Micah and her.

"I can show you from this side," he said.

Krista stepped closer to the separation. Martin looked to the rest of us and nodded toward the way we'd entered.

"Why don't we let the young ones talk for a while," he said.

Grace hesitated at the suggestion, the protectiveness about her showing.

"She'll be fine," Martin assured her. "You can hear from out there."

The promise came from a stranger. A stranger who'd seen to our taking by force. But he was also the one who, if any consequences of our lie were to be suffered, had spared us.

"Okay," Grace said, putting a hand to her daughter's back. "I'll be in the room we came through, sweetie."

Krista acknowledged her mother's words with a cursory nod, her attention almost fully fixed on Micah as the boy pointed to different radios and computers, explaining what each was, and what each did. Martin slipped from the room beyond the barrier, and so did we, exiting the way we'd come in with the chatter of little voices behind us.

Twenty Eight

Martin emerged from the right side access to the clean room, no full body suit and respirator this time. Just the same jeans and sweatshirt we'd just seen him in beyond the thick plastic barrier.

"My apologies for the precautions," he said. "The bio suit is a necessity until I'm sure anyone I meet is relatively healthy."

The man was worried about contamination. Not of himself, but of the boy.

"What's his condition?" Grace asked for us.

"He has an immune system disorder," Martin explained. "Which wouldn't be such a mountain to climb if it wasn't for his heart."

His heart...

A memory rose. Images that had been broadcast from the Denver station, before Neil had reached my refuge. Strangers had gotten the cameras and transmitter working, sending out a message intended for Eagle One. One of the people, her name was Jennifer, I remembered, she was the one on camera, and at one point she displayed a photo. A grisly picture of an open chest cavity, instruments spreading flesh and ribs to reveal a, presumably, still-beating heart. She'd said then that what was on the picture was what they could bring. That bit of pulsing, vital human muscle.

"Does he need a transplant?" I asked.

"Not anymore," Martin answered. "He had it two months ago."

"Wait," Grace interjected. "Your son in there had a transplant? A heart transplant? Here?"

The incredulity pouring from her was obvious and intense.

"Yes."

For a moment her mouth hung slightly open. As a nurse, what she was hearing strained not only the limits of the possible, but also the prudent.

"Do you even have a hospital?" she asked.

"A functioning one? No. But we have a couple doctors in town. One of them is the surgeon who was supposed to perform the transplant on Micah before the world fell apart. He brought his wife with him here when we were able to assure some sort of safety to him. And to others."

"And the heart?" I asked.

Martin quieted for a moment. A too long moment.

"Where did you get the heart?" I pressed, and still he did not answer. "I'm only curious about this, you understand, because I saw people broadcasting from a Denver television station with a picture of a heart still very much inside someone, and they were saying they could bring that. And they were talking to you. To this place."

For another few seconds the man stood silent. But this interlude seemed to come from a place of contemplation, not avoidance.

"Some people took what we were asking for too literally," he said. "They were desperate. Ready to do things that no person should just to get here, to the safety we could offer. We were just requesting medical supplies, instruments, things like that. Things we didn't have but that the surgeon said we would need. That's all."

"Quid pro quo," Neil said. "You bring us what we need, and you can stay among us."

"Basically," Martin confirmed. "We have had to turn some away. They weren't compatible with our community. I doubt they would have been compatible with any community that didn't include bars and guard towers."

That was not surprising. Criminals, or those with such tendencies, were just as likely to survive as anyone. Maybe more so, actually. When morality was discarded, doing what one needed to survive came easier.

"You still haven't said where the heart came from," I reminded him.

"A child," Martin said. "One of our own."

His mood turned grim with memory. Some dark moment rushing from the past to the here and now.

"It could have happened two years ago, three. Just a ten year old boy climbing a tree. Nothing odd about that. Except the tree was like all the others. Dead, brittle. The limb he was crawling out onto snapped and he fell."

The rest didn't need to be told. Head injuries. Brain death. An awful decision.

"His parents let him go so that Micah could live," Martin said. "My son had maybe a month left in him when that happened. Now, he has more."

I thought on what he'd just shared. The absurd normality of it. When the entire planet was dying, the extremes of saving and extending life still did work. That said something about us as a species. Our resilience. Even our love.

"You have power," Neil said, gesturing to the fixture above.

"We have a hydro setup in the river," Martin explained. "The Coquille. It's rudimentary, but we're improving it. One of our residents was an engineer at the Hoover Dam. We have solar, wind, diesel generators for backup."

"You have diesel?" I asked with some doubt. "It's not contaminated by now?"

"We make our own. Another resident who came to us with her family worked in petrochemicals. She designed and helped build a processing unit for what we pump from a couple existing wells to the south of town. It's small, but we have hopes to expand that."

"How many people are here?" Grace asked.

"I believe we are at four hundred and eight," Martin answered, smiling as he caught a mistake. "Make that four twelve. I'm assuming you want to stay."

I'd been master of my own destiny, reliant on myself for more than a year, with Neil and Grace joining that effort to stay alive not long ago. Here I, we, would be assimilating into an already existing band of survivors.

"Everybody helps out," Martin said. "Different things. There are committees, all the usual things that crop up when people try to run things together."

It was all useful information. All to be expected from a place that had established itself as a sanctuary for those of some moral fiber robust enough to seek out Eagle One and find it. But there was a massive piece of the truth missing from what Martin had shared.

"And what about food?" I asked.

"You'll be well supplied," Martin said. "Nothing extravagant, but not bad."

"And where does it come from?"

He smiled at my questioning, maybe amused at my attempt to drill down to a nagging fact.

"I mean," I began, "you somehow guided people to hidden food caches across the country and—"

"Micah did that," Martin corrected, interrupting. "Not me."

"Right," Neil said. "We heard him on the radio."

"No," Martin said, shaking his head slightly. "He didn't just tell people where to find the food lockers. He found them."

What the man was telling us made no sense. It was clear he noticed our reaction, and the extent of our disbelief.

"Micah," Martin began, "for all the issues he's had with his health, he's a remarkable boy. Brilliant. Even more than that. The only real way to describe him is beyond genius."

"So he's smart," Neil said.

Martin shook his head mildly at the gross misstatement.

"Smart is something that schools try to measure," Martin said, with the tone of a father marveling at his child. "No one has ever been able to quantify him. They've tried since he was four."

"He's a savant," Grace said, picking a term of art to describe the child.

"He's something," Martin partly agreed.

"Okay, he's off any chart of brain power ever conceived," I said. "How does that get him to knowing where those food caches were?"

Martin glanced over his shoulder, toward the space where Micah was schooling Krista on the operation and interconnection of computers and radios.

"He's spent most of his life isolated in places like that," the father shared. "Sealed rooms with purified air. By himself much of that time. Thinking, experimenting, probing."

Probing...

The word had a connotation beyond mere acts of curiosity.

"Remember the NSA snooping scandal a year or so before the blight hit?"

Who couldn't? The instruments of the nation's intelligence apparatus had been turned inward, with the capability to poke into virtually every aspect of a citizen's life, mostly without restraint or accountability.

"Micah was infuriated by that," Martin said. "We talked about it at the time. He's a child, and his brilliance doesn't equate with maturity, but he grasped that issue with an understanding that...well, it actually moved me. He seemed like such an old soul when we discussed it, the ramifications to freedom. Even what freedom meant."

Then Martin paused, smiling through a slight shake of his head, marveling again, but in a different, a more serious manner.

"But he was doing more than talking, I learned," Martin said. "He didn't tell me until after the blight had hit and things started to get bad. It was a couple weeks before the Red Signal when he fessed up."

"To what?" I asked.

"To hacking the NSA."

A look volleyed between us. I half expected a laugh from Neil, one that I would certainly join in on. But there was no hint from Martin that what he'd just shared was anything close to a joke.

"I didn't believe it either," the man said. "Then he showed me. He'd found a way into a secure communications node. The way he explained it, it was like a hub where satellite and radio and land communications all passed through. And I asked him, wouldn't that stuff be encrypted?"

"It would," Neil said. "Everything sensitive from where I worked at the State Department was."

"I know," Martin said. "He showed me stuff from State, from the Department of Defense, the White House, other agencies. From just about everywhere."

"Wait, what?" I asked, losing track of just what his son had supposedly done. "You said he hacked the NSA, not those other places."

"Right," Martin confirmed. "He didn't have to hack them—the NSA already had."

There'd been news reports of possible illegal snooping directed at civilians, and even some toward elected officials. But what Martin was suggesting pushed that toward another realm entirely.

"You're saying the NSA had routine access to every government communication?" I asked.

"Yes," Martin said. "Once Micah had them, he had everybody."

"Okay, okay," Neil said, still trying to get a grip on the one small detail of this that pushed it from disturbing to fantastical. "Micah, your son, that eleven year old kid in there broke into the NSA, and cracked their encryption?"

"Actually," Martin corrected. "He was nine at the time he did that."

Our silence signaled a mix of disbelief and almost frightened awe.

"Look, I didn't actually believe it at first," Martin said. "I thought maybe that Micah had concocted the whole thing to entertain himself. You know, something because he was suffering from an adolescent version of cabin fever. Being isolated like he was, like he is, it does affect him."

"But he did something to convince you," Grace said, reading the man correctly.

Martin nodded, the event flooding back, a sense of wonder blossoming for him again.

"He said something was about to happen," Martin said. "From all the intelligence he was seeing. That's how he was acting—like his own little intelligence agency. From all this, he could tell there was a tipping point being reached. Assets were being moved. He said it was like a countdown had started."

"To the Red Signal," I said.

"As it turned out, yes," Martin said. "I needed to know how real any of what he was saying was. One of the things he showed me were the locations of the supply lockers. The ones he ended up guiding people to. There was one supposed to be close, just up past Coos Bay, so I drove up there with a shovel, and I stabbed it into the ground, and I hit metal. I cleared it off and opened the red lid up, and it was full. Food, water, chemical light sticks. I didn't doubt Micah after that."

There was no reason to not believe what the man was telling us. But there was every reason to find it completely implausible.

"How the hell did your nine year old son break the most secure encryption known?" Neil asked. "Governments can't do that."

"You're asking the impossible," Martin said. "He tried to explain it to me, but it's so beyond me, so technologically esoteric, that I realized I'd never had a full grasp on just how special Micah is. Then, I stopped questioning, because it didn't matter. What he was allowing with the information, the intelligence he'd hacked, was a way for us to survive. For him to survive. It allowed us to save Bandon as a community and to make it a sanctuary for people like you."

I let what Martin had told us sink in for a moment. There was no point in trying to discredit what he had shared. The proof was on his side. Except for one thing.

"You're the one in charge here?" I asked.

"People look to me because of what Micah's done. And what he's still doing. Sometimes difficult decisions have to be made, and it falls on me to do that."

So he was the head honcho. The shot caller. That meant he had to know the answer to the question nagging me.

"You have four hundred people here," I recalled. "And you've been feeding them for over a year."

"Basically, yes."

"How?" I asked. "With what? If you gathered every one of those food lockers in the country, maybe. But you didn't."

"No," Martin said. "We didn't."

"So where does the food come from?"

Martin considered my question for a moment. Not as if he was deciding how to answer, but how *not* to.

"Don't take this wrong," he began, "but you're not entitled to that information just yet. Tomorrow you might be, or the next day, or next month. We just need to see that you're going to fit in here, first. Fair enough?"

I didn't think 'fair' had anything to do with it. He could have just said the location of some obviously huge food cache under their control was secret, but he didn't. He dangled the possibility of knowing out there with a subtle hint to play along if I really wanted to know.

"We appreciate you letting us stay," Grace said, sensing there would be no more exchange between Martin and me on the subject at hand.

"You're very welcome," Martin said, then glanced back toward the room where his son and Krista were. "Micah needs to take some medication and get some rest."

"I'll go grab my daughter," Grace said, and disappeared up the hallway.

Alone with Neil and me, Martin seemed to study the two of us. I thought he might be making an appraisal of our usefulness to the town.

I was wrong.

"No more bullshit from you," he said, quiet and firm, like a man who didn't need to raise his voice to get an understanding across. "You lie again like you did to get on the ground here, and I'll send you out into the wasteland."

He didn't wait for either of us to acknowledge or agree to his admonition. There would be no discussion of it. He'd drawn a line in the sand and warned us to never cross it.

"Head on out the way you came in," he said. "Someone will get you set up with a place to stay."

He left us then, making his way back into the clean side of the space beyond.

"Tough love?" Neil wondered aloud.

I didn't know if it was that. Or something hinting at a darker part of the man's nature. Possibly he'd come to believe that an iron fist was sometimes necessary, or that the simple implication of its existence would be enough to avoid trouble down the road. Whether it was either possibility, or something I could not yet see, the fact remained that we were here. We were alive. We were safe.

I hoped that that would last.

Twenty Nine

We came out of the Meeting Hall to find Burke and Elaine waiting for us, all the weapons and personal gear we'd been forced to surrender upon landing before us again, neatly gathered on the sidewalk.

"Anything still in the plane you can get in the morning," Burke said, his abrupt officiousness on full display.

Elaine took the small coat that was bunched with the rest of the items and spread it open, bending slightly as she held it out to Krista.

"Better get this on," the woman said.

Krista slipped her arms into the garment. Grace crouched and cinched it tight against the chill, looking up to the woman who'd just shown a modicum of kindness.

"Thank you," Grace said, a wary gratitude about her.

"Keep your weapons ready and in good order," Burke instructed, the direction delivered matter-of-factly. "Everybody in town has to be ready at a moment's notice."

"For what?" Krista asked.

Burke looked to her, then back to each of us, skipping the child's question.

"You on your own?" he asked me.

"Excuse me?"

Burke gestured to Grace.

"Do you need a place of your own?"

I understood his question now. The gist of it, at least. Exactly where it was leading I still wasn't sure.

"We've all been together, but, sure. I'm flying solo, if that's what you're getting at."

"And you, ma'am?"

Grace grinned lightly at the respect he was showing her.

"Something for the three of us," she said, taking Neil's hand in hers.

"Okay," Burke said. "I'll get the three of you set up. Elaine, you get..."

"Eric," I prompted him.

"Elaine will get you situated."

I gathered my things, slinging my pack and shouldering my AR. Elaine pulled my Springfield from the back of her waistband and handed it to me. I holstered it and watched Neil and Grace walk off with Krista, Burke leading them through the fog. My friend looked back to me and gave a thumbs up. I wasn't sure if he was signaling that everything was all right, or that it would be. The difference between belief and hope.

"You ready?" Elaine asked.

The woman who'd held a gun on me not an hour earlier was now my guide.

"I still have some questions," I told her.

"I know."

Her acknowledgement was just that, and she offered no opportunity for me to seek answers. At least not from her.

"Come on," she said.

She headed off in the same direction my friends had just left with Burke. I stayed close, trying to take in as much of the town we passed through as I could with the misty night blotting nearly everything out.

But not everything.

As we crossed a street, a light resolved on the far corner, its beam angled up, into the fog. Drawing nearer I began to understand its purpose. And I began to feel just a bit less apprehensive about the town, and our welcome, and the warning words we'd received from its de facto leader.

All because of a flag. The flag. Old Glory. Its stars and its stripes flapped lazily atop a pole where two roads met, the gentle breeze moving it.

The people here, it seemed, still believed in it. Still believed in something I had my entire life. Freedom mattered.

I only hoped the banner that symbolized it wasn't being flown just for show.

Thirty

Elaine slipped a key into the lock and opened the front door. She reached in and flipped a light switch of before stepping to the side.

"Welcome home," she said.

I looked past her from my place on the porch. A single lamp burned within the space that had been dark just a moment before, its ability to throw much light muted by a thick shade that topped it. The table it sat upon rested next to a wooden rocking chair, paisley cushion tied to the seat. I didn't actually see any doilies from where I stood, but I was willing to bet that I'd find some once I was inside.

"It belonged to an older lady," Elaine said, sensing my mild amusement at the interior décor.

Belonged...

As with so many things after the blight, possession had become more fluid. My truck was taken by a woman in the north of Montana trying to get her son to safety. An anonymous elderly lady in Bandon, Oregon had surrendered her house to me.

"She died?' I asked, though I was really asking the specifics of her passing.

"I assume so," Elaine said. "I was told she left with a son or daughter from out of state. They came to take her with them when things got bad."

That moment was when I began to understand Elaine. The quiet compassion she'd shown to Krista while we were being escorted to the Meeting Hall after landing should have been my first clue, but it had taken until now, when she'd shared that she was '*told*' of the reason for the old woman's absence. The woman standing with me on the porch of the pretty house was an outsider. She was no Bandon local. Like me, and others, she'd come here. Maybe drawn by Micah's broadcasts.

"Try to keep only one light on at a time," Elaine said. "That way we don't put a strain on the power system."

"Understood."

I put my rifle down against the wall just inside the door, then shed my backpack and let it come to rest next to the wooden rocker. The pistol I left on my hip for a moment as I wandered into the space, back through the kitchen, to the pair of small bedrooms and the single bathroom. I turned the faucet over the sink on and water came out. Cool, fresh water. When I returned to the living room, Elaine was still standing there, waiting.

"You have water," I said.

"Cold only, for the time being. If the power stabilizes there's talk of converting the water heaters to electric that already aren't."

"When you say there's talk of it..."

"Improvement Committee," she told me. "It's just talk right now. There are bigger projects to tackle before we all get hot showers again."

I supposed it was a luxury item, considering. But it was hard to let that be too much of a black mark against the place when compared to what was already being offered. Shelter. Power. Food.

Food...

"Where does the food come from?"

Elaine looked past me in a failed attempt at avoidance.

"You'll have plenty in your kitchen for a week," she said.

"That's not what I meant."

"I know," she told me.

"Martin wouldn't answer that question either."

"Then maybe you should stop asking it," Elaine suggested.

So we were trusted. To a degree. The people of Bandon had accepted us into their community, without yet accepting us completely. I supposed that was fine, except for the fact that they were the ones who had advertised for people to join them. To build up their numbers, presumably.

"Take tomorrow," Elaine said, sidestepping the brief burst of awkwardness. "Get used to things. Then we'll slot you into an assignment."

"Assignment?"

She regarded me with a look that doubted I was too stupid to understand the obvious.

"This isn't summer camp. Everyone pulls their weight."

"Of course," I said, trying to erase the impression of idiocy I'd given.

Elaine looked to my rifle where I'd leaned it next to the fireplace.

"Burke will probably put you on the wall."

The wall...

"That sounds ominous."

"Weeks of boredom interrupted by seconds of terror," she said, almost smiling. "Or so it's told."

She turned and went to the door, stepping out and looking back as I followed, standing just inside the house. My house.

"If you need anything, have any questions, your neighbors can steer you right."

"Thank you," I said, and she left the porch, heading down the walkway, stopping once again halfway to the sidewalk.

"I'm two blocks over if they can't help you."

I nodded a thanks and she left, walking up the dark sidewalk. No different than anyone might. Except for the submachine gun slung across her back.

"Wait," I said, leaving the house and porch and going to where the walkway ended, waiting as she paused and looked back to me. "Elaine..."

She smiled. It was a good smile, if somewhat measured. She wore it well, the sort of expression offered only when truly felt.

"Morales," she said. "Elaine Morales."

"Eric Fletcher."

"Glad to meet you, Eric Fletcher."

"You, too."

She turned away and continued up the block. I watched until she rounded the corner and was gone.

* * *

Two hours later I was sitting in a chair in the living room, staring at a clock atop the mantle. A cord ran from it to a wall outlet. Its hands moved, second hand ticking time away. I smiled at the simple sight. At the reminder of a once mundane device now made amazing by the relative abundance of electricity. I might have marveled at it for hours to come, but the knock at the door ended my distraction.

A knock at the door...

My door. How odd was that? How long would it take for that sound, and the concept of a visitor, to seem normal once more?

"Hello, Eric."

Martin stood on the porch, rifle slung over his shoulder. An AK, I could easily tell. On his belt a pouch hung low with two additional magazines. Thirty rounders. The man wanted to be ready wherever he was.

"Martin..."

"Can I come in?"

I didn't need to offer a 'yes'. I simply opened the door fully and stepped aside. The man entered and immediately leaned his rifle against the wall near the entry. Right next to mine.

"Ready to grab and go," Martin commented, seeming pleased at the placement of my weapon. "You're a good addition to the town."

"Let me guess, a common defense?"

Martin nodded and gestured a chair near the cold fireplace.

"May I?"

"Please," I said, sitting once my guest had.

"Common defense," Martin repeated. "Very founding father of you. I like that. And, yes, we ask that those who decide to stay be prepared to defend the town."

"That's necessary?"

The man nodded, a tiredness to his affirmative response.

"I wish it weren't," he said. "Burke will give you an assignment. Probably on the wall."

"Right. Elaine said the same thing."

"Elaine..."

He let her name hang there for a moment, a hesitant prelude in how it was delivered.

"Did she share her story with you?"

I shook my head.

"Didn't ask," I told him.

"In time you should."

His suggestion did make me curious. Everyone who'd survived had a story. Little was ordinary anymore. Not in extraordinary times. Which made me wonder what set the tale of Elaine Morales apart from what others had experienced.

"And how about you," I said.

"Me? I'm an open book."

"When you choose to be."

He smiled at my soft shot across his bow.

"That wasn't meant for you," Martin said, a note of apology in his tone. "It was for your friend's benefit."

"Neil?"

"I didn't want to create a rift, so I laid it out to both of you."

"We were all in on saying we had things to offer so we could land."

"I know," Martin said. "It's not about what you did. It's about what he might do."

I was at a loss. The man had spent all of ten minutes, maybe twenty, in the presence of the best friend I had, and he was peering into some dishonest part of his nature.

"Just what do you think he's going to do?"

"He's with the woman," Martin said. "And the girl. Yes?"

"He is."

"I thought so."

So he'd pegged Neil and Grace as a couple, and Krista as part of their blended union. What possible bearing that could have on his trusting of my friend was beyond me.

"A man will do anything for his family," Martin said. "Anything to keep them alive and safe. Steal. Lie. Cheat. Kill. I know I would."

"Neil is as decent as they come," I told him.

"So was I," Martin said. "Then the world changed. Rules went out the window. We're trying to reestablish some of that here. Some people can't hack that. Life out there has changed them too much."

"Not Neil."

"I hope you're right," Martin said.

I sat back in my chair. The man before me was no James Layton. He was no dictator laying down *his* law under the threat of death. I really didn't know what he was. But I might be able to know more of who he was.

"Where is Micah's mother?"

"Probably dead," Martin said, knowing he'd had to offer more to fill in the huge blanks his answer created. "She ran off with my best friend when Micah was two."

His best friend. It began to dawn on me why some pre-judging might have occurred. Though it seemed that any animosity or suspicion by proxy should have been directed at me. The friend of the one who was spoken for.

Or, maybe, I was just reading too much into what the man was saying.

"She couldn't handle Micah's issues," Martin said, no melancholy, no regret in his manner. "All I can say is she missed out on one great kid."

Single father. With a son whose life included the extremes of a parent's dreams and nightmares. Excellence and illness.

"Life wasn't always peaches before the blight," Martin said. "And it's not now. But it is good."

He was an odd one, I thought. Tough. Tender. Realist. Optimist. But not one whose intentions were transparent.

"Why did you come here tonight?"

"Micah said I should," Martin told me.

I half snickered at his reply. The little guy was pulling some pretty big strings. Or so I thought.

"The truth is, I was thinking about stopping by anyway. You seem like a level-headed sort, and we really need that moving forward."

That was his reason, maybe. Just the desire for a chat. But his reason did not exist in a vacuum.

"Why did you son zero in on me?"

Martin shrugged and shook his head slightly, more amusement than confusion in the gesture.

"Hell if I know," he said. "Another mystery of Micah."

I wasn't sure how comfortable I was having a prepubescent super genius place his attention on me. Especially so soon after arriving in a place that appeared to place great deference on anything he said. Or suggested.

Martin stood, waiting by his chair as I rose.

"Don't let yourself get overwhelmed," he said, reassurance true in his voice. "This really is a good place. We just want to keep it that way."

He left after a handshake. I walked him to the door, but no further, and closed it before he'd even made it off the porch.

I didn't know what to expect of Eagle One before reaching this spot on the coast of Oregon. That place, imagined, had been but a destination. A hope. In many ways, it had delivered on its promise.

The rest would come. That was what I told myself.

Thirty One

It was a park. An honest to God park, with play equipment and children laughing and grass so green it almost hurt to look at. That it was made from some recycled plastic and, as I'd been told by a neighbor that morning, pilfered from a college football stadium, mattered little. To look upon it and connect the image with a still familiar memory of the real was a pleasing diversion.

Krista tugged at Neil's hand as the three of us entered the park, pulling him toward the swings and monkey bars and slides, a row of manufactured greenery beyond, fake plants taken from the waiting rooms of medical offices and hair salons.

"Come on!" she commanded him.

He tossed a glance back at me as the child dragged him off.

"Guess I'll be seeing you," he said, stumbling forward.

Stumbling and smiling. A true smile.

"Fletcher!"

I looked toward the voice and saw Burke sitting at a picnic table, Elaine across from him. A red plastic cup sat before him, and a bottle, smoky contents within nearly half gone. The man waved me over, his hand gesturing vigorously. Social niceties were something I was having to reacquaint myself with, including the act of being polite to one I'd rather ignore.

But I could not dismiss the invitation. And, in any event, it was not just Burke at the table. Elaine balanced out the bombast certain to greet me with a quiet normalcy.

Again Burke urged me over, and I moved to join them, taking a seat on the bench next to Elaine.

"Good morning," I said, looking to each of them.

"Morning," Elaine said.

She wore a pistol on her left hip, but her MP5 was nowhere in sight. Burke's AK was leaning against the end of the table. Though I could not see it, I was certain he had a pistol in the thigh holster I'd noted on him just after we landed, and I imagined another small handgun hidden somewhere on his person. Probably a knife as well. And I wouldn't have been surprised to see him take a grenade from a pocket and place it on the table for effect.

"You settling in okay?" Burke asked.

"Getting used to things," I said. "It's been a while since there was this much life around."

I noticed several people approaching Neil and Krista at the play equipment, four adults offering greetings, two children among their number. The little ones joined Krista in climbing and swinging, slipping into behaviors that, thankfully, had not been erased from their nature.

"Where's..." Burke struggled for the name.

"Grace," Elaine prompted him.

"Grace," Burke said. "Where is she?"

"Neil said she wanted to get the house organized."

We'd spent the previous day just getting acclimated. I'd left Neil and Grace alone, giving them a chance to spend what would pass for family time with Krista. I'd mostly wandered through the house, my house, arranging things to suit my taste, marveling at the cabinets full of food in the kitchen.

And I'd slept. Fleeting thoughts of exploring the town, of strolling outside, were superseded by an insatiable desire to close my eyes, and keep them closed. As often happened,

I dreamed of the green world. Not places like this with its manufactured homage to the past. No, during my first full day in Bandon, until the afternoon crept toward three o'clock, my subconscious had placed me in a vast, open field, with stalks of alfalfa tickling my shins as I walked through it. Then ran through it. The dream was soundless, but my mouth gaped giddily, as one might when laughter burst forth uncontrollably.

When I woke, I remained in bed for a good half hour, trying to remember every piece of the placid and silly dream, then trying to make myself forget it. I needed to face the day, embrace this place, without letting pleasant shadows of a past long gone make me wish for more.

"It's not easy moving into someone else's place and making it your own," Elaine commented.

I nodded. But Burke snickered breathily at her observation.

"First night here, I slept like a baby," he said. "Haven't moved a damn thing in the house since then. Still sleep like a baby. Whoever lived there before is just dust now."

Elaine glanced at the cup and bottle, her silent appraisal of this part of the man's being verging on harsh. Burke poured a splash of whiskey into the red plastic cup and slid it slowly across the picnic table toward me.

"Little early for me," I said.

"Suit yourself," he said, keeping the cup and taking a long sip. "Best thing to come from the blight—no laws against drinking in public."

I couldn't tell if the man was a crazy optimist, seeking some good in any situation, or if he was that far out on the edge of society that this new world had come to resemble one he'd imagined before it all went to hell.

"Gonna miss this when it's gone," Burke said, lifting the bottle to admire the smooth brown contents, gone by half after his pour. "Just five or six bottles left in town."

"And he has four of those," Elaine said.

"Four and change," Burke corrected her, tipping the bottle her way in offering.

Elaine looked to me, grinning dismissively.

"I don't touch the stuff," she said. "Burke considers that a character flaw."

He nodded and gave his cup another splash before twisting the lid back on the bottle and setting it aside.

"Nothing even close to this at the supply center," Burke said.

"Supply center?"

"In the old Post Office," Elaine clarified for me. "If you need something that's not food you can pick it up there. Toilet paper, a flashlight. Similar things."

"Everything our patrols can scrounge that's useful is funneled there," Burke explained.

"Smart," I said.

They were organized. I'd realized just how much the night we landed as the coordinated force, led by Burke, made it impossible for us to execute any threat against them, if that had been our intent. That type of regimentation clearly also existed in how they gathered and maintained supplies for the population.

"Excuse me...Eric, right?"

I looked up to see a man and a woman standing near, two of the same who'd offered greetings to Neil and Krista. They had the look of a couple about them. Each wore wedding bands, and I guessed they were pushing sixty.

"Eric, this is Doc Allen," Elaine said. "He's the one who saved Micah's life."

"You're the surgeon?" I asked.

"Yes. And, please, it's Everett. This is my wife, Carol."

"So pleased to meet you," Carol said warmly, taking my hand in both of hers. "I hope you've been made comfortable."

She flashed a look toward Elaine.

"He's settled into a nice house," Elaine assured the woman.

"The Readiness Committee worked hard to make sure we can accept new arrivals," Carol explained. "We want to see people enjoy the fruits of our labor."

Burke lifted his cup and took another long sip, adding some volume to the swallow this time for effect. The doctor's wife shifted her gaze momentarily to him, maintaining a smile with some effort.

"Well, we just wanted to say hello," Everett said to me. "I'm over on Franklin near Cross if you have any medical needs."

"Thank you," I said. "I appreciate that."

The doctor gave a nod to Elaine, and to Burke, then headed off with his wife.

"Burke, you're a piece of work," Elaine said, openly judging the man now.

He laughed softly and looked to me.

"Some people, like the good doc's wife, think all that needs to be done to get the world working again is to have committee meetings and flash tight smiles to those *lessers* who live among them." He took another drink, draining his red cup and tapping his own chest. "This lesser thinks it would be in their best interest to remember just who it is who keeps the Horde from cooking them up for Sunday dinner."

The Horde...

My confusion must have been more obvious than I'd intended. Elaine tried to fill in the blanks.

"That's our pet name for the psychos from up north," she said. "They congregate in and around Seattle. Every once in a while they send some raiders our way."

"Drug addled cannibal scum," Burke commented, draining the last of his whiskey and turning the empty red cup over before smashing it atop the table. "Not a worthwhile mouth breather among them."

Elaine made sure his mini-tirade was over before going on.

"They're the main threat we face," she said.

"Main outside threat," Burke added, the amount of drink he'd consumed that morning working on him, a tinge of slur to the edge of his words.

"You have inside threats?" I asked.

The man laughed sloppily and gestured to the space around us, sweeping a hand in a 360 like a lasso.

"Yeah, we have inside threats," Burke said, the pronouncement almost oozing past his lips, liquid and thick. "You're a threat."

Next to me, Elaine straightened, seeming ready to offer up some defense of me. Before she could, Burke raised a hand and wagged a single finger in her direction.

"And you're a threat," he said, pointing next across the park to woman and a young boy. "They're a threat. Everybody in this town is a threat."

Whatever inebriated logic there was that was fueling his accusations eluded me. Burke seemed like the kind of blowhard whose bravado could be measured and predicted by the fluid ounce. He was used to neighbors and associates letting him have his say, expecting that the moment would pass.

I was not going to.

"If I'm a threat," I began, "why don't you deal with me now?"

Burke focused on me, his mouth hanging open with slack amusement. His head tipped backward, the man regarding me like a bully might a potential new victim, trying to pick out a soft spot he could aim for.

"You're a funny one," Burke said. "You and your pal and his lady and that little snot-nosed—"

"Burke!"

Elaine's admonition cut off what the man was about to say. But it didn't stop me.

"Go ahead," I urged him quietly. "Finish what you were going to say."

The smile went away now. Drained to nothing. Just a darkness remained, in his eyes, his expression, all for my benefit. After a moment he swung his legs over the bench seat and stood, his balance surprisingly solid. He reached out and snatched the bottle, gripping it by the neck like an upturned club.

"You're on the wall tonight," Burke said to me. "And I'll see you there."

He walked off, a straight line exit through a few residents just arriving at the park, not a wobble or a weave to his step. The man could hold his liquor in that respect, it appeared.

"Ignore him," Elaine said.

"That's going to be hard for me to do."

"It's just the BS factor," she told me, and judged by my lack of reaction that I was missing something. "Burke Stovich. His name. BS."

So the man was to get a pass because of alcohol and a crudely apt pairing of initials. Clearly, I was quickly coming to understand, the residents of Bandon had learned to look past, way past, the faults in each other for some greater good, which I suspected Burke Stovich was a particularly important part of.

"Is he former military?" I asked.

"He's former something," Elaine replied.

"What does that mean?"

She stood and regarded me for a moment with a casual wariness. It was a trait that seemed natural to her. Not borne of events, such as what Grace had endured, but simply part of her being. It was possible she was alive because of it.

"It means you've been here less than forty eight hours," she said. "You don't get to ask questions yet. And you certainly don't get to judge."

She turned away and followed the same path out of the park as Burke, leaving me there among the lush façade of the old world.

Thirty Two

Elaine and I waited on the corner for Neil to join us. I'd been informed by a messenger, a kid struggling to sprout a goatee, that I was to meet Elaine two blocks over at seven, armed and ready for duty. It was seven on the dot, night settling full and the first wisps of mist creeping in from the ocean.

"Is your friend prone to being late?"

The same messenger had been tasked with rousing Neil from whatever sleep he'd been able to catch that afternoon so that he could join us. I'd managed a full six hours.

"No," I told Elaine, surprised myself. "He's not."

Fog rolled across the dark street, washing out the houses beyond like an eraser leaving misty streaks in its wake.

"Go hurry him up," Elaine said, the words hinting at some authority she'd once wielded.

But before I could move, a figure began to resolve through the fog, moving right at us from the direction of Neil's house, emerging from the damp grey haze, bolt action rifle slung.

Elaine looked to me, then to Grace.

"Where's Neil?"

"He's watching Krista," Grace told her.

"He's supposed to be here," Elaine said.

"We decided I would go."

We?

The doubting look I laid on Grace pushed some button I was about to wish hadn't been.

"I don't control him, Eric. He's not some puppet with strings I pull. You, of all people, should know that. If I'm going to be part of this town, then I'm going to pull my weight and do my time, and not just dust and sweep. Okay?"

My response didn't come immediately. When it did, a smile of apology accompanied it.

"You do know he sucks at keeping a house clean," I said.

She smiled back, suppressing a laugh.

"I'm becoming aware of that, yes."

Elaine took in the exchange with her own amusement obvious, though it did not erase the impatience that preceded it.

"We've gotta move," Elaine told us.

"Okay," I said.

"Okay," Grace agreed.

Elaine started up the street. Grace and I followed close behind, walking side by side. The way good friends did.

* * *

The wall was a miles-long barrier of chain link, scrounged from towns up and down the coast as the blight took hold. It surrounded Bandon on the north, east, and south, the ocean providing what protection it could to the west.

"We're covering a section of the north wall tonight," Elaine explained. "The only bridge into town crosses the river there."

"It's the only one?" Grace asked.

"The only one left standing," Elaine clarified. "We have an observation post there on the second floor of a structure that we built. It's reinforced, with good views in all directions. A double gate blocks the bridge just beyond the OP. Our job is to make sure nothing crosses."

The task seemed simple enough, though that did not negate any danger. Hand grenades were simple devices, and they could turn a person into hamburger.

We walked up the highway, once a two lane route numbered 101. The signs that labeled it still stood. One, I saw as we approached, had been defaced. Eyes and a mouth had been scrawled inside the '0' making a face, and each of the '1's to either side had been turned into middle fingers. I wasn't sure what it was supposed to mean, if anything, but it certainly seemed fitting when I heard the voice call out to us from atop the OP.

"You're late," Burke said.

We were. Two whole minutes. Elaine tossed a thumb toward Grace. Burke considered the assignment of blame for a moment.

"I'm coming down," he said.

He disappeared from the top of the OP, its four sides open under a sturdy roof, and reappeared at ground level, coming out a door to meet us.

"Where's Moore?"

It was 'Moore' to him, I thought. Not 'Neil'. Elaine was just that to him, but the newbies seemed to be on a last name basis. I was seriously beginning to think the guy had been a drill instructor somewhere, spewing curses at recruits, telling Jones or Pinkerton or Landry to drop and give him fifty. Or he might simply have been a foreman on some construction crew, abrasive to the point of abusive. The truth was, all I knew for certain about Burke Stovich was that I wasn't going to be having him over for dinner anytime soon.

"They switched places," Elaine told him.

"We don't do that," Burke said, focusing on Grace.

"We didn't know," Grace said.

Burke thought it through, the rigid mask he'd flashed at us seeming to soften, if just by a degree.

"Relieve Ben and David," Burke said, looking only to Elaine and me. "I'll take the lady with me to the river bend OP."

"The lady's name is Grace," Grace reminded him.

The oddest thing happened then. Burke smiled. A stone-cold sober expression of admiration.

"The lady named Grace has some spunk in her," he said, looking me next. "Enjoy your time on Checkpoint Chuck."

I snickered lightly.

"A play on Checkpoint Charlie," I said, recalling the name of a road connection between East and West Berlin, a potential flashpoint during the Cold War. "Cute."

Only it didn't resonate with any amount of humor.

"No," Burke said. "Guy named Chuck Clemmons was killed here while watching the bridge."

I'd walked into that.

"A Horde sniper got a lucky shot off," the man told me. "It'd be shame if we had to name something after you."

Despite Burke's abrasive persona, and his drunken reproach of me earlier in the day, I was still an outsider. I knew virtually none of the history of the place, before or after the time of the blight. This verbal misstep I decided was as good a reason as any to listen, and to think, before flapping my gums.

Burke headed off, taking a worn footpath to the east. Grace followed, flashing a smile back at me as she left. In just a few seconds she was lost in the fog.

* * *

"Coming in," the radio crackled soft at the base of the sandbag wall.

Elaine picked it up and looked behind the bunker, in the direction of the town. We'd relieved the residents who'd kept watch before us, and were thirty minutes into our shift when the call came.

"Copy," she said.

I tracked her gaze and saw a figure approaching through the drifting mist.

"Keep your eye on the bridge," she told me.

I faced the foggy span again as the sound of boots neared.

"Hey," a male voice said.

I glanced back and saw a familiar face. One from the force who'd met us when we landed. A young face, the kid maybe twenty one, AR similar to mine slung on one shoulder and a bag over the other. His name was Mikey, if I was remembering correctly.

"Eric, this is Mikey Winthrop," Elaine said.

"How ya doing?" Mikey asked, reaching into his bag and removing a thermos and two cups.

"Just taking it all in," I said.

Elaine took the thermos and cups, setting them on a crude wood table in the back corner of the OP's top floor.

"We your first stop?" she asked.

Mikey nodded and gestured off to the grey night to the east.

"Jeff and Ross are roving the river," Mikey said. "I'm dropping theirs off with the one for the point."

"Roving the river?"

Elaine opened the thermos and poured us each cups of steaming coffee as she answered my question.

"The fence has sensors, but we keep a patrol moving at night along the northern line."

"The Horde will try swimmers sometimes," Mikey said. "They all drown. They're all doped out of their heads, so, what would you expect?"

"You never know," Elaine said. "All it takes is one to get across to cause trouble."

"Have any gotten into town?" I asked.

Mikey shook his head, pleased.

"Micah has this warning system set up," the kid explained. "Even has sensors hidden on the north side of the river."

"There's been more movement up there recently," Elaine said.

"Seattle is a long way from here," I said. "Wouldn't Portland be a closer base if they're into big cities?"

Mikey looked to Elaine, surprised that I was even asking that question.

"You didn't fly over Portland on your way here?" she asked.

"We were on the coast."

"The place is nothing but ashes," Mikey told me. "Burned to the ground. Everything. Every single thing."

Images of what I'd caused in Whitefish flashed in memory. Most everything turned to cinder. Cars. Buildings. People.

"How did it happen?"

Elaine hesitated for a moment before answering.

"We did it," she said, the barest hint of regret in her voice.

I didn't press the issue as to why. If anyone knew that such a thing might be necessary, it was me. As it was, Mikey was in the mood to share.

"If we'd left Portland standing, the Horde could have done just what you thought—moved closer to us."

"Scorched earth defense," I said, understanding. "You make the survivors from Seattle have to travel all the way down here."

"Not survivors," Mikey corrected me. "The Horde. Survivors are people. Survivors deserve to live. These things don't."

"Things?"

"He's being dramatic," Elaine said.

"I am?" Mikey asked defensively, fixing on me, wanting to drive some point home. "The Space Needle is an appropriate landmark for the place now. That's all those psychos do—shoot up, snort. Somehow they landed the mother lode of pharmacopeia and, believe me, they put it to use."

"Some people choose to escape from reality rather than accept it," Elaine offered.

Mikey shook his head at her, the point she was making not new. There was a history here, not harsh or damaging, just points of view that would never meet.

"Elaine has a bit too much compassion for the Horde," Mikey said. "Considering they'd eat her raw if they could."

She laid a look on him, signaling that he was precariously close to a line he shouldn't cross. He seemed to get the mild warning and dialed back the rhetoric as he continued.

"Every once in a while they send raiding parties down. It's been happening more lately."

"Their food is running out," Elaine said.

She sipped from her cup of coffee and handed me mine. I set it on the bunker's sandbag wall and scanned the bridge, noting nothing through the fog.

"This one time, they dragged this catapult thing that they'd rigged up onto the bridge and—"

"The rovers are out in the cold," Elaine interrupted him, nodding toward his bag.

"Yeah. Right. You're right."

The young man reached out and shook my hand.

"We'll catch up later," Mikey said. "Lotsa good Horde stories to tell."

He made his way down to the first floor, then out, his form dissolving into the thickening mist as he moved northeast toward the point.

"A thermal sight would be nice about now," I said, wishing that the piece of optics that could register heat signature through both darkness and fog was available.

"We have one," Elaine said. "Just one."

"I'd think this would be the best place for it."

"You'd be wrong," she told me.

So it was somewhere else. The only other 'someplace' that made sense for a piece of equipment like that to be utilized would be at the most vital place in Bandon—where the mystery stash of food was kept.

"Stay alert," Elaine told me. "It's almost midnight."

"Does that time mean something?"

"It's when the Horde prefers to make their moves."

She was facing the bridge, scanning, her MP5 held against her chest. I brought my AP up and rested the suppressed barrel atop the sandbagged opening. We watched, saying nothing, until just after midnight when all hell broke loose.

Thirty Three

The burning woman emerged from the shifting fog and threw herself at the chain link stretched across it.

"Jesus!"

I shouldn't have let the exclamation slip out, but the sight of a woman, her lower half engulfed in fire, jogging nonchalantly across the span was about the most startling thing I'd seen. Flames licked upward, over her face, hair atop her head smoldering as she grabbed at the porous fence and began to climb it.

"Take her out!" Elaine ordered, grabbing the radio quickly. "We have contact, Checkpoint Chuck. One—"

"Elaine," I said, calm but firm, and she looked to see what had seized my attention.

A staggered line of people, all on fire, were charging across the bridge, lighting the foggy night like a moving funeral pyre.

"Take them out!" Elaine shouted, then got back on the radio. "Multiple attackers at Checkpoint Chuck!"

I drew a bead on the first we'd seen, the woman, screaming now, wailing, her hands just reaching the top of the fence as I fired. A single shot. There was no chance I would miss from the hundred foot distance, and I did not. Her body slipped, feet losing the purchase they'd found on the chain link, hands struggling to hold her up until finally she succumbed to the wound and fell, flopping backward onto the bridge, flames leaping from her body.

The others rushed toward her. Toward the fence. Toward us. I fired, picking my shots, watching the attackers drop one by one. Some fell to their knees and tried to continue on, crawling even as fire swirled about them.

"How are they doing this?!"

"They're hopped up on every pain killer you can imagine," Elaine said, firing now, short bursts from her MP5.

More of the attackers fell, two tumbling from the bridge and into the river, their bodies continuing to burn atop the waters as the current carried them toward the ocean. Then, from the right, more fire joined in, spraying the bridge from the east.

"The one on the left," Elaine said.

I found the mark she was directing me to, a solitary individual, a man, his body a rolling ball of orange about to crest the fence where it doubled back toward land. The sight of him, dying already, was mesmerizing. Two shots from my AR dropped him, his blazing remains tangled with the chain link, hanging there, a dead inferno.

In less than two minutes there was no more movement and nothing to shoot at. Bodies continued to burn on the bridge, two more caught in the fencing. From below, boots slapped the stairs urgently, followed by softer, though no less urgent steps.

"What was that?"

It was Burke, and behind him, Grace, her rifle at the ready. She slipped past the head of security and joined me looking out over the failed, insane attack.

"They doused themselves in something and set themselves on fire," Elaine explained. "That's a new one."

"Yeah," Burke agreed, the slightest hint of nerve showing about him.

"Was that you shooting?" I asked.

"It was Jeff and Ross," Burke said. "We came to reinforce you."

Elaine looked to Grace, then to me.

"Baptism by fire," she said.

If the pun wasn't intended, it still made an impact.

"That was pointless," Grace said.

"No it wasn't," Burke challenged her.

"They were probing," I said, taking Burke's side.

"And now they know how we'd react to a headlong charge," he said.

Elaine backed away from the front of the OP and slid to a sit against the side wall.

"That means they're planning something," she said.

Burke surveyed the smoldering carnage strewn across the bridge and nodded.

"Something big," he said.

Thirty Four

"Hello."

The boy's voice drizzled down through the speaker mounted on the ceiling just this side of the clear barrier, and the child himself stood very properly just beyond it, regarding me with subdued appreciation. He did not smile, but I had the distinct feeling that, were the barrier not there to separate us, his hand would be outstretched, offering the greeting to me.

"Hello again, Micah."

A chair was already placed for me on the 'unclean' side of the barrier. The same messenger who's summoned me to duty on the wall the night before had come again to my house, in the afternoon this time, waking me, this time with a request from Micah. The child wanted to see me.

"Please, sit," the boy said, taking a chair from his computer workstation and rolling it close on the 'clean' side.

I took the seat left for me, and he sat to face me.

"You've done an amazing thing here," I said.

Micah glanced behind to the array of electronics he'd acquired and linked together.

"This?" he gently scoffed. "The real magic you can't even see. Satellite dishes to intercept communications, antennas hidden on hilltops. I even have an antenna thirty miles away working off a hardwired repeater so anyone tracking my transmissions won't be able to pinpoint the source."

I... My...

He used the singular, claiming status over what had been accomplished. To be certain, I'd commended him just a moment before, but whatever electronic wizardry he'd performed still required others to manifest in some tangible way. In the old world, one might brand him just short of precocious. Now, in this time, I wasn't sure how to classify him beyond boy genius.

"So, I have a few questions," he said, opening a notebook on his lap and clicking a pen open. "Krista said when we talked the other day that a pilot you shot down spoke another language."

"Yes. French."

"French?" He made a series of notations in his notebook. "Interesting."

"Why is that?"

Micah finished writing and looked up, pausing in thought for a moment.

"Three days after the Red Signal, I started picking up communications over secure satellite channels. Ones that *our* military used. All those communications were in French. It was both verbal and encrypted written messages."

"Encrypted," I said.

"Yes, but I broke that long ago. Or didn't my father tell you what I've been able to do?"

"No, he told me. Most of it. Everything except where the food to keep all this going is coming from."

Micah considered me for a moment through the barrier, the gentle ripple of its structure distorting his youthful features as air moved against the material. He was eleven, looked younger, but spoke of things beyond those who were twice his age.

"You were on the wall last night," he said. "Right?"

"I was."

"There was some excitement, I understand."

If watching a woman and dozens of others self-immolate before being shot could be termed 'exciting', I supposed he wasn't wrong. When I didn't confirm or comment on his observation, he continued.

"There's been an increase of activity from the Horde. My expectation is that they will try something major soon."

"Your head of security seems to think so," I told him.

"They will fail. I've seen to our intelligence and defense activities. The town is ready."

I marveled quietly at the boy. The child. His short life had been filled with distress, illness, operations, confinement. Yet he had placed himself at the center of an effort of survival beyond what I had expected when imagining what Eagle One might be. Whatever shortcomings he might exhibit in terms of personal humility, I had to look past.

"Why did you ask if I'd been on the wall when I asked about the source of your food?"

"New arrivals always have wall duty before they get to guard the cache."

His answer opened the door for yet another question. But I didn't get the chance to voice it.

"Don't ask what or where that is," the boy told me. "You'll find out tonight."

"I see."

I didn't, really, but if an answer to that nagging question was but hours away, I could wait.

"You're sure that this pilot was speaking French?" Micah pressed me.

"Absolutely."

"Hmm."

"What?"

The boy shook his head a bit and opened his notebook, flipping back through pages, heavy notations everywhere, precision scribbles. Numbered. Connected.

"I'm a little surprised they've made it this far north in any appreciable number," he said.

"Are these French military?" I asked, and Micah giggled.

"Please. Do you think France invaded under the cover of the blight?"

"I don't know what to think about it," I told him. "I'm just curious. I'd like to make sense of why French speaking troops are on our soil trying to kill people. I'd like to know why my government abandoned me. I'd like to know what the plan is to make the world whole again."

"Beaucoup de questions," Micah said, his accent feigned and overly dramatic. "Une seule réponse."

I shrugged, letting the child be the master he wanted to be. And that he was. For the moment.

"Many questions, one answer," he said.

"That's very philosophical."

"Is it?" Micah asked, genuinely unsure. "I thought it quite accurate. It all comes back to the blight, you see."

"It does?"

Micah smiled at me, as if regarding a child who'd just expressed confusion in the most precious of ways.

"Thousands of lockers filled with food and supplies are buried across the country," he said. "French speaking paramilitary forces are used to restrict civilian movement. The earth is scrubbed clean of all but the heartiest survivors."

He stopped there, for a moment, letting his statements of assumed fact settle.

"You believe that the blight was just some random appearance of a biological nightmare?"

It had always been at least plausible that some form of bioweapon had gotten out, by accident or design. But what was Micah saying here?

"Those supply lockers were buried six months before the blight even appeared in Poland," the boy said.

I eased back in my chair, studying the boy, wondering just how much of the surety he'd expressed in everything he'd said was real. How much of it was quantifiable. Provable. Like his father had at one time, I was finding it difficult to accept not the gist of what he was saying, but him as bearer of the information.

"My father told you how I hacked into our communications systems, correct?"

"You were upset at the spying the NSA had been doing on American citizens," I recounted.

"And so I took action. I hacked them. What did I have to lose? What were they going to do with a sick child—throw me in jail? I was untouchable."

"I imagine they were preoccupied," I said. "Too busy with more pressing matters to make much of your intrusion."

"I thought the same," Micah said, accepting and complimenting my premise.

"You knew how bad the blight was going to be before it exploded."

Now the boy shook his head, correcting me. Keeping me from going too far down a still tenuous road.

"I knew that something was coming," he said. "There were signs. Those food lockers. Officials communicating about a small unit of former French Foreign Legion troops at a reunion in Colorado when the blight was taking off. Do you know what nationality makes up a large portion of the foreign nationals serving in the Legion?"

I didn't.

"Poles," he said. "Where did the blight first appear?"

Near Warsaw. He knew I knew this, but was asking for effect. To make certain his prowess as finder and keeper of a terrible knowledge was apparent.

"Do you know what those same former Legionnaires did when they were on active duty during the Gulf War in nineteen ninety?"

"What?"

"They captured Al Salman Airport in Iraq," Micah explained, as a teacher would to a clueless student. "The very place an Iraqi biological warfare scientist named Al Siduq was trying to flee the country through. He was never seen after reports of his presence there."

Iraq. Bioweapons. French troops gone rogue. Connections to the most fertile region in Europe. What the hell kind of operation, or conspiracy, was this?

"This is sounding..."

"Like a plan gone awry? You're right."

"So our government got in bed with all of these elements to do this?"

The question seemed to disappoint the child.

"Our government?" he scoffed. "The only thing they knew was they couldn't stop it. So they tried to prepare. They buried food and supplies to help essential personnel have a chance to reach safe zones. Probably bunkers originally designed for survival during the cold war. Totally inappropriate for this sort of thing."

"You think they're all dead," I said.

"The plans of theirs I saw were laughable. They were counting on the military to protect a civilian leadership that was writing off ninety-nine point nine-nine percent of the nation. How many true soldiers do you believe would lay down their lives for people like that?"

I'd witnessed what bureaucratic control of a military operation could lead to, near Arlee in my home state. That had spun out of control. All Micah was proposing was the same, on a larger scale.

"So who the hell is actually behind this?" I asked.

"Does it matter?" the boy countered. "Shouldn't you be asking 'why' instead?"

"All right, why?"

He stared at me, and for the first time I sensed a crack in the veneer of certainty the boy wore as if it were armor.

"I don't have it down as provable fact, but I am comfortable with my analysis," he began.

"Which is?"

"Someone wanted to start over. From as close to scratch as you can get."

I didn't say anything right away. I simply took in the horrific totality of that possibility.

But I did begin to think something. To wonder something.

"You didn't ask me here to talk about the French pilot," I said, the realization rising. "You already knew that. You knew they were targeting us when you told us to get off the radio."

Micah closed his notebook and stood, taking it to the computer and communication tables. He placed it there, pen atop it, then turned back toward me.

I stood, too, eyeing the boy through the barrier. Looking down at him.

"What was this all about?" I asked.

He replied with his own question.

"What did the French pilot say to you?"

The child is a liar...

Could I say that to Micah? To the child? Or, was the question actually, could I not?

"He said you were a liar."

Micah grinned, unsurprised. He turned and walked toward the door to his bedroom.

"Thank you for your time," he said. "You should find tonight fairly interesting."

He passed through the doorway and closed the door behind, leaving me beyond the barrier. Alone and wondering what this had all been about.

Thirty Five

I was able to catch a few more hours of sleep after the odd exchange with Micah. All that he'd told me, and what he'd withheld, had been in the back of my thoughts all night. The possibility, or likelihood as presented by the boy, that the blight had been an orchestrated act of global cleansing was hard to fathom. And, I had to remind myself, futile to dwell on. If it was that, if the world had been turned grey and dead by a madman, or collection of them, the deed was done. If the plan had gone awry, with survivors hanging on despite attempts to contain populations by force, and strike out at them if they had somehow survived, then the architects of the apocalypse could very well be among the billions and billions of dead.

'Does it matter?'

That was Micah's response when asked who had done this. And he was right. Even the why, as postulated by him, mattered not at all. I was here. We were here. Neil, Grace, Krista. We breathed the air of an earth not scrubbed clean. We had defied whatever plan had been set in motion. Life went one. And that was what mattered.

"Either of you get seasick?"

Burke's question as we rode in the back of a pickup, Mikey Winthrop at the wheel, caught both Neil and me off guard. We'd been picked up just a few minutes earlier, told to arm up, and were now cruising through Bandon as the afternoon crept toward evening, heading to pull our first duty guarding the main cache of food that supplied the town.

"No," Neil said.

I shook my head similarly, adding the question to the data points feeding my wondering as to the location of the food storage. Sea sick? That would hint at a boat trip. Were there islands off the coast of Oregon here? The geography I'd retained since high school didn't offer any immediate answer to that question.

The pickup moved through town and stopped at the town's small harbor, a sheltered port where the Coquille River spilled into the Pacific. A small collection of boats was maintained there, remnants of a fishing fleet that no longer had a bounty to pull from the ocean. The blight had sent its destructive tentacles from the top of the food chain to the bottom. It was possible that some creatures still lived in the deep waters off the coast. Would plankton still thrive? Would krill? Enough to feed baleen whales that would filter the tiny creatures and consume them as nutrients? I didn't know, but it was clear from the lack of any netting visible that what the fishermen here had once found plentiful in the waters offshore had disappeared.

We climbed out of the pickup and, with a wave to Mikey as he drove off, followed Burke not to one of the wide wooden fishing vessels, but to a long, narrow skiff, the craft's driver already aboard, readying it to cast off.

"Gentlemen, this is Jenny Martell," Burke introduced.

The grizzled old woman, if a woman could be termed as such, nodded and fired up the boat's big outboard, the exhaust blast tossing her wild white hair. Neil and I climbed aboard, Burke bringing up the rear, the three of us taking a position on the benches at the middle of the craft as we pulled away from the dock. We swung westward, dodging old pier pilings in the small harbor, and picked up speed. The bow of the skiff rose up, taking us over waves and swirling water where the Coquille and the Pacific jousted for supremacy.

"All right," I said, my voice loud above the outboard. "How about you fill us in now?"

"No point in that," Burke said. "You'll see soon enough."

He eased off the bench and slouched to a sit on the hull, back against the side, wind rushing past.

I looked to Neil, his own attention fixed forward as well. In the distance the sun was settling toward the horizon. He stared at it, letting his eyes close for a moment, soaking in the fading warmth, some peace seeming to fill him. Some contentment.

"I could get used to this, Fletch," he said without prompting.

I could understand his feeling, even if I could not yet relate.

"Relax," Burke told me. "You're about to be handed keys to the kingdom."

Behind, Jenny Martell laughed. I looked to her and saw a nearly toothless mouth open, bellowing with glee.

"See, Jenny agrees," Burke said.

An hour we raced across the water, sun slipping below the defining line of the earth in the distance, the last of its yellow light beginning to reveal something in silhouette. A shape. Of a ship.

"What is that?" Neil asked.

"The supermarket," Burke said.

"With no waiting on any register," Jenny joked, her gummy laughter bellowing again.

The skiff leapt over the rising chop, nearing the hulking orange ship.

"She must be twenty miles from shore," I said, hanging on, the hard wooden seat absorbing little of the impacts each time the boat came off the crest of a wave and slammed back onto the churning sea.

"Thirty," Burke corrected.

"You want to provide some context here, Burke?" Neil asked.

Burke looked back to us. The rifle slung across his back swung back and forth with the motion of the skiff.

"The *Groton Star*, courtesy of Micah's magic," Burke said. "And the United States government."

"The feds just parked this out here?" Neil asked, doubtful.

"Not willingly," Burke answered, flashing a smile before looking again toward our destination. "The day before the Red Signal, Micah intercepted orders that the ship had received directing it to deliver its cargo to a naval base up in Washington where nuke subs are based. This was supposed to supply the boomers as things went to hell. At least that's what Micah figured."

What Micah figured...

It seemed that if Micah decided something, it was to be seen as gospel. Being bothered by the level of near worship afforded the boy would have been easier if he'd actually been wrong. But, as yet, I hadn't learned of that happening.

"So what Micah came up with was pretty damn brilliant," Burke said.

"Is anything he does *not* brilliant?" I asked.

The question was mostly compliment, with a bit of resistance to the minor cult of personality that surrounded the eleven year old.

"What did he do?" Neil asked.

Burke smiled and shrugged admiringly at the simplicity of what had transpired.

"He gave them new orders."

"Before the Red Signal?" I asked.

"The day after," Burke answered. "He broke through that, too."

That it was possible to defeat the nationwide, maybe worldwide, jamming of all communications, radio, internet, telephone, and television, did not completely take me by surprise. The television station in Denver had managed it, broadcasting after its engineers discovered some loophole in the forced silencing. Was it any real wonder that the boy genius was capable of less?

"He sent text signals over an official frequency and told the ship to moor thirty miles off our coast and wait for a supplemental crew," Burke explained.

"The supplemental crew being your people," I surmised.

"I wasn't here at that point," Burke said. "I only learned about it when I pulled into town a month later. But it was pretty damn beautiful to imagine. The town sent out ten people. The crew helped them aboard. Then the guns came out. There was no resistance. This wasn't Somalia with pirates firing RPGs. Our people just loaded the crew onto a couple boats and took them up to Coos Bay and dropped them off. Not a shot fired."

It was a calculated act of piracy. Knowing what I did now, particularly how the nation's leaders had abandoned the populace, justified was the only label I could append to the action. Beyond that, Burke was right—it was brilliant.

But not every question about the source of the town's food supply was answered by what we were seeing, and what we'd been told.

"So why haven't you offloaded what's on board?" I asked.

"Look around you," Burke said, sweeping his hand from horizon to horizon, the shore not even visible from this far out. "Who's going to sneak up on you out here even if they knew you were here?"

I realized then where the lone thermal sight Elaine had hinted at was.

"Good visibility night and day," I said.

"Absolutely," Burke confirmed. "It's secure, and it's accessible. We send boats out twice a week to bring food to shore."

My curiosity as to the location of the town's food cache might have been answered earlier if I'd spent any time near the port. Seeing ships come in and out, with decks loaded down, would have provided enough information for an educated guess.

"With those deliveries, and the ten day supply we keep in town in case weather prevents us from running the convoys, we're pretty set."

It was a fairly foolproof way to keep the precious supply secure. How anyone could get within miles without being seen was hard to imagine.

A few minutes later we neared the ship, the skiff slowing and pulling along the smooth side of the large vessel, a rope ladder dropping quickly over the railing above. The skiff driver kept the small craft close to the ship as we hauled ourselves up, the three guards we were relieving meeting us.

"All quiet?" Burke asked.

One of the people filled him in, as the others introduced themselves to Neil and me. By the time they were climbing down the rope ladder and speeding away with Jenny steering them toward land, I could only recall their first names—Lou, Victor, and Damian. The rest of what had been shared was gone, the sheer scale of where I was standing somewhat overwhelming.

The *Groton Star* was easily six hundred feet in length. If I'd known anything about cargo ships, I could probably have made a guess at the tonnage. That wasn't necessary for me to appreciate what was shifting gently beneath my feet.

"She's anchored at four points," Burke said as he led us toward the stubby superstructure rising at the aft of the vessel. "We brought material from shore, pound by pound, to make the two weights that anchor the stern."

I glanced over the rail and saw one long, stout cable stretching from a hole in the hull and disappearing at an angle into the sea. A quick passage through a steel door took us to a set of stairs that switchbacked up four decks until we emerged on the bridge.

"The beast is dead in the water," Burke told us, pointing to a portable generator at the center of the bridge. "If we need power, we have this."

I went to the forward facing windows, a bank of dead electronics below them, the array functioning now as a shelf. Atop it rested the thermal sight, switched off. The stubby device, appearing like a short, fat telescope, had a bit of heft as I lifted it.

"That mounts to tripods on either wing," Burke said.

Just outside the bridge, to either side, were platforms that hung out over open water, placed to give maximum visibility of the vessel's port and starboard sides when maneuvering in to dock. Which this ship would never do again.

"We're here how long?" Neil asked.

"Twenty four to thirty hours," Burke said. "Two awake at all times, one sleeping."

An efficient system, but one that would play havoc with sleep cycles once back on land.

"You'll pull this duty once every three weeks," Burke said.

That spacing of time on the ship would mitigate the disruption to day and nighttime schedules somewhat.

"Moore, bunk room is one floor down," Burke said. "Fletcher and I will take the first watch."

Neil nodded and looked to me.

"Nighty night," I said to my friend.

He shuffled slowly down the steep stairs, a door opening and closing below after a moment, leaving me with Burke.

"You want to see it?" Burke asked. "The food?"

I did. If just to put the last piece of the puzzle in place in terms of my understanding how Bandon had survived thus far.

"I would."

"Same stairs we came up on, two decks below, through a door forward and you'll see the aft hold."

I followed Burke's directions, letting myself through a watertight door and securing it behind with a spin of the wheel that locked it. The space was pitch black, sealed from the world outside, not a wisp of the fading daylight outside seeping in. I turned on my small flashlight and found my way along a short corridor, metal grating for a floor beneath, the passage ending in a sort of balcony beyond a bulkhead. Stepping onto it and shining my light below, I saw only air beneath through the breaks in the metal flooring. I shifted my light, directing it over the railing ahead, tapping its switch to up the brightness, finally seeing what it was we were here to protect. The precious cargo. The life blood of the town.

Pallets and pallets of food cases were stacked below, the cargo hold stretching out before me, a hundred feet at least. It looked empty by maybe half, the supply less than I had imagined. Then I remembered this was only the aft hold. Judging by the size of this one, there could be two or three more of similar size. How full they were I didn't know, though I suspected those responsible for transferring the food to shore would try to keep the weight even among the cavernous holds, lest the ship become unbalanced. Keeping it in place through the winds and waves that storms would throw at it would be test enough for the anchors without any unwanted listing, or having the bow or stern riding high.

I swept the space with my light, noting a set of steps to the right, and to the left, leading down into the hold from the balcony where I stood. Ropes and pulleys had been affixed to exposed steel spanning the hold above.

Everything here was being done by hand. By muscle. Every box of food was raised and grabbed and carried from this space and then lowered to boats bobbing on the water next to the huge vessel. Nothing about this was easy. Just like life as it now was.

I made my way back to the bridge. Burke stood at the window, staring out at the darkening sea. His AK lay upon a table behind, one that I could imagine covered with maps and charts, and in his hand he held a small flask, uncapped. He looked back to me as I entered, noting my attention on the container in his grasp.

"You disapprove," he said.

"I really don't care," I replied. "Unless that puts anyone in danger because you can't perform."

Burke lifted the flask and sipped, smiling.

"I know my limits," he said.

"Yeah, no one with booze in their hand has ever said that before."

He took no obvious offense at the minor shot I'd just taken at him. Instead, he looked back out to the Pacific and smiled.

"You seem to have adjusted to the world quite well," Burke said, bringing the flask to his lips again, sipping slow, swallowing, his gaze never shifting from the tranquil view outside. "I haven't."

It wasn't a sob story. Just a statement. Maybe one more telling than what I'd anticipated.

"I haven't adjusted to anything," I told him.

He looked to me and held the flask out slightly.

"And you don't need this? You don't need anything? You're a bigger man than me."

He capped the flask and tucked it into a pocket on his tactical vest, facing the black water again.

"You didn't leave anyone behind, did you?" Burke surmised more than asked.

"I left plenty behind."

"But no one person," he said, reading me, correctly as it turned out. "No one perfect, wonderful person."

He seemed to want a drink right then, tongue sweeping over his lips, but he didn't. Beyond the glass that encased the bridge, the last hint of day drained away on the western horizon. Night surrounded us.

"Who was it?" I asked.

Burke turned and snapped a chemical light stick, tossing it to the floor, its soft green glow providing enough light to allow us to maneuver without tripping.

"No one to you," the man said.

He picked up the thermal sight and turned it on, a blue-grey glow spilling onto his face as he brought it to his eye and surveyed the darkness.

I pressed him no more. There'd been no expectation on my part that our time guarding the town's food supply would turn Burke Stovich into a friend. He wasn't. I didn't know if he could ever be.

But I knew now that he wasn't simply an ass by nature. The hardness about him might be real, but it was sharpened by the reality that had been thrust upon all of us.

Many questions. One answer.

Micah had said that to me. Here, for Burke, the same applied. The blight had done something to him. Taken something. Someone. It had left him damaged.

He was haunted.

Part Five

The Horde

Thirty Six

I settled into a routine, as did Neil. And Grace. And Krista. We did our part in town, pulled our weight. Spent time guarding the ship. Watching outward from observation posts along the wall. There'd been no further attacks from the Horde. The feared 'big' move coming from the north hadn't materialized.

Yet.

In the calm of the moment I tended to my house. I met my neighbors. The town held pot lucks in the meeting hall, the shared fare an interesting demonstration of what could be crafted from preserved foodstuffs. Three more people arrived in Bandon, individually, all coming from the south. Only one survived, the others too malnourished and diseased to hang on.

Christmas came. We celebrated. We went to church, the two ministers in town, one Lutheran and one Presbyterian, offering a services for those of the faith, and those whose beliefs might not be represented with any familiarity.

Burke scoffed at the adherence to any dogma other than the sheer will to live, preferring in his downtime to sample further from his supply of booze that always seemed on the verge of being exhausted, but never ran dry.

He and I had come to a quiet acceptance of each other. Me more than him. We were in a time of adaptation, and writing off anyone because of personal failings was an easy way to live a solitary existence.

New Years passed with a party plentiful on noise, but light on alcohol. There was singing, most of it bad, but not all. One voice slipped seamlessly free of the off key shackles surrounding it as *Auld Lang Syne* was sung at midnight.

Elaine's voice.

Her eyes closed, the tune rose from her lips, perfect and pure, sung not for want of accolades, but for love of the music, the lyrics. Voices around her quieted, clearing the soundscape so that only she could be heard. When it was done, the revelers applauded. Elaine accepted the appreciation with a smile that was half embarrassed, half surprised.

I asked her then in the first moments of the New Year if she'd always sung, and she hinted at a life where music had been central to her existence. Hinted. That time when the world was whole was gone now.

"I don't see the point," she'd said to me then.

But there was a point, I told her. Anything that could make a crowd of people stop and take notice, stop and savor a moment in time, was worthwhile. Was good. More than good, even. It was necessary.

She seemed to accept my premise, but I didn't hear her sing again as winter wound down.

Spring was on the horizon. The chill was lifting. In another time, flowers would have awakened from their slumber, green stems sprouting blooms, painting gardens with color. But all that hinted at that in this place was still false. A trick on the eye, on the mind. Imitation plants. Plastic grass. The people of Bandon wanted the world to be what it was. They were trying to make it work again.

I just didn't see how that was possible. Not while living off canned and packaged foods from a supply that was not eternal.

But there was good. There were signs of hope. The perfect example of that came into my house in early March. On a day I'd almost forgotten.

My birthday.

Thirty Seven

I'd tagged along on a patrol the previous week that was searching south of town, scavenging anything and everything of use. But I'd gone along with some specific need in mind, and what I'd found, a screen door on a house near the beach, now hung at the entry to my house. I preferred to leave the door open, even in the wet chill of winter winding down, letting the crisp ocean air flow in.

So when I heard the footsteps on the porch I didn't have to get up to open the door to know who had come by.

"Nice work, Fletch."

Neil opened the screen door, testing its swing back and forth before letting it settle gently closed. He held something in one hand, a tall, slender gift bag, red ribbon wrapped perfectly around its looped handles.

"Happy Birthday."

He held the bag out to me. I stood and took it from him, sensing the liquid weight within.

"Grace insisted on the bow," Neil said.

"I sure as hell knew you didn't add it."

I peeled the ribbon away and reached into the bag, pulling a bottle of scotch out.

"You been raiding Burke's bottomless supply?"

Neil grinned and sat down.

"Actually, I traded him for it."

I eased myself back into my chair and eyed my friend with curious appreciation.

"Thanks," I said. "I hope he didn't take you for too much."

"Well, I was prepared to part with my Benelli."

Neil loved that shotty. There were plenty of weapons around for the taking, but that was the thing that had come with him across the country, first to my refuge, and then on to Eagle One. To Bandon.

"But I didn't have to."

"Come on," I said. "I've gotta know what Burke Stovich considers a fair trade for one of his liquid lovers."

"Nothing," Neil said.

"Nothing?"

"Nothing," Neil repeated. "He wouldn't take anything when I told him what I wanted the bottle for."

"You told him it was for my birthday and he just handed it over?"

I was perplexed, doubting that Burke had grown suddenly fond of me.

"Well, this is sort of a two birds with one stone deal," Neil said. "This is also a best man gift."

I felt the smile build slowly on my face.

"Burke's a softy for weddings, I guess."

"When?" I asked.

"Next week," Neil said. "I have to work out a time with Reverend Morris, but I don't think there will be too many scheduling conflicts."

"Yeah," I said, setting the bottle on the end table and standing. "I'd think not."

Neil stood, too. We walked toward each other. I reached out and pulled my friend into a bear hug, not some faux embrace that men sometimes attempted. After a moment I let him go and stepped back.

"I'm happy, man," I said. "Seriously, completely happy for you."

"If I'm settling down, I want to do it right."

Settling down...

That term held many meanings. One of them implied putting down roots. Making a home. A life.

Staying.

There was too much joy in the moment for me to share with Neil what I'd been feeling. That my time here, in Bandon, was running out. Not because of the people, or the place, but because I felt there was no way to move the ball forward here. I wasn't even sure I could explain it to Neil if I'd wanted to. I'd come to not only believe in hope as a thing, as a sentiment, but also as a motivator. A thing to drive what was left of humanity, be it one town, or one man, toward some solution. Some fix for the barren world. Staying would not allow that. Out there, somewhere, was an answer. Maybe *the* answer. I wanted to find it.

"You picked a good one," I told my friend.

"I know."

Grace had already made him happy, and would continue to. Krista was a light to cut through the darkest days. My friend had them now. His reason to stay. I had mine to go.

"You gonna bring a date?" Neil asked, a slyness heavy in the question.

"Really?" I said. "You trying to marry me off now that you're taking the plunge?"

"You could do worse than her," Neil told me.

Her...

I knew who he meant. Elaine. She'd become a friend. A good friend. But nothing more. Neither of us had pushed to change that.

"Come on, Fletch. What did you tell me back at your place? That I shouldn't look past the opportunity for happiness? You were right. I wish I'd realized that sooner. And I wish you'd do the same."

"Neil, come on."

"Whatever you saw in Grace that convinced you she cared for me, I see that in Elaine when she's around you."

"You're seeing things," I said.

"That doesn't mean I'm wrong."

Could I admit to myself that I did feel something for Elaine? If I probed the deepest part of myself, where I locked away nagging truths?

Yes. I could admit that. But I wouldn't. I knew where my future lay, and where hers did. Like Neil, she had chosen Bandon as her home. She was connected to it now. More than I could ever be.

"How about we get through one wedding first," I suggested, deflecting his line of discussion.

He knew it was not the time to push the notion, much as I'd had to accept the need to back off and let what would happen between Grace and him come at its own time. When they were ready for it to be real.

"Okay," Neil said, beaming, the happiness about him palpable, though it dimmed for an instant as an impossible want surfaced. "I wish my dad could be here for this."

The blight had taken so much, but Dieter Moore's fate was sealed before the grey death spread upon the earth. That didn't make his absence any less meaningful.

"Me, too," I told my friend.

He didn't let emotion overwhelm him. Didn't let the memory of loss set aside the joy to come. Nothing, I knew, would diminish the special day to come.

That didn't mean, however, that the days until then would pass without danger interjecting itself.

Thirty Eight

Word spread quickly. Not by text messages or email, as once might have happened, but by neighbors dashing from house to house and knocking on doors to share the news. An infiltrator from Seattle had been caught after sneaking past the town's defenses.

One of the Horde.

I slung my AR and stashed two spare magazines in the cargo pockets of my pants and sprinted out the door, past Mrs. Heller from across the street who'd brought the word. As I jogged down the block I could see Neil up ahead, coming out of his house, pistol on his hip and Benelli in hand, Grace watching from the doorway as he ran into the street to meet me.

"Why didn't the alarm sound?" Neil wondered.

The town had a general alarm, a siren that could be activated to summon everyone tasked with defense to their assigned stations. But it hadn't sounded here.

"Sounds like a single infiltrator," I said, looking to my friend. "Why don't you hang back? If you die two days before your wedding, Grace will kill you."

"And miss the fun?"

"It's just one person," I said, trying to minimize any need for my friend to be present.

Neil didn't slow, keeping his pace as quick as mine.

"If there's one, there could be more," he said.

He was right. In the brief time we'd been in Bandon, there'd been the one overt assault from the north, flaming members of the Horde hurling themselves at the perimeter fencing. Probing, we knew. Possibly for what was transpiring right then.

We ran to the meeting hall. Our first introduction to the essence of Bandon had been here, at gunpoint, with Martin sizing us up through the dark lenses of a respirator mask. He was there now, too, along with Burke, Elaine, and Mikey Winthrop, the latter keeping the muzzle of an AK pointed at the back of a man bound to a chair in the dim space.

"One more time," Martin said. "What is your objective?"

The man, the prisoner, was already bleeding from the mouth, the left side of his face swollen, and a spray of red erupted when Burke backhanded him with the butt of his pistol as his silence dragged on.

Elaine broke away from the group and met us as we approached.

"He's not alone," she said, gesturing to a pile of items on the floor. "We pulled all this off of him."

I crouched next to the collection. A 9mm Beretta, two spare magazines, a knife, a plastic water bottle half empty. And one other thing. One bit of technology that said to me, to all of us, that the intruder, regardless of silence or lie, had not come on his own.

Neil knelt next to me and took the small walkie-talkie in hand.

"It was in that plastic bag," Elaine said, pointing to the clear container, the outside of it still damp.

"He swam across the river," I said.

"His clothes are drenched," Elaine told us.

"This thing has a five mile range," Neil said. "Max."

"He's got friends out there," Elaine said. "Waiting to hear from him."

"Yeah," I agreed. "Waiting to hear what?"

Thwack!

Another blow sent the intruder's head snapping the opposite direction, Burke's hand already drawing the pistol back, readying the next strike. Neil and I stood and approached the interrogation, Elaine hanging back as still more residents came into the hall. All armed. All ready to supplement the night's outposts if the word was given. By Martin.

"Your silence is only going to mean more pain," Martin said. "What is your objective here?"

The intruder's head tipped up, swollen eyes finding his inquisitor, lips curling and peeling back, revealing a jagged-toothed grin. Burke moved to strike the man again at the act of defiance.

"Wait!" I shouted, all eyes snapping to me.

Burke, especially, laid a hard, burning stare upon me. The look Martin gave me wasn't far removed from that degree of animus.

"What the hell are you doing?" Martin demanded.

From behind, I could sense movement among the residents, all who'd been part of the Bandon community far longer than me. They were inching closer. To me.

I stepped toward Martin, between him and the intruder, and reached down, grabbing the front halves of the man's soaking wet shirt and jerking them apart. Buttons popped. His chest and stomach were exposed, revealing an emaciated horror.

"They're coming for food," I said, giving voice to the obvious.

Martin eyed the man. His jagged ribs pressed against sallow skin. Then, he turned to me again.

"With me," Martin said, gesturing toward the plastic tunnel to his house. "Now."

He walked that way, and I followed, the both of us stopping where light from the hall's single ceiling fixture ebbed, leaving us mostly in shadow.

"You think I don't know they're after our food?"

"No," I said. "So give him some."

Martin eyed me, genuinely puzzled. As if I'd given him a mathematical answer to some question of philosophy.

"Instead of letting Burke beat his teeth out," I began, "give him a meal. He's starving. You think he won't talk if we actually give him the very thing that will let him live."

Slowly, Martin's expression changed. From puzzled to amused. He regarded me with precious pity before he spoke.

"You've been here a couple months," he said.

"Three," I corrected, like a prisoner might, marking the time of their sentence.

"If you want to make it to three and one day, I suggest you listen," he said, glancing briefly toward the intruder, the man's head hanging forward now, chin against his chest. "I've heard your little tales of the head cases you've come across. Guys trying to fry up a few fellow travelers in a shack. Some hippy woman ready to cleave a pound of flesh from you when you landed your plane. There are a lot of pure crazies out there. People driven past the edge of anything sane, anything moral, by the blight. Well, if you sprinkle a fair dose of evil on top of that and add the world's biggest drug den, you've got the Seattle Horde. And he's one of them."

He paused, but just long enough to step close to me. Dangerously close.

"Your morality will get you killed in this new world," Martin almost hissed, words spilling past his lips, hot and threatening. "Our goodness begins and ends with our own."

He walked back toward the intruder, leaving me standing in the dim half-light. I followed, stopping outside the circle of locals who'd crowded in toward me. Across them I could see Neil, eyeing me, worried and annoyed. As if I'd just stepped into a minefield that was plainly marked to avoid.

"Look at me," Martin said.

The intruder didn't oblige the command. Martin reached to the man and grabbed a bunch of his thinning hair, jerking his head up, the jaundiced gaze drifting finally toward his interrogator.

But Martin didn't say anything. Not immediately. He glanced over his shoulder to where I still stood, then again faced their prisoner.

"We have food," Martin said. "If you tell us why you're here, we'll give you something to eat."

Just beyond the prisoner, Burke looked up, surprised, his gaze shifting to Martin, and then toward me. I could feel the man's ire. I'd upset the order by planting the idea of an alternate approach to getting the prisoner's cooperation. Or, I considered, it might just be that Burke enjoyed beating the crap out of people when the need arose.

"Tell me," Martin said. "I promise you a good meal."

It seemed that as soon as the word 'promise' was uttered, the man began to laugh. Not some normal burst of joy, but a rolling wet cough, bits of bloody saliva dragging reddened stalactites of spit past splintered teeth, leaving them hanging from his chin. A smile, defiant and dirty, accompanied the mocking expression. Martin needed to hear or see no more.

"Take him for a swim," Martin said to Burke.

In an instant Burke swung the butt of his pistol across the man's face, harder than the previous times, knocking him into unconsciousness before grabbing him by the arm. Another man came forward and took the other arm, the both of them dragging the bleeding prisoner across the floor and out the door.

Martin turned to where I stood. The crowd between us thinned, residents drifting away and out the door.

"Satisfied?"

I wasn't. But I didn't say that to Martin. I'd been wrong, but it wasn't wrong to try.

"People here like you, Eric," he said. "Don't piss that away with idealism that should have died with the rest of the world."

He walked away from the bloodied chair, past me, and through the door to the tunnel.

"Fletch."

I turned. Neil stood by the door, waiting. I approached, pausing before exiting.

"He's right, you know," my friend said to me.

"No," I countered. "He's not."

"We're part of this now," Neil said. "Remember that. This is our home."

"You really feel that way?"

Neil thought for a moment, then nodded.

"I do."

He said nothing after that. Maybe waiting for me to concur, or to offer the same sentiment. But I couldn't.

I walked past my friend and back to the house that wasn't really mine in the town where I didn't really belong.

Thirty Nine

Reverend Morris officiated, speaking words that were familiar to most everyone. The blight had not stolen the ceremony from what remained of civilization. People still could commit to love, honor, and cherish. They could still say 'I do'.

My friend and Grace did just that with half of the town in attendance for the late afternoon wedding. Martin gave the bride away. Krista pulled double duty as maid of honor and flower girl, casting brightly colored cutouts of paper up the aisle as she went to join her mother near the altar. I stood with my friend, as his best man. He was happy. They were perfect for each other, proof that that standard of measure could still exist in the world.

They kissed. Those in attendance clapped, Krista slapping her palms together with such happiness that the act of revelry drew its own wave of applause from the crowd.

Neil and Grace stepped from the altar as man and wife. They took Krista by the hand, the girl between them, the new family walking up the aisle for the exit.

That was when the town's alarm sounded, wailing its warning beyond the walls of the church.

"Stay here," Neil told Grace.

She nodded reluctantly as I sprinted past them, joining the crush of guests rushing to grab their weapons and gear. I'd left mine in the building's foyer, as had many, the necessity to be ready at a moment's notice deeply ingrained. Even Neil had come prepared. We grabbed our vests and weapons and ran from the church.

"That was a short honeymoon," I said as we hurried north toward our assignment.

"We'll hit Vegas next week to make up for it," he said.

It was a light moment, and it lasted just a few seconds, as the sound of gunfire began to cut through the siren's scream.

Forty

It was another pointless attack, minus the self-immolation of the previous attempt to test the town's defenses. Twice as many attackers charged the fence on the northern perimeter of the town this time, nearly fifty people, sprinting across the bridge, charging into the river, swimming madly for the far shore.

Not a single person made it.

Gunfire rang for twenty minutes. Most came from our side, the armed members of the Horde spraying their weapons seemingly without aim, bullets impacting far from the protective structures positioned along the perimeter. Neil and I occupied Checkpoint Chuck, the both of us firing straight down the long span across the Coquille, dropping everything that moved.

"I don't get this," Neil said, his suit jacket shed but tie still in place, loosened with the shirt collar now unbuttoned. "It's like they're not really trying."

"Another probe?" I wondered.

"It's a lot of people to sacrifice to get essentially the same intel they got from the last try."

Neil was right. What the Horde had learned from their flaming assault months earlier had shown them how we would deploy our defenses. Some modifications had been made in the plan since then, with an additional patrol on foot able to respond as a sort of ready reserve, but if testing had been their purpose, this repeat performance made little sense.

"Maybe they are just drugged out lunatics," I said.

"Patrol Two, take over at Checkpoint Chuck," Burke's voice ordered over the radio. "Neil and Eric, rally at Old Glory on the double."

Odd, I thought. It wasn't 'Moore' and 'Fletcher' from Burke.

"What's that all about?" Neil wondered, knowing I was as in the dark as he was.

Out the right side of the observation post we could see the patrol running to relieve us.

"Let's find out," I said.

* * *

Neil and I reached the intersection where the flagpole stood to find a dozen people formed in a circle, warily surrounding two figures at the center.

"Dear God..."

It was all I could say when we saw who the two were at the same instant. Or the one that truly mattered. Krista. Her tiny form was clamped against a rabid looking man, waif thin, his arm across her neck, pinning her to him as he held a small revolver to her head.

"Let her go," Burke said, his AK slung, pistol in hand pointed at the ground, fearful of taking a bad shot.

"Short brown hair," the man from the Horde said, seeming to blabber. "Thin face. Blue shirt."

Neil approached the group encircling the man and Krista.

"Neil," she whimpered, and the man pressed harder against her neck, looking directly at my friend.

"Black hair, over the ears, wide shoulders," the man muttered, as if describing who he was seeing.

"If you hurt her..." Neil warned.

The man spun to the left, fixing his crazed gaze on another person in the swelling crowd, easily two dozen now surrounding him.

"Really blue eyes, really blue, and a shaved head, not very tall."

"What the hell is he doing?" Burke asked aloud.

There was no answer. Not to that question.

"How did he get here?" I asked.

"Came up from the south," Burke said. "The whole thing was a diversion."

A diversion so that one man could slip into town and grab a little girl while he chattered incoherently? That didn't make sense. What was the payoff? What did the Horde hope to achieve through this?

From behind, Martin jogged up, getting between Neil and the abductor. Krista began to cry and the man pushed the barrel of the revolver hard against her head, tipping it sideways as she sobbed quietly.

"It's okay," I said. "Krista, everything's going to be okay."

Neil couldn't restrain himself anymore and tried to push past Martin. I grabbed him, wrestling the Benelli from his grip.

"We've got to do this carefully," I told my friend, his enraged gaze locked with mine.

"Krista? Krista!"

It was Grace, still in the dress she'd worn for their wedding, running up the street, having just seen where her daughter was.

"Go stop her," I told Neil. "There's no way I'll let that scum hurt her. You know that."

It might have been the urgency of the moment, or the realization that I was right, but Neil quelled the anger within almost instantly and directed his energy to intercepting his new wife. He pulled away from me and grabbed her, holding Grace back, burying her wailing face against his chest.

I rejoined the circle, Elaine there now, standing next to me, pistol in hand.

"I can make the head shot," she said.

"And his dying brain sends a signal to every muscle to instantaneously contract, including the ones in his trigger finger," I reminded her.

She knew that already, I was certain. It was a simple fact that every single person standing near, whether urging the man to stop, or consoling Krista, wanted to end this. Elaine wanted to do that with a bullet. So did I.

As it turned out, so did another.

"It's time to end this," Martin said to the man. "You can't get away, and the little girl has done nothing to harm you. This has to stop."

The man ended his descriptive babbling and looked straight at Martin.

"You're right," the abductor from the Horde said.

Then, for me, time slowed. All the world narrowed down to a tunnel where I could only see the man holding Krista as he pulled the gun away from her head and put it to his own. Before anyone could do or say anything more, he squeezed the trigger and the side of his head opposite the revolver opened up with a shower of crimson and grey.

Krista screamed as the man's body folded down upon itself. I sprinted to the girl and snatched her up, no blood having splattered on her. Grace and Neil ran to meet me as I carried Krista away from the hellish scene. They both took her from me, holding the girl between them, parents, mother and father, in every way that mattered.

"I left her at the church to get my rifle," Grace said, the weapon discarded up the street where she'd dropped it when coming upon the terrifying scene. "I thought she'd be safe there."

"I'm sorry, mommy. I went looking for you. And the man...the man..."

She dissolved into tears against her mother's shoulder.

"Take her home," I said.

Neil looked to me, tears filling his eyes. He nodded and put a hand to my cheek, some measure of gratitude being offered. For keeping him from doing something rash, I expected. After a moment he and Grace walked away, up the street, heading for home.

"Eric."

It was Elaine. She was crouched over the dead man, Burke and Martin standing close, others a few steps back.

I moved to join her, stopping next to Martin and looking at what Elaine had discovered under the dead man's shirt.

"A radio," she said. "Transmit button is taped down."

"He was describing us to someone," Burke said.

"Marking us," I suggested, a supposition at best. "Targeting specific people."

"For what?" Elaine wondered.

Martin had nothing to add to the guessing game we were engaged in. He crouched and ripped the radio from where it was attached to the dead man's belt, bringing it up to his own face, holding it there, as if to say something. But he didn't. He squeezed the device in his hand and whipped halfway around, launching the radio at the wall of the corner building. It shattered and dropped to the ground as Old Glory flapped above.

Forty One

The town was on edge. People waited. Expecting something to come after the attacks and the infiltrations. Patrols were increased. The observation posts were reinforced. But nothing happened.

Nothing on land.

"They're not answering," Burke said past the half open door, hints of fog swirling in the street behind him. "The ship."

It was late, or early. One in the morning by the clock on the living room wall. I blinked the sleep from my eyes and nodded.

"Give me twenty seconds," I said.

I made it out the front door in closer to fifteen, all I'd need for such a response kept just inside the front room. Boots. Jacket. Flashlight. Binoculars. Vest. And my weapons.

We jogged up the street in the dark, a thin moon hanging high in the west, mist that might have blotted it from the sky dissolving in the night.

"Who's on the ship?" I asked.

"Elaine, Mikey, and Ross."

Elaine...

It shouldn't matter any more that she was there. The potential danger faced by the others was no less real. But, still, a sharp pang stabbed at my gut when I heard her name listed among those aboard. That was the moment I knew. Like Neil must have known at some point in his travels with

Grace. Beyond any ability to rationalize what I felt away, I couldn't. Not right then.

But I had to force the feeling down. All the feelings. There was no indication that Elaine felt anything similar toward me, despite Neil's claim that he could see it in her. The complications of some one-sided romantic desire could wreak havoc on too many things. Especially when heading out to see just what was going on thirty miles from shore.

Halfway down the block, fast steps behind made me look back. It was Neil, slipping into his vest as he ran, shotgun in hand. Beyond him, silhouetted by a dim light from within, Grace stood on their porch, watching us sprint up the block.

"This ever happen before?" I asked.

Burke shook his head, saving his breath to keep up the pace as Neil caught up with us.

"Who's got ship duty?" Neil asked.

I filled him in, none of us saying any more until we reached the dock. Martin was waiting there with Jenny Martell, the latter getting the skiff's outboard fired up.

"They have three damn radios," Burke said to Martin. "How does this happen?"

"Micah said he's picking up some sort of jamming," Martin said.

Neil turned to me, memories rising of the radio screeching at my refuge the day before the helicopter attack obliterated it. We both were thinking that, but here it made little sense.

"Could it be the Horde?" Burke wondered.

"I don't know," Martin answered.

Burke started to get aboard the skiff, but a hand against his chest stopped him.

"Not you," Martin told the head of security.

"What do you mean?" Burke protested.

Martin looked to Neil and me, a grim truth in his gaze.

"We can't risk all three of you," he said.

It was a harsh assessment. A game of numbers. One that we could make no argument against. Neil and I had become integral members of the force defending the town. We'd been tested before arriving. We'd seen death. We'd killed. And we could so again.

But I wanted things on our terms.

"She stays," I said, gesturing to Jenny.

The woman looked to Martin, not used to taking orders from anyone else. He turned to me, allowing an explanation of my thinking.

"Neil and I can run the skiff," I said. "All she's gonna be is another person to worry about out there. Another potential target."

Martin didn't even have to think on what I'd said. He knew I was right. As right as his limiting of the risk was.

"Go," he said.

* * *

We ran the skiff at full speed, through sporadic remnants of fog that had earlier clotted the night, until the first hint of the ship became visible, the shadow of its bulk jutting up from the sea, spreading a black scar upon the starry horizon.

"Get the paddles," Neil said as he cut the outboard, giving us a chance for a silent approach.

I took one and handed the other to my friend. We dug into the water beside the skiff, pulling the boat forward, foot by foot, until, a quarter mile from the *Groton Star*, we could hear it. A growling cough, like a huge beast trying to catch its breath.

"Someone's trying to start the engine," I said.

"Will that work?"

"It shouldn't," I said. "That doesn't mean it won't."

Neil and I crouched low, paddling steadily in the light chop, the skiff riding easily over the ocean rolling low.

"Can you see anything?" Neil asked.

We had no night vision equipment. My personal one had been lost in the attack on my refuge. The only piece of optics able to cut the darkness, a thermal scope, was on the very ship we were approaching, potentially watching us at that very moment.

As Neil paddled, I took my binoculars in hand and focused in on the ship.

"She's dark," I said. "Blacked out."

That was not unexpected. To keep the vessel invisible at night, the most illumination to be chanced in an open space, like on deck or in the glassed-in bridge, was a chemical light stick. I couldn't even make out the green glow one of those would show off when activated.

"I have no movement," I reported. "Not a th—"

Thud.

The impact was gentle, the sloped flat bow of the skiff seeming to ride up upon something it had struck. Neil stopped paddling. I crept to the front of the craft and peered over it, into the water.

Mikey Winthrop's dead face stared up at me.

"Jesus..."

Neil scooted forward and looked with me as I grabbed the young man's jacket collar and held him close to the boat.

"Shot in the head," Neil said.

My friend was right. By starlight and the scant glow of the slivered moon, the dark circle in Mikey's forehead was stark against his pale, ghostly skin.

I looked back to the boat, two hundred yards from us now as we bobbed gently on the water, my unaided vision detecting something now. A hint of movement at the rail where the rope ladder would usually be deployed.

"Someone's on deck," I said.

Neil looked, nodding a second later.

"I see them."

There was no telling who it was from this distance, in this light. It might have been Elaine, or Ross Lane. But we doubted it.

I looked down to Mikey a final time, putting my hand to his cheek as I let him go. His body drifted off to the side of the skiff and disappeared in the black water.

"We need to get aboard," I said.

"We need to get close first and see who's at that rail."

My friend was right. Impatience was not a strategy here. A killer was aboard the ship. Or killers. Rushing to stop them would likely only add to their body count.

"Let's head aft of the ship," I suggested. "We can get a closer look up the side."

The starboard side, I reminded myself. That was the right side. We paddled steadily ahead, aiming for a point near one of the rear anchor cables, reaching it in less than five minutes.

"You see it?"

Neil nodded at my question. Tied to the side of the *Groton Star*, at the bottom of the deployed rope ladder, was a boat not unlike the one we occupied. A skiff too close in appearance to be coincidental. It was empty, riding high on the light sea, banging occasionally against the big ship's steel hull.

"If we try to get to the ladder, whoever's on deck can pick us off," Neil said.

He wasn't wrong. We'd have to find another way onto the ship.

The answer to that dilemma presented itself hardly ten yards away.

"You remember the rope drills Macklin had us do?" I asked.

Our high school football coach, a tough and lovable SOB, had often worked us and our teammates almost into the ground, with a favorite drill to toughen us up being climbing ropes suspended from the ceiling of the gymnasium. Neil caught on, but eyed the angled cables doubtfully.

"That was straight up," he said. "This is a wet piece of steel. It's basically a zip line we'd have to ride in reverse."

"It's also the only option."

He thought for a moment, then put his paddle back into the water. I did, as well, and we moved the skiff close to the anchor cable, tying to boat off to the thick wire. I slung my AR and maneuvered myself under the cable, grabbing it with gloved hands and wrapping my legs around it as I pulled myself up the incline. Neil followed, our bodies suspended beneath the cable as we crept upward, foot by foot, closing in on the ship, the cable disappearing through a smallish hole cut in the hull.

"Hang back for a minute," I told my friend.

Neil paused, anchoring his body to the slanted cable with the hook of his elbow latched over it. I wriggled my body close to the hull and wrenched myself over the top of the cable, groping for balance as I put a hand to the solid steel of the ship.

That was when I slipped.

My hand slid off the slick, moist steel, the rest of my body twisting over the top of the anchor cable and dropping like a rock toward the water.

"*Fletch!*" Neil shouted in a hush.

My right hand clamped onto the cable, a death grip that kept me from falling into the cold Pacific.

"I'm okay," I assured my friend, though I wasn't certain of that myself.

I got my other hand onto the cable, then swung my legs up and over it, repositioning myself for another try at getting aboard the *Groton Star*. The deck was maybe five feet above the penetration where the cable disappeared into the ship. With more attention to balance I again planted a hand against the hull and eased my feet onto the cable, positioning myself like a circus wire walker.

"Careful," Neil urged, maybe prayed, just to my rear.

I teetered back and forth, sliding my front foot toward the cable hole, finally planting it there for a solid foothold, allowing me to reach upward and slip my fingers over the edge of the deck. Slowly, I raised my head until my eyes could just peer over.

The fantail at the rear of the ship was empty, no sign of life there. But forward, past the vessel's superstructure on the starboard side, I could now make out more clearly the shadowy figure at the rail. A man, I thought, tall and rail thin, a rifle in hand, held low as he paced back and forth near the rope ladder's anchor point.

I pulled myself carefully over the rail, staying low as I reached through the cross members. Neil slid forward on the cable and repeated the process I'd just completed, taking my hand. The boat rumbled, engine chugging, pistons throbbing deep in the hull somewhere, metal slamming against metal.

"That's not going to start," Neil said as I helped him over the rail.

"Keep hoping that," I told him.

We moved to the rear corner of the superstructure, a door there that I knew would let us in. But that was not the first move we were going to make.

"Can you take him from here?" Neil asked.

"We're sure that's not Ross?"

It certainly wasn't Elaine. Ross Lane was tall like the figure along the rail, but not as thin.

"I'd bet cash money on it," Neil said.

That was good enough for me. I raised my AR, bringing the suppressed barrel in line with the target. The dim orange triangle in the sight danced lightly over the figure, settling to a point between his shoulder and his waist. The safety was already off. The selector was set to semi-automatic fire. My finger eased onto the trigger. I inhaled.

Held the breath. Let it seep slowly out and put pressure on the trigger.

The front of the weapon bucked slightly, just a quick rise as the bullet flew downrange. It struck the man, though I could not see precisely where. His body spun and crumpled, just a slight whimper cutting across the twenty yards to where he'd stood. I readjusted aim to his now horizontal form and fired a second shot, then a third, the final round penetrating enough to raise a spark and a quick *clang* from the metal deck as it exited his body.

"Headshot," Neil said.

He might have been right. There was no further movement.

"Inside," I said.

We turned to the rear door, both of us familiar with the layout of the ship's interior after multiple times serving guard duty aboard.

"Ready?"

I nodded to my friend and reached for the door handle.

Forty Two

We stepped into darkness and closed the metal door behind, as quietly as we could, taking positions to either side of the short corridor we'd just entered. For a moment we stood still, letting our vision acclimate to the internal night. Listening for any hint of what might be happening.

Neil heard it first.

"Laughing," he mostly whispered.

I could just make out Neil pointing forward and down. Toward the hold.

We advanced, stepping carefully, the barest ambient light trickling down the stairs from the bridge four decks above. At the base of the steps we stopped, our choice to move down toward the sounds, or up to the bridge. As it turned out, the choice was made for us.

The bunk room door swung open just behind us. Reacting quickly, Neil and I turned in unison, seeing the woman step into the corridor as she saw us. Her face was marked with sores and cuts, hardly any flesh upon her. Bits of red chunks clung to her chin and stained the front of her threadbare clothing. In her right hand was a knife, its blade dripping something thick and liquid.

Her mouth opened to scream, or yell, but she never got the chance. Neil slammed the butt of his Benelli across her face, knocking her into the wall. She bounced off of it and dropped to the floor, gurgling. Alive.

Until he drove the butt again into her skull, cratering her head. She twitched for a few seconds, then went still.

He looked to me, and then to the bunk room, its door still open. We eased toward it. I took my flashlight out as Neil covered the opening. A flick of my thumb on the switch lit the space up, revealing what we knew would be there—beds, communal table—and what we feared.

Ross Lane lay face down on the table, his jeans removed and piled on the floor, a long strip of the flesh removed from the back of his thigh. All around him was a bloody horror, evidence of a meal interrupted.

"Christ," Neil said. "A whole ship of food and they do this."

"They have a taste for it now," I said, my stomach sickening. "We have to find Elaine."

Neil nodded. I turned off my flashlight and stowed it. We moved forward again, to the stairs, and descended, coming to the catwalk level that gave access to the rear hold. The laughter was louder now, and with it we could hear the tearing of cardboard and the ripping of plastic.

"They're at the food," I whispered.

Neil moved a step ahead, taking point. Every few seconds I glanced behind, wanting no more surprises. We passed through the watertight door that was left open, our boots scuffing along the grated flooring. Just ahead the corridor opened onto the balcony over the hold. The level of noise increased, laughter and ripping and metal banging, indications of more than one person awaiting us.

I wondered how many that skiff could have carried out to the boat, forcing down questions as to how they'd gotten aboard, much less close to the vessel. Some trickery, to be certain. In concert with the jamming Micah had detected. All seemed to point to a plan well thought out and perfectly executed.

We reached the balcony, a light spreading beyond, flickering and yellow. A fire. Neil crept onto the overlook, crouching. I did the same, looking below to see a minor bonfire burning, pans placed close, water boiling. Packages of MREs were open and scattered at the feet of three men, each gorging themselves and dumping the contents of large cans of rice and dried beans into the frothing water.

The ship shuddered again, engine sputtering through loud and angry death throes.

"Get it started already!" one of the men below shouted between bites and howls of laughter.

The Horde had made it onto the ship. Their intention was to take it to feed the crazed masses in Seattle. I needed no playbook to make their plan apparent to me.

Again the engine rumbled, then stopped with a jolt that shook the ship.

"Can't he do any—"

The man below never finished his damning question, his gaze catching sight of something in the light spread by the fire.

Us.

The yeller was the first to reach for his weapon. Neil made sure he never got a finger on it, firing three times from his Benelli, the buckshot shredding the man, half his face turning to mist.

The other two went for their own rifles. I dropped the first with a half dozen quick shots, his comrade getting to his AK and bringing it to bear without aiming, finger mashed on the trigger, rounds spraying upward toward us.

Sparks danced off the metalwork around us as we ducked. Neil rolled to the left, tumbling onto the stairs. I moved right, too quickly, my foot catching, tripping me up as bullets ticked off the bulkhead above.

Below, the man was shifting his fire left and right. Neil squeezed off two shots, both wide, shotgun pellets tearing into a pallet of MRE cases. I tried to bring my weapon to bear, but the suppressor slammed against the railing support as I swung it toward the shooter. We were pinned down. Vulnerable. Sitting ducks.

More fire came. But it sounded different. Then a scream. A man screaming. The man below, firing at us. Who *had* been firing at us. His weapon was now silent, laying across the bonfire.

"Fletch!"

Neil was calling out to me from across the hold.

"Neil, are you okay?"

"Yeah! Did you take him out?"

"I did," the answer came, the voice familiar and welcome.

Elaine stepped from the shadows beyond the pallets at the far side of the hold, MP5 in hand, trained on the downed shooters as she advanced toward them, limping.

I got to my feet and made my way quickly down the stairs on the right side of the hold as Neil did the same on the left. Elaine half fell against a pallet of cased food, but never let her weapon come off of the shooters.

"What happened?" I asked, getting an arm under her so she wouldn't fall.

"There's one more," she said, looking past Neil, to another door up the stairs. "In the engine room."

Neil covered that door while I lowered Elaine until she was sitting on a small stack of cases. A dark spot had spread upon her jeans just above the knee, hole in the denim on the outside of her thigh.

"I caught a ricochet," she said. "I fell back to here to guard the food. They got Mikey."

"And Ross," I said.

Her face sagged. She hadn't known. She kicked one of the pans of water with her good leg, dousing the cooking fire.

"How'd they get aboard?" I asked, pulling a bandage from my vest for her leg.

"The radios went out, and it was foggy. Mikey said the skiff was coming up. They looked like people from town."

Another piece began to fall into place.

"The guy who grabbed Krista," I said. "He was describing us to his pals so they could disguise themselves."

Elaine nodded and winced silently as I tied a dressing over her wound.

"Their hair was died, they padded their clothing to not look thin. When the first one came up the ladder he shot Mikey. I fired, then a bunch of them fired. It was chaos."

"Drugs didn't kill all their brain cells," Neil said, almost admiring the operation they'd nearly pulled off.

"How many were there?" I asked.

"These three and three more," Elaine answered.

"We got two up top," I told her. "That just leaves your engine room guy."

She nodded, then tried to stand. I put a hand on her shoulder and guided her back down with some force.

"You stay here," I told her, gesturing to the balcony above. "Shoot anyone who comes through either of those doors."

"Even you?" she joked through a building wave of pain.

"No, just Neil."

My friend tossed me a look and a smile.

"Let's go hunting," he said.

We started toward the stairs.

"This prey shoots back," Elaine said from behind, reminding us just what we were about to face.

* * *

The engine room was one floor below the level of the balcony, in the belly of the ship. No sound of the engine throttling futilely had been heard since our shootout in the cargo hold, the sound of that exchange certainly alerting the last member of the Horde to our presence.

The door to the compartment was almost closed, an inch of space between it and the steel frame. We listened, a soft jostling sounding in the distance beyond the door.

"We can't wait him out," I said.

"Okay," Neil said, bringing the muzzle of his Benelli to the edge of the door and pushing it inward.

A volley of automatic fire rained through the open portal immediately. I ducked left, and Neil right, the fire from within stopping after a few seconds, the sound of a magazine dropping coming next.

"Go!" I shouted.

We took the opportunity to rush through the door, a distant flashlight resting on the floor giving the space some shadowy definition. I found cover behind a lacework of thick pipes. Across from me, Neil was crouch-walking behind what appeared to be some sort of tank.

A click signaled that the man had reloaded, and the fire began again, wild shots spraying, ricocheting off metal, slicing into ductwork. Dust and sparks flew, and once more the fire ebbed, another magazine dropping.

I moved again, along the outside wall of the space, huge diesel engines to my left, a smoky stench hanging over them. The pistons had seized, burning through whatever inadequate lubricant remained after more than a year of non-use.

Click.

Another magazine was ready. But no fire came this time. The man was holding back. Lying in wait.

"You don't get to live!"

It was the voice of a young man. A crazy man.

"I get to live!"

To the left of me. That's where I tagged the origin of the shouting. On the far side of the engines.

"I will kill you and then I get to live!"

Clang!

The sound was sharp and reverberated across the compartment, something heavy and metal striking something heavier and metal. A diversion, I knew, Neil taking some initiative to draw the man's attention. It worked. Gunfire erupted again, the crazy man firing, his lone mode of fire seeming to be holding the trigger down until his weapon ran dry.

His weapon went silent, but no magazine dropped. Instead, a solid thud echoed, his empty rifle hitting the floor this time, all his rounds and spares expended. For that weapon.

I came around the far end of the diesel and heard another sound. A click, though not like before, then a fast, sizzling hiss, like a fuse being lit.

No...

I sprinted toward the sound, clearing a bank of electrical vaults just as the crazy man drew his arm back in the open space beyond, fragmentation grenade smoking in it. His aim was directed toward the sound that had drawn his fire just a moment ago. A sound that I knew Neil had made.

"Neil!"

The man looked my way even as his arm began its forward arc, grenade launching from it as I fired, a half dozen shots finding their target and an equal number flying wide. The man fell sideways, the grenade's trajectory wobbled by the hits he'd absorbed. It flew low and banked off a pipe tracking across the ceiling, then dropped to the floor and rolled right at me.

I was about to duck behind the engine I'd just passed, but across the space, between a wall of rising pipes, Neil appeared, the grenade between us.

"Get to cover!" I screamed.

Neil spun away as I did, my body making it around the corner to the cover of the massive engine when the device detonated. A flash filled the compartment, shrapnel peppering every exposed surface as choking smoke swirled. I was on the floor, I realized, not remembering diving or falling, my back stinging. I reached back and felt a piece of my vest ripped away, torn by shrapnel. But there was nothing wet. No sticky blood oozing. I'd gotten a very lucky kick in the side and no more.

But I had no idea if Neil had been so lucky.

"Neil!"

I scrambled up, steadying myself, shaking off the effects of the concussive blast wave as I caromed off the engine, the electrical vaults, pipes and fittings, mostly stumbling toward my friend. I took my flashlight out and turned it on, the one that had been lit obliterated by the detonation. A wide scorch mark blackened the area where it had gone off.

"Neil!"

"Eric!"

I looked left and saw Elaine hobbling into the compartment.

"I can't find Neil!" I told her.

She cut through the warren of equipment with me, rounding a corner where pipes dove through the floor. That was where we found him.

"I don't think that guy liked us," Neil said, looking up from where he'd been knocked to the floor.

"Are you okay?" I asked him, the question urgent, almost a demand.

He coughed through the smoke and nodded. I reached down and helped him up.

"Let's get back to dry land," he said.

"Seconded," Elaine agreed.

We moved to the door, then out of the engine room. A few minutes later we were on deck, the stars bright above.

"God, it's beautiful," Elaine said, looking skyward, her voice cracking just a bit. "How can it be so beautiful after all that?"

I knew what she meant. And why it troubled her.

"Because we want it to," I said, and she collapsed, sobbing, against me.

Forty Three

A full week it took, running the skiff and two other boats back and forth to the freighter, night and day, burning through a full three-quarters of the fuel the town had stored. But by the end of the effort, every single box, can, and package of food left on the *Groton Star* was on land, secured in multiple locations around town.

The day after the final trip was made, a few minutes after noon, timed charges planted strategically on the freighter detonated. From shore there was nothing to see, but a sound did reach land, roaring low after a series of sharp cracks. Without seeing it we knew that the ship was at the bottom of the Pacific.

That night a meeting convened, as many of the residents who could make it jammed into the Meeting Hall. It was standing room only. I arrived to see Neil, Grace, and Krista in the front row, listening to Martin talk about measures to ensure the security of the food supply. From my place at the back of the hall, I took in the sight, some form of democracy in action, with a mix of martial law expectedly flavoring the results. To a person everyone seemed satisfied. Everyone was onboard. A consensus had been unanimously reached.

And I was sickened by it.

I left the hall with the meeting still in session, wandering away, no destination in mind. The world felt airy and empty, like the town was already gone and I was the last man standing.

But I wasn't.

"Too officious for you?" Elaine asked.

I turned toward her. She sat on a bench across the street. Behind her was an empty storefront, faded lettering announcing that it had once been a candy store. How many times had children come to the place and slapped their money down, then hurried out to savor sweet treats on the very bench where she now sat? The thought of those anonymous children wasn't even a memory. It was an echo of a time that would never be again. Not with what was being discussed inside the Meeting Hall.

"I don't understand them," I said. "I don't understand this."

Elaine absorbed what I said, seeming to contemplate it for a moment, deeply and fully.

"You're leaving, aren't you," she said, no question in her tone.

I could have answered in the affirmative, but something kept me from being honest. From being forthright with her. A something that was no mystery to me.

I didn't want to leave her.

"This can't go on," I said. "Everything here has an expiration date that comes when the last MRE is eaten."

"You're not wrong," she said. "But does leaving change that? For you or for anyone left here?"

"Probably not," I said.

She stood, teetering for a moment on her bad leg. I reached out and she grabbed my arm for support. Her hand remained there for a moment after she'd already steadied herself. She looked to me, just looked, saying nothing for a moment.

Then she eased her hand from my arm.

"If you have no destination, no prize to put your eye on, isn't that just running away?"

I didn't have an answer for her. And she didn't wait for one. She smiled softly and turned away, walking up the street. I could have followed. Maybe I should have. But I didn't.

Forty Four

"What now?"

Neil didn't answer me right away. Instead he stared at the street from where we sat on his porch. Behind, in the house, Krista and Grace were doing some crafty thing with paper and colored markers they'd gotten from the supply center. Later they were planning to go for a walk on the beach to collect rocks. An impossibly normal day.

Except it wasn't.

"Why does there have to be some decision?" he asked me. "Can't we just live?"

"Live?" I parroted. "This is the life you want?"

"Fletch, what the hell do you want? This is the world we live in. What else is there? Do you think there's something better out there?"

There might be. I didn't know. But I was aiming at a more concrete point.

"This can't go on," I said. "You know that."

Neil didn't offer any comment to my statement. Not right away. He lifted his glass of water and sipped. In a month, spring would be half over, summer on the horizon of seasons. Martin had said there would be power available to run a communal ice maker. Someone, Burke maybe, would break out a hoarded bottle of liquor and there would be drinks on the rocks. But that, too, would end.

"Everything here is going to run out," I reminded my friend.

"Then it runs out," he said, an edge to the statement. "I have a life here, Fletch. I know that sounds impossible, but Grace, and Krista, without the blight I would never have found them. I would have never found this kind of love and acceptance."

"Neil..."

"No," he said, stopping me. "Maybe, just maybe, it was all meant to end. Maybe this is the last flourish of humanity. If that's the case, I don't want to spend it looking for something better that might not even exist. I can live, really live, right here, with the two most precious people in the world to me. Why would I want to jeopardize that?"

There was no point in trying to convince my friend. My best friend. Our paths had diverged. This was his be all, end all moment and place in time.

The front door burst open and Krista came out, a brightly colored and sweetly crafted paper flower in hand. Its petals were yellow, stem and leaves below a lush green.

"Do you like it?" she asked, showing her creation to Neil as Grace came out, witness to the warm moment.

My friend took it and examined it, turning it slowly in his hand before giving Krista a satisfied nod and a smile. He brought it to his nose and sniffed playfully.

"Can't tell it from the real thing," Neil said.

Krista beamed at him, then at me.

"I'm going to give it to Micah," she said, then spun toward the steps and bounded down to the walkway, nearly sprinting up the street.

"I guess we're delivering it now," Grace said, and followed her daughter.

But as she turned from walkway to sidewalk, she glanced back toward the house. Directly at me. It was as if she sensed something. In me. My unease with the town's placid march toward oblivion, maybe.

"They're happy here, Fletch," Neil said once Grace and Krista had disappeared up the block.

"This place is a death sentence, Neil. For you. For them."

He didn't respond to my words. My implied plea.

"You're killing them by staying."

"And what about out there?" he challenged me. "After what Krista went through, a gun to her head, what do you think we'd face out there? I can't chance anything happening to them. I couldn't live with that."

"There's no future here, Neil."

"Stop it, Fletch."

I leaned toward my friend, wanting desperately for him to accept what I was saying. To understand. To agree.

"They're your family, Neil, for God's sake!"

"I know what they are!" he shouted, standing too fast, the chair he'd been sitting in toppling.

Silence raged between us for a moment. He reached down and righted the chair, glancing up and down the neighborhood to see if anyone had witnessed the outburst.

"I'm right," I told my friend.

"I don't care."

"Neil..."

"Leave," he said, uttering a word I'd never heard him say to me. "Now."

I hesitated, stunned and stung by the moment.

"Now, Fletch," he repeated, emphasizing his desire to be done with me.

I stood, slowly, wanting to say something, anything, to fix what had just transpired. But I couldn't. The only way to do so would be to deny the truth and accept the fading fantasy my friend had embraced.

Forty Five

He wants to see you...

There was no need to ask who the 'he' was. Burke had simply knocked on the door of my house and said those words as I opened it. I followed him down the front walk and up the street, keeping pace a few feet behind. As much as I had been accepted by the Bandon community, there was still a separation. They felt it, and I hadn't done much to conceal my feelings since the *Groton Star* went to the bottom of the sea.

In fact, distance did not only exist between me and them. The rift between Neil and I had widened to the point of fracture, like tectonic plates bursting apart in a cataclysmic quake.

"Is Neil coming?"

Burke glanced back toward me.

"He didn't ask for Neil."

We continued up the street. The day was warming. Windows were open and curtains were flapping in the soft wind rolling in from the Pacific. If one could forget the previous year and a half, the serene moment would seem almost normal.

But what had transpired, be it in the past eighteen months, or eighteen hours, was indelibly etched on every fiber of my being. Neil's too, I was certain as we passed the house he shared with Grace and Krista. Down the side I could see the child running across the yard, dirt where a putting green lawn had once been. Her bare feet kicked up puffs of the dusty earth as my friend, my best friend despite recent events, chased her, both giddy with the moment. With some semblance of what passed as normalcy.

I also saw Grace. Standing just inside, staring out through the fine mesh of the screen door, her gaze set upon me. Staying with me as I continued down the street. I turned away first and did not look back.

She'd been the skeptic, originally, when it came to deciding whether to seek out Eagle One. My refuge was a place of safety. Until it was not. Now she saw Bandon much as she had the place we'd fled from. As did Neil, though I knew, I believed, that his embrace of this serenity was based more upon his love for Grace than it was on a rational review of circumstances.

Part of me did understand their desire to accept the stability of the community we'd come to. It was the closest thing to the old world that we'd experienced. Or that we were likely to experience.

But it was not that world. Not that time. And it would not be that just by planting our flag in a locale and wishing blindly that it would be so. Comfort was not interchangeable with progress. Bandon was a place in waiting. Just like every other spot on earth where human beings still drew breath. Death was marching toward the town, and it was getting closer. Not in the form of psychotic hordes from the next state up, but from the simple concept of inevitability.

Wishes did not fill stomachs.

To be certain, Micah, and Martin, and even Burke, along with most of the town, had done a wondrous job at creating a community of like-minded souls who had seized on the good 'now' to the exclusion of the terrifying 'tomorrow'. A sort of shared amnesia toward the future. I didn't understand my place in that. I, *we*, had come to this place, to Eagle One, wanting it to be where the new world would begin. Instead we'd found a sort of living mausoleum, of people meaning well, and doing good, but with no way to spread that beyond the border they'd established, or beyond the fleeting moment of plenty they now enjoyed.

I had to get away from that. I had to find a place, or make one for myself, that pushed toward some larger salvation. The hope that Neil had long ago made me believe in, I had to carry that to an actuality. The future, one not limited by dwindling stores of food, must be made. And if it could not be, I wanted to die trying to make it happen.

This would be the moment I declared that to Martin. I would be leaving, striking out on my own. There would be no attempt to stop me. Nothing beyond words, at least. Bandon was not a prison, and the people, as misguided as they were, did not fancy themselves as sentries necessary to keep the unwilling within any metaphorical walls.

"Go on in," Burke said as we reached the Meeting Hall.

I paused before entering. The guard seated just outside on a plastic patio chair stood and opened the door for me.

"He didn't say anything?" I asked.

"No," Burke said, a caustic tinge to his tone. "But apparently you're the one he wants to say something to."

It wasn't jealousy that was fouling Burke's mood. It was reality. At his best, the man was muscle. In this place, facing the threats that were prevalent in the dying world, Burke Stovich was recognized as an asset.

But every situation did not require a fist, or a bullet. Sometimes a word would suffice, and Burke did not know how to operate in that arena.

"He's waiting," Burke said, and I entered the Meeting Hall.

The single light burned within the empty space. Across it was the door that led to Martin and Micah's house. It was propped open, which seemed odd. Though it did not lead to the sanitized clean portion of the living quarters beyond, it had always been closed to maintain a sort of seal between the Meeting Hall and the house. I passed through it and down the plastic tunnel that crossed the street, mounting the steps as I had before. Once inside I walked down the hallway and through the strips of plastic, emerging to the room where the transparent barrier cut the space in half.

Only it was not there.

"Come in," Martin said, standing near Micah's radios and computers, just air between us.

"Martin, what..."

I didn't know what to ask. What to say. The sturdy plastic that had maintained an environment of cleanliness for Micah was gone, left on the floor to my left, rolled up haphazardly. Remnants of it still clung to the ceiling and walls, rough edges showing. It had been cut down and discarded.

Martin stared at the array of electronics, humming quietly in some digital slumber.

"Martin, where is Micah?"

The man, the father turned to face me, and without a word led me to his son's bedroom door and opened it for me.

Micah lay on his bed, still and silent, his eyes closed, hands clasped lightly upon the top of the blanket that covered him to the chest, softly clutching the flower Krista had made him. Its false green leaves and hand colored petals were forever.

He was not.

"I knew it could happen," Martin said, looking at his son's body, no tears or grief yet apparent. "He wasn't supposed to live past two. That's what the doctors told us when he was born. They just didn't know what a tough little guy he was. I mean, really, he beats those predictions, does all he's done to help us, survives a heart transplant under the conditions we're all having to endure...the will this kid had to live leaves me in awe."

Now the first hint of tears came. Martin's eyes glistened as he looked from his son's body to me.

"I'm so sorry, Martin."

The sympathy I expressed, and the grief I was witness to, made me feel very connected to the man. And very alone. Because I was. No one else was here, and it seemed to me that none had come before me.

"I'm the only one you've told," I said.

"Yes."

"Why?"

Martin composed himself. A look of apology, maybe shame, washed over him.

"People believed too much in him," Martin said. "That was my fault. And now that he's gone..."

"He was a child, Martin."

"I know. But they expected him to be more. They expected him to provide. To have the answers."

That was too much to lay on one person. Micah, from what I had seen, never felt burdened by the vague worship bestowed upon him. It drove him, I thought. Corroborated his genius.

"I wish he was here," Martin said, looking to me now. "He'd be so much better at this than me."

"Better at what?"

Martin looked to the electronics room beyond the door.

"Come with me."

We left the boy's room and stood once again before the devices which had helped Micah work his magic.

"Do you know what fast scan TV is?" Martin asked me as he moved to a monitor hooked to one of Micah's radios.

"I can't say I do."

The screen was blank on the powered-down device, though the radio's digital display was lit up, with glowing blue and green readouts pulsing. It was receiving a signal. This much I knew from observing Del's obsession with his similar gear.

"It's a way of transmitting video signals over amateur radio frequencies," he explained. "In essence, your own personal television station. Any radio operator with the right gear to receive it can watch whatever you decide to broadcast."

I understood the concept, but wondered as to the usefulness of such a thing, particularly in the world as it was now. Was Martin hoping to send out video messages from Eagle One, much as Micah had simple voice transmissions? If so, to what purpose?

Unless...

"Did you pick something up?" I asked, realizing that we could be on the receiving end as much as the sending.

"Micah did," Martin said. "Just before you arrived in Bandon. Someone out there was transmitting a video stream, and Micah was trying to zero in on where it was coming from."

"Another group of survivors?" I asked.

Martin shook his head.

"Just an image," he said. "No voice. No sound at all. Just the image."

"Of what?"

He reached to the monitor and powered it up. The screen fuzzed to life from a single point at its center, image upon it resolving through intermittent bursts of electronic noise. But even with the interference, I had no difficulty making out what I was seeing. My pulse quickened.

"Oh my God..."

Martin nodded, looking with me.

"I know."

The image came to us not in grainy black and white, but in color. And that color was green.

Green leaves. Green stem. The green of a plant. A living plant.

Maybe...

"How do you know it's real?" I asked. "We have a park two blocks away plastered with fake greenery."

"We know," Martin said.

He took a few steps to where a computer was running. I followed, standing next to him as he clicked an icon on the screen.

"That feed has been recording since Micah first picked it up."

The image that was on the live feed appeared on the computer monitor, mirrored there. Martin moved the cursor to the bottom of the screen and clicked on the digital equivalent of the REWIND button. The picture began tracking backward, time running in reverse. He clicked the same button again, speeding up the trip into the past. And again, and again, time receding at ten times normal speed. Then twenty. Thirty. Forty.

And that's how I knew. How he knew. We watched together as the green miracle on screen grew smaller, and smaller. Days passed, columns of sunlight sweeping across the space where the plant grew, over and over, night following, only to be replaced by the previous day. It was like looking into a time machine. Bursts of moisture periodically sprayed onto the soil where the plant had sprouted, that process witnessed in reverse now, leaves curling back into stems, stalk shrinking, a flash of something, until finally we were at the beginning.

"Watch," Martin said, stopping it there and playing it again as it had happened, at normal speed.

At first there was dirt. And light. The warmth of the sun drizzling down from above. And then there was a hand. Little more of the person it was part of than that and a few inches of forearm.

"This was six months ago," Martin said.

The hand was gaunt. Thin skin over emaciated flesh, both barely concealing the bones they covered. It reached to the dirt and scooped a small hole, then withdrew. A moment later it reappeared, index finger and thumb pinched together. Holding something. It shifted position closer to the camera to reveal what it held.

A seed. A single, solitary seed.

It gingerly placed the seed into the hole and filled the void once again, patting the dirt flat over what it had just planted before it withdrew from sight.

"We never saw the hand again," Martin shared.

A moment after the hand's disappearance, a trickle of water from above moistened the soil.

"It's some sort of automatic watering system," Martin said. "Micah calculated out the timing, the amount of water it was dispensing. He said it was set to deliver precisely what the plant needed as it grew."

"What kind of plant is it?" I asked, my past knowledge of horticulture limited to how many potted plants I could kill in a year's time.

"Tomato," Martin said, looking to me and nodding. "Food."

He advanced the image again, speeding it up, pointing out details as we watched the plant grow.

"See the leaves move?"

"Yeah," I said.

"Micah figured this is in some kind of greenhouse setup, with openings for ventilation, but protected overhead with a glass covering, or something similar. Watch the sunlight track across the space. You can see the shadows of thin frames on the ground."

I did. And then the image stopped its rapid advance. We were back watching a live feed of the transmission. A view across the miles to a here and now that was wondrous in its simplistic reckoning of the old world.

"Tomatoes," I said.

"Slow growing," Martin observed. "It's something different. Maybe that's why the blight doesn't affect it."

Martin reached out and put a finger to the electronic image. He wanted to put a hand through the monitor and seize the once ordinary plant. Seize it and bring it here. He wanted that desperately. Needed it more than anyone knew.

Except, maybe, for me.

"The food will be gone in eight months," Martin said, easing his hand back, fingers curling, a fist forming. "Eight lousy months."

He thumped his knotted hand against his hip, softly, some muted form of punishment. The admission he'd just made mirrored what I'd come to understand. Bandon was dying. Slowly, quietly, certainly.

"I knew," he said.

"Everyone knows," I told him. "They just don't want to see it."

He looked to me, embarrassed. Ashamed. Weak. It was a state I had never seen infect the man. Not even moments before, when he stood stoically over his dead child.

"We have to find that plant," he told me, the words edging toward a directive. "Where it's growing, there might be more. Whoever planted it might have found a cure for the blight."

"They're already dead, Martin."

He knew that. It was plain from the image of the hand, and the automatic setup of watering, that the person who'd planted the miracle seed had known they would not live to see it mature. Would not see it bear fruit. Would not taste the bounty of the singular crop.

"Micah had been working on locating where this is," Martin said. "He said by measuring the angle of the shadows at specific times on the feed, then comparing it to conditions in Bandon, he could do just that."

Once more, the emotion rose in the man. The father. It choked him up.

"He never finished," Martin said, settling into Micah's chair at the computer table.

I stared at the image. The amazing green image. Even fouled by pulses of electronic noise, it was mesmerizing, rivaling even the vast fields of cool grass and swaying trees that filled my dreams. Except this was real, and it was out there.

"You said he never finished. But he started. Right?"

"Right," Martin confirmed.

"Did he get anywhere with what he had? Did he have a general idea?"

Martin thought for a moment, the question seeming to puzzle him. Then he stood and walked past me, back into Micah's bedroom. I followed after a few seconds.

On the far side of the bed, just beyond his son's pure and peaceful body, Martin bent over the boy's bedside table, searching through notepads and individual slips of paper, scouring them with his eyes. Searching.

"You had to have something," Martin said, the words, the certainty offered to whatever ethereal trace of his son that might remain. "I know you. You had to have something."

He tossed papers aside after studying them. Pushed notepads to the floor.

"Martin..."

He grew more determined. More frantic. Wanting, *needing* to find that last bit that his son had accomplished.

"Martin, stop..."

But he couldn't. He continued, scanning every sheet, every notebook page, until finally he stopped. His hands each held an edge of a piece of paper, calculations covering it, lines and arrows intersecting, numbers jumbled in equations. All meaningless.

All except two words. A name. A place. An oval circle drawn around it. Marking it as important.

"Cheyenne," Martin said, looking to me, tears over the proud smile on his face. "Cheyenne, Wyoming."

He held the paper out to me and I took it, eyeing it for a moment as I stood next to the body of the child who'd come to this conclusion. I looked to Micah, wondering if this was the last thing he'd done, or just another in a string of incredible acts beyond his years. Beyond what any of us could have accomplished in ten lifetimes.

"He chose you," Martin said.

I lowered the sheet of paper and puzzled at the statement.

"Excuse me?"

"The day you came to talk to him, about the French pilot, he told me after that that you were the right one to find where the plant is."

So, as I'd suspected, it hadn't been just an odd debrief. Even then the little guy had been thinking, planning, choosing.

"He was the one to say we had to find a sustainable source of food," Martin said. "Long before you arrived. The broadcast of the plant images gave him the starting point to make that happen."

"Why me?"

"He said you were honest."

The child is a liar...

I'd told Micah that, giving him the answer when asked, choosing truth over avoidance. I still didn't know what the purpose of the French pilot telling us that was. It was as likely a lie as what it purported to be fact. Supposition instead of truth.

We walked back to the gathering of radios and computers.

"Someone has to get to it," Martin said, staring at the image of green on the screen. "You won't have to do it alone. I know others will volunteer. But Micah wanted you to lead the search."

What the man was saying, and what my own feelings toward the stasis I thought prevalent in Bandon had developed into, were aligned in ways I could not have imagined, and would have never believed. Until now.

"Here," Martin said, taking a small black notebook from his pocket and holding it out to me. "This may help."

I took it and turned back the cover, flipping slowly through the pages within. Nearly half were covered with precise notations, latitudes and longitudes, accompanied by more generic directions.

"Two hundred meters due west of bridge end," I read, puzzling at the significance.

"Those are the food storage lockers Micah didn't tell anyone about," Martin said. "Some may have been used already by the people they were intended for. But some will certainly be full."

I would need these. We would need these. Whoever the others in that equation turned out to be.

Forty Six

Virtually all the town was there, watching the handcrafted casket sink slowly into the earth. The simple headstone was already planted in the soft dirt, speckled granite crafted in haste, but not without loving detail, the name Micah Robert Jay chiseled precisely upon it.

I stood just behind Martin, the man dressed impeccably, black suit crisp. It had likely been in a garment bag for years. He didn't shed a tear as Reverend Morris spoke, talking lovingly of Micah, his challenges before the blight, and how he rose to the occasion to help his neighbors and strangers in the dark times that came. There were stories. Someone, I do not know who, read from a poem, supposedly penned centuries ago by an Englishman. Only a few minutes had passed since the verse had been recited, but I remembered not a syllable of it. Only the sentiment.

This life was but a step toward another.

I didn't know if that was true. I hoped it was. But then I'd been reduced to hoping for many things. That I would find success in the task I'd agreed to undertake. That there would be a tomorrow beyond the time when the last of the food stored in town ran out. That the earth again would be green.

But mostly I hoped that Neil and I would find a way back to our friendship.

He stood with Grace and Krista across the hole from my position. When the casket was fully lowered and the

Reverend had finished, Krista stepped forward and tossed more flowers that she'd crafted into the void. She quickly scurried back to her mother and buried her face against the front of Grace's dress.

Neil didn't move. Didn't flinch. He showed no emotion. But worst of all, he wouldn't look at me.

When the services were over, Neil turned away and walked off, Grace and Krista with him. The little girl looked behind, in my direction, and brought a hand up, fingers flapping slowly in a quiet wave. I returned the gesture, smiling, and then they were gone.

I strolled across the cemetery, dirt where lawn should be.

"I hear Burke's going with you."

It was Elaine. She'd come alongside me without me knowing, her gait improving by the day.

"Doc Allen does good work," I said.

"Doc Allen gives good drugs," she countered.

We continued across the patchy earth, weaving between tombstones. She seemed to want to say something. To talk.

"Elaine, do you—"

"I'm going with you," she said, blurting out the last thing I'd expected to hear.

I stopped, then she did, the both of us facing each other, a twinge of wonder on her face.

"What were you going to say?"

I sidestepped the question and moved to my own.

"Martin's okay with this?"

"I have no idea," she said. "I just decided now."

"Now?"

"Right now," she said, pointing behind to a spot on the ground. "About fifteen feet that way."

My thoughts stuttered.

"This isn't the kind of thing you decide on the spur of the moment," I told her.

"What were you going to say?" she asked again, putting me on a spot I wanted to avoid, especially now.

"What? Wait. Elaine, you—"

She started walking, away from me.

"Cheyenne's a long way," she said without looking back. "We'll have plenty of time for questions and answers."

I was at a loss. She'd outmaneuvered my desire to bury any feelings toward her by outright trying to pull them from me like a trout from a stream. And the only thing *that* could mean was...

The smile came without me trying to summon it. Happiness and hope and possibilities coming on the most unlikely day, in the most unlikely place.

Among the dead, I'd begun to feel alive again.

Forty Seven

The door opened before I ever reached the porch. Grace stood just inside, looking out at me as if I was already a ghost.

"He's not here," she said.

I stopped where the walkway ended and the steps began.

"Where is he?"

"I don't know," she said, worried. "Eric, don't try to talk him into anything."

"Grace..."

"You don't need him. You have Burke, and now Elaine is going. You have everyone you need."

She was pleading. Almost begging. Yet still, in her vulnerability, a stoic defiance flourished. She and Neil had come through hell together. They'd found life, and *a* life together. They had Krista. They had time, no matter how limited.

"I do need him, Grace."

Tears began to build upon her beautiful eyes. She shook her head slightly and they spilled.

"I need him more. Krista needs him more. If that's selfish, I don't care."

There was little I could say to change her mind. I knew that before I'd taken a step out my door on the way over. But she needed to hear from me that Neil, her husband, my friend, was important. Was needed.

"Will you tell him I stopped by?"

She shook her head again, no tears cascading now. A quiet fury had dried them.

"I'm sorry, Grace," I said.

She watched me walk away. I could feel her stare. She loved me like Neil did, but, at that moment, I could tell she wished she'd never met me.

Forty Eight

The plan was to head south, just past the California border, then inland, zigzagging our way east on minor highways and back roads until we reached Interstate 80, probably somewhere in northern Nevada. It was a route chosen the night before, during a sit down with Burke and Elaine. I'd returned home from my stop at Neil's to find them on my porch, maps in hand.

What was the saying? No battle plan survived first contact with the enemy? Well, this might not be a battle in the literal sense, but it would be a fight to reach our destination. The enemy was every obstacle we would come across, most inanimate, but no guarantee that we would not find ourselves facing varying versions of Major Layton, or the Seattle Horde. Or, the vehicle Burke had chosen, and which the town's best mechanic had prepared, might simply stop working a hundred miles from Bandon. Or run out of gas.

In the middle ages this might have been termed a quest. A journey to seek some fabled treasure. It was not far from that, I thought.

Burke and Elaine arrived just before sunrise as the town slumbered. My gear was ready. Weapons checked. I loaded all but my AR and my pistol into the shell-covered bed of the four by four that would carry us and slipped into the back seat of the crew cab with my weapons, Burke at the wheel, Elaine next to him. But before we pulled away from the curb, Burke looked over the seat back to me and lifted a nearly empty bottle of bourbon. Hardly a sip or two remained within its thick glass.

"Last liquor in town," he said, holding the bottle out to me. "A final drink for luck."

I took the bottle and unscrewed the cap, taking a swig, holding it back toward Burke. It was intercepted before he could take it, Elaine seizing it.

"I thought you never touched the stuff," I said.

"I don't," she said, and tipped a swallow back.

She passed the bottle back to Burke and he put it down on the seat.

"Aren't you joining in?" I asked the man.

"When we get back," Burke said.

"I thought this was the last bottle in town," I said, smiling.

"Last, next to last, who knows?" he said.

"You do," I told him.

"Damn right I do."

Burke drove away from the curb, taking us past Neil's house. I wanted to look, but didn't. It wasn't sadness, or disappointment, that filled me. Knowing my best friend would be here simply left me feeling incomplete. He'd saved my life by warning me about the coming blight. I trusted him. He trusted me. Facing what I knew we would, and things which I couldn't yet imagine, was not something I relished without him by my side.

"What the hell?"

Burke's mild exclamation coincided with the four by four slowing, then stopping, just short of the intersection. I looked through the windshield to see what had brought us to a stop.

It was Neil. He stood in the middle of the street. His Benelli was over one shoulder, backpack the other. He walked toward the truck, down the side where I sat, and stopped at the window. I rolled it down.

"I was at the airport when you came by yesterday," my friend told me. "There was a plane there I had to get ready for a trip."

"A trip?" I asked, playing along.

"Little hop over to Wyoming," he said.

"I hear Cheyenne's nice this time of year."

Elaine looked back from the front seat, smiling at me. For me.

"Short flight versus a long drive," Neil said. "Anyone want to join me?"

Burke looked back to him.

"Hop in. Just so happens we're heading for the airport."

Neil nodded, then put his gear in back, and came around the truck to join me in the back seat. Burke pulled away and through the intersection.

We were on our way.

Thank You

I hope you enjoyed *Eagle One*. Please look for other books in *The Bugging Out Series*.